Liz Here Now

Liz Here Now

A Novel Inspired by True Events

Todd Connor

Journey Media Productions

ISBN 978-0-9978593-0-0 (print)
ISBN 978-0-9978593-2-4 (eBook for iPad and Nook)
ISBN 978-0-9978593-1-7 (eBook for Kindle)
Library of Congress Control Number: 2016949331

www.LizHereNow.com

Journey Media Productions
P.O. Box 756
Danville CA 94526
925-837-4404

To Liz

Chapter 1

Summer, 1966.

My hands were numb and my head was throbbing from pressing my fingers into my ears, trying but failing to drown out my sister's screams. Even muffled, Chrissy's cries were blood curdling, as her terrified and panicked voice pleaded for mercy. "Mommy, please, Mommy. I'll be better, Mommy. Please! No, Mommy!"

I wished I had a better place to cower than under my bed in the room next to hers. I struggled against my own tears, knowing loud shrieks always came when I cried. That would make me the next target. My older brother Mark could cry without making a noise. I couldn't. I wished Mark was here, but he'd stayed overnight at a friend's. I wished Liz was here.

My fingers felt like they were going to break off. I pulled them out to slap my palms over my ears, and in that unmuffled instant heard my mother's raging voice scream, "You need to be punished!" My tears burst and I yelped, then quickly bit down hard on my lip to stifle my noise. Bad idea. It only increased my urge to scream.

So I squeezed my eyelids closed and tried quashing the impulse by remembering my birthday. It was the day before yesterday. I was four, almost a big boy. I got nice presents. But best of all, it was a Liz day. She made me a big cake with lots of whipped cream and strawberries on top. She knew it was my favorite. Liz loved me. Liz made me feel safe.

"Look at you, little man," she said as she placed the cake on the table at lunch. My dad wasn't there. He was a doctor. People said he was "important." To me, the word only meant "gone all the time." Mom wasn't there either. She hardly ever was on a Liz day. "You gettin' so growed up," Liz crowed. "Now you make a big ol' wish and blow out all them candles, Todd. You can do it, little man!"

When I blew out all four candles in one breath, Mark and Chrissy clapped and Liz laughed as she pulled me close and wrapped her pillowy arms around me.

"I loves you, baby. I am so glad you was born. God gave me the best gift ever, when he gave me you." She kissed the top of my head and then pointed at Mark and Chrissy, "And you, and you too!"

All three of us absolutely glowed, wrapped in Liz's universal embrace. Until I saw Mom standing at the kitchen door. Her eyes were crazy. Mom got mad when Liz told us how good we were. She got really mad when Liz, the maid, acted like she was the one who was our mom and we returned the warmth of her love.

Chrissy didn't see Mom. She scooted onto her knees on the chair and asked, "Can I cut the cake?"

Mom strode into the room and Chrissy went silent as she made herself as small as possible in her chair. Mom yanked open a drawer and grabbed a sharp knife. She slashed it into the cake as if she were butchering an animal, then slopped pieces onto three paper plates and shoved them at us. She held the knife up and stared at Chrissy. "Don't be silly. You're five. Five-year-olds don't get to use knives. Only grownups do."

The jovial mood went as flat as the birthday balloon I'd popped that morning. Liz's heavyset body seemed to get smaller too as she took a step away from the table. She quietly asked, "Anything I can do fo' you, Mizzuz Connor?"

Todd Connor

"No!" came Mom's sharp, angry reply. She slapped the knife into the sink as fearful stillness seemed to freeze the room. She turned to Liz and pointed at the cake. "Save that. We'll have it with dinner tonight." Then she left the room.

After Mom was gone, Liz held her finger to her lips, the signal to be very quiet. Her eyes sparkled as she cut each of us another slice of cake, plus one for herself. Within minutes we were all laughing again. We didn't see Mom again until after Liz went home when it got dark. It was the best birthday I'd ever had.

"Mommy! Please, Mommy!" Chrissy's screams crashed me back to the present. My palms were not muffling enough sound. So I drilled my thumbs hard into my ears. With that shift, a strange sound leaked through. A woman's voice. It wasn't Mom's. The lady was shouting. It sounded like she was in the laundry room, near the back door. Chrissy was still pleading and Mom was still screaming. Then all of a sudden both Mom and Chrissy went silent. Mom must have smashed her hand onto Chrissy's face to make her be quiet.

Jane?" a woman's voice called out. "Is everything okay? Hello? Jane? It's Kay."

It was Mrs. Wagner, from way over at the next house. I held my breath in relief. Through the bedroom wall I could hear Chrissy whimper again. "Quiet," Mom growled lowly. "You keep quiet or you'll get it worse."

"Jane," Kay called more calmly, more politely. "Jane, dear? I heard some noise. I thought I'd make sure everything is okay." Her voice grew louder as I could hear her entering the labyrinth of hallways to the bedroom wing of our home. "Hello, Jane? Is everything all right?"

Chrissy and I loved visiting Mrs. Wagner. We often wandered over to say hello. We weren't supposed to but, because Mrs. Wagner was so nice to us, we often forgot. We thought she looked like the mom on the Donna Reed TV show. Mrs. Wagner always gave us cookies and talked to us for a while before shooing us back home. It was also daring to visit her because her house seemed so far away. We were forbidden to leave our yard, which seemed to go on forever.

Our neighborhood was called Woodland Estates. Everybody had big houses surrounded by big yards with lots of trees and manicured lawns. What I realized much later was that Woodland Estates—a quiet, exclusive enclave in the Oakland Hills, twelve miles from the fashionable buzz of San Francisco— was reserved for those who had climbed high up the ladder of the American Dream. Most people were friendly. Most of the men were handsome and the women beautiful.

The country was booming. President Lyndon Johnson's "Great Society" had launched the biggest economic expansion in U.S. history. LBJ was attempting to continue the youthful prosperity espoused by his predecessor, John F. Kennedy, the youngest president ever to sit in the Oval Office. Kennedy's "Camelot" had changed America forever. The post-war American Dream was bursting out of imagination and into reality for most people. Music by The Beatles and the Beach Boys blared from every radio with upbeat, youthful sounds. *The Donna Reed Show, Father Knows Best,* and *Leave It to Beaver* all brought understanding, successful parents and cheerful siblings into every living room through the television. Everything about America promoted youthful vibrancy. Everything about Woodland Estates reflected the same image.

Seemingly, my parents, Dr. Frank and Jane Connor, were poster models for the American Dream. Our rambling ranch house, larger than most in the neighborhood, was equipped like all the others with the latest in mid-1960s modern conveniences, such as an all-electric kitchen and automatic dishwasher. Since it was assumed there would be day help, every Woodland Estates home had a second back entrance for the maid through the laundry room. Lush lawns surrounding each house stretched into nearly two acres of thickly planted shrubs and trees, creating the almost reclusive feel of a small estate. All was great for America. All seemed great for those who lived in Woodland Estates. Even at four, I knew our life there was supposed to be very different, even special.

Chrissy's door slammed and, along with it, jolted my mind back to the present. Mom's footsteps rushed past my room and around the corner toward the laundry room and back door. Knowing she was gone was my signal to check on Chrissy, but first I crept halfway down the hallway and peeked around the corner. Standing a few feet away from Mrs. Wagner, Mom's normally perfectly coiffed dark brown hair was messy. Sweat was on her forehead and her eyes blazed with rage. Her hands were thrust into the pockets of the apron she was wearing. I could see her fists clench and unclench, bulging through the flowered print fabric.

"What do you want?" Mom snapped. "What are you doing in my house?" Then, seeming to remember social decorum, she visibly struggled for composure. She raised her hands to smooth the front of her ruffled apron, as if in pretense she had been innocently baking a cake. Taking a deep breath and forming her lips into a well-mannered smile that her eyes didn't reflect, she murmured, "Kay, dear. What a surprise."

Mrs. Wagner took a step forward, as if to try to walk deeper into the house, but Mom quickly stepped in front of her, blocking further entry. Mom's back was now to me and I had my chance to get to Chrissy. I got down on the floor and started to crawl away.

"It's a bad time right now, Kay," I heard Mom snap. Her voice got louder and more shrill. "A very bad time. The children are acting up." I glanced at Mrs. Wagner as I quietly inched away and saw the worry and fear on her face.

"Well, I heard some loud … um … noises." Mrs. Wagner spoke slowly. "I wanted to see if I could help in some way."

Mom barked, "Help? We don't need any help!" Then, more calmly and almost syrupy, she repeated, "We don't need any help, dear. The children are just acting up again. You know how kids can be." Mom chuckled. It sounded so fake I wondered if Mrs. Wagner was fooled.

"Well. I just want to be a good neighbor," I heard Mrs. Wagner say sweetly as I slipped into Chrissy's room.

She was curled up on the bed, sobbing, with her face buried in her pillow. Her yellow dress was wet with red. I didn't know what the red was but I didn't want to touch it. I climbed up next to her and tried to pull the pillow away. "Chrissy, it's me," I whispered urgently. She just grabbed the pillow tighter and continued crying, harder than I'd ever heard her cry before.

I panicked. What if this time it was so bad that she would forget about me? I knew what that was like, the times Mom went after me. All I wanted then was to disappear and never come back: to let shock and despondence float me away, to float me to someplace where I could not feel anything anymore—not pain, not terror, not anything.

On the floor I saw a large pair of scissors, wet with red like on Chrissy's dress. That must be it, I thought. Maybe Mommy wasn't hurting her this time. Chrissy must have been playing with scissors and got hurt. Maybe that's why Chrissy got into trouble, I thought. I wanted to believe that. I needed to believe that, at least for that moment. Scrambling off the bed, I swooped up the scissors and ran down the hall toward the laundry room.

The muffled voices of Mom and Mrs. Wagner continued as I rounded the corner and called out, "Mommy! This is how Chrissy got hurt! Look, Mommy, she had scissors!"

As soon as I held up the scissors, I realized my mistake. Her crazy eyes, forgotten in my brief delusional moment, darted at me like a predator discovering its next meal. Before my mind could register another thought I felt her stinging slap across my face and the sudden ache of my head hitting the wall. Stunned, but also keen on escape, I ran, scuttling back to the safety under my bed, hoping Mom would not find me and do to me whatever she had done to Chrissy.

She didn't come back down the hall. Thankfully, for both Chrissy and me, Mrs. Wagner seemed to have halted Mom's rage, at least for that day.

Forty years later: May, 2006.

The Christian Tabernacle Church of God in Christ was packed. Several hundred brown faces stared up at my white one from the pews in the large red brick building on 84th Avenue in East Oakland. The neighborhood was known as the "Killing Zone," helping bring Oakland the dubious title as one of the most violent cities in America. White faces were rare here. Yet here was mine, at the funeral of their beloved church member Elizabeth Baxter. The faces stared at me, kindly but puzzled, not knowing what to make of me or the story I had started telling them. A story about some woman named Kay Wagner and the Connor family from Woodland Estates, a white neighborhood in the Oakland Hills, a world away from their own. Suddenly I didn't know what I was doing here either. I stood in catatonic silence with my mind racing on what to do next.

The pastor, Reverend PT Williams, stepped to the pulpit that I gripped tightly. "Son, maybe this isn't the time. We want to celebrate Mrs. Baxter and her life. Your story doesn't exactly seem to be doing that."

"I'm sorry, Pastor," I choked out through my tears. "I have to tell this. She asked me to. Please, if I could try again?"

He looked at me reluctantly but acquiesced. As he returned to his seat at the side of the stage, I began again.

"I'm sorry." My voice echoed from the microphone off the solid walls of the massive church. "My name is Todd Connor. I was the little boy in that house. Liz—I mean, Sister Baxter, was our family's maid for many years. You knew her as a mother, friend, and a choir member who sat in these pews to sing and pray. I knew her as a savior, a heroine of monolithic proportions."

A stately old gentleman, tall and thin, nodded his approval from the front row. Now a grieving husband, his usual broad smile was gone from his face, but his nod to me was strong and confirming. Speaking to him directly, I said, "Yes, Claman, we both knew her in a way these people did not." I looked out at the mourners who had gathered. "She told me shortly before she died that she wanted me here, to tell you this story. She needed me to tell it. She wanted you to know." Reclaiming my grip on the podium, I began again.

"That's the way it was behind the front door of our family home. For me, my sister, Christine, and older brother, Mark, that was our whole world. Except for Sister Baxter."

As a child, at first I hadn't known she was named Elizabeth. We children knew her only as Liz. She worked on Tuesdays, Thursdays, and every other Wednesday. With her came the precious nutrients of love, of which my siblings and I lived in complete deprivation when she was not there. For us, kindness, joy, caring, hugs, and laughter—lots and lots of laughter—arrived every one of the mornings that beautiful butterball named Liz walked through the back entrance. On days she didn't come, I'd sneak the refrigerator door open to stare at the bottle of Aunt Jemima syrup. Liz and the lady on the syrup bottle were the only brown faces I'd ever seen in our house when I was very little. The syrup bottle lady was round and heavyset and full of smiles. She looked like Liz, I thought, except Liz's dresses weren't long and her hair wasn't covered up. I'd look in the refrigerator and beg the lady on the bottle to come to life as Liz, as my magical fairy godmother.

My voice trailed off as my mind searched for the joyful remembrances one is supposed to share at funerals, trying my best to exclude the dark realities I had started with earlier. There was so much joy and love from her, so much to share. However, none of those stories could be told without the dark backdrop of our family's reality: violence, and despair.

Liz and I had talked about this moment when she was sent home from the hospital. Cancer was measuring out her remaining lifeline in only weeks, or maybe days. "It's time you told yo' story, Todd," she instructed me on one of my visits to her bedside. "You been holdin' it long enough, too long. It's time. An' you tell it all, Todd. Every part of it."

She stroked my hand as she pushed me to commit to her dying wish. I loved her touch. I loved her calling me "child," even though my forty-fourth birthday was just a few weeks away.

"I been holdin' it all in too, baby. Because you ain't been ready. We been talking 'bout this fo' a long time, Todd. You knows my part of the story now, and you lived your part of the story. So you tell it all now. It's time, child."

Her soothing eyes stared into mine as her words poured into the deepest part of me, crushing all resistance. Tears bathed my cheeks. I clung to every word, knowing these might be the last I would ever hear from her.

"Promise me, Todd." Still holding my hand and staring at me intensely, she insisted, "You gonna tell the story, the whole story. Promise me, child."

I had tried to speak but a silent, tearful nod was all I could deliver. It was all she needed. She let go of my hands and fell back onto her pillow, exhausted of all energy. Her breathing soon relaxed and sleep overtook her.

In and out of wakefulness for several weeks after that, she never asked again. She knew I had promised. Each day, she faded a bit more until the morphine drip stole her consciousness. From there, we waited for life to take her somewhere else, somewhere better suited for her, a more worthy world. With Claman, her sons, and me at her bedside, we planned her memorial service.

So now, here we were at her funeral, and here I was in the middle of it, struggling to fulfill her dying wish.

Claman slowly pulled himself up from his pew. All eyes turned to him as he steadied himself with the side railing to climb the steps to the pulpit. The church remained silent, as did I. I felt relief. I assumed he was coming to reprieve me. I stepped aside, offering him the microphone, and whispered, "I don't know how to do this, Claman."

He gripped my arm, looked straight into my eyes, and said, "Yes, you do, son. You strong. She made you that way."

Claman looked at the crowd. I realized how the last few months had aged him. Nonetheless, the steadiness so characteristic throughout his life beamed from his dignified face as if emanating from a much younger man.

"Thank you, everyone, fo' attendin' today. We're all here celebratin' my wife, Elizabeth. We all loved her. That wasn't hard to do." Grace exuded from him as he spoke. A smile lit up his face, and smiles beamed back at him from those recollecting their own images of her widespread kindnesses. "We all knew her in different ways. Fo' me, she was my wife of near seventy years and mother to our two fine children, sitting right there in the front pew. Fo' some a you, she sang in the choir. Fo' others, she come along side you and helped in any way she could. An' fo' some a you, she got after you." He paused, lowered his head, and looked out over the top of his eyeglasses. "An' some a you needed gettin' after."

The crowd chuckled as people looked from side to side, teasing those around them. "Now, don't you go pointin' fingers. You know who you are! Yes sir, she done left me a list an' I'm gonna call each one a you and continue gettin' after you. So don't think you hidin' now!" Roaring laughter broke out. It took some time for the noise and banter to die down.

His countenance then weathered and Claman's voice became serious. "But they is some things y'all don't know about my Elizabeth. An' you oughta know. Now, you never heard about it, 'cuz it never happened here, at this church. An' it never happened in this neighborhood, where we got lots a crime and violence goin' on. But the real story about my Elizabeth, the story that shows who she really was, happened in a place where it ain't never 'spose to happen. An' it happened to children, babies really, who ain't never 'spose to have this happen to 'em. An' the only one cared enough to do somethin' 'bout it was the one person who weren't never 'spose to be able to—my Elizabeth. An' the only one who can tell the story, the true story 'bout my wife, is this young man standin' right here."

Turning to me, Claman continued, "Now, son, I know you're strugglin' 'cuz you're tryin' to say somethin' nice an' sweet about my wife. These folks already know all about her bein' nice and sweet. You and me, we know the whole truth. She was much bigger than nice an' sweet. You the only one who can tell the truth, all of it. Me an' her filled in the blanks fo' ya, the parts you didn't know when you was growin' up. So now you have it all."

I held my head down, shaking it slowly, feeling completely inadequate.

"Look at me, son. I know the story's dark, Todd. But darkness always shows off the light at its best." Claman looked at Pastor Williams. "Ain't that right, Pastor?"

The pastor's face still registered confusion, but also a curious questioning. "Amen, Brother Baxter," he murmured. "That's right."

Turning back to me and gripping my arm tightly, he said, "So, it's okay, son. The dark parts a yo' story gonna show off her light. An' they gonna tell the true story 'bout her fo' the first time ever. So you tell it all now, son. We're all gonna be right here with you."

Claman stepped to the side of the podium, gesturing for me to move into position again. He then motioned for a young man to bring him a chair so he could sit by my side. His presence comforted me as I proceeded.

"Okay, Claman." My voice shook from my effort to shed my fear and also keep the tears away. I took a deep breath. Feeling as if Liz was standing right there with me, I seemed to hear her voice say, "You done promised me, child. Now, go on." Her imagined voice brought a wave of her deep love that washed my fear away. I began again.

Chapter 2

Mrs. Wagner witnessed one of Mom's "crazy-eye days" on a Saturday. There were many such days when Liz was not there. But Mrs. Wagner never saw what had happened that day. No one did, except Christine and Mom.

Mrs. Wagner and even our relatives knew Mom was unstable. Some of the family members called her "restless." Others ventured to say she was "sometimes troubled." She was all of those things, and so much more. It would not be inaccurate to call her crazy. It's not a nice word, really. Mostly, people use it when they want to discredit someone. I don't mean crazy in the schoolyard teasing kind of way. I mean really crazy.

We knew it: my brother and sister and me. Even when we were very young, we knew it—not in an intellectual or medically diagnosed way, of course. We knew it because we watched her. We had to, for sheer survival. We saw it first in her eyes, as she started slipping from reality. Her pupils dilated. Her eyes glazed over and eventually went completely vacant. Her jaw clenched. Her voice changed pitch, becoming louder and piercing in its shrillness. Her pleasant countenance was overtaken by some sort of demented darkness. Sometimes it took hours. Sometimes it happened in a matter of seconds. Once the process completed itself, Mom was someone—or something—else. What remained was a mutated personality filled partly with fear, partly with tension, but without question, a whole lot of violent rage. Her "crazy eyes" told us something else was then in control.

We were children, powerless to stop the beast that consumed her. We could only watch it coming. The force of her transmutation was paralleled by the terror in our souls. Our minds screamed with the only viable instruction available: Run. Hide!

Her crazy eyes made any real peace and tranquility impossible in our home. Even on days when she seemed normal, we never knew when her crazy eyes would kick in, when Mom would travel somewhere far from the reality of our home to some frighteningly distorted place only she could see. Our constant level of fear was a stark contrast to the veneer of the American Dream others outside of our home saw.

Years later a friend at school mused about his "rich uncle." The conversation went like this. Him: "My rich uncle came over last weekend. You know, everyone has a rich uncle." Me: "I don't think I have a rich uncle." Him: "Todd, your family is the rich uncle."

It was true. Our house was large, even for our wealthy neighborhood. Two matching blue Cadillacs, new every year, waited obediently in the garage. Money and flash radiated from our parents' frequent and lavish parties, which were louder and livelier than anyone else's. Mom and Dad were the picture of all that was young, vibrant, and impressive in America. By the time I was in grade school I realized Mom was a dead ringer for the 1950s bombshell Jane Russell. We were seldom in public without a stranger calling out, "Excuse me, Miss Russell, may I have your autograph?" It was so commonplace that she simply scribbled autographs to avoid arguing with offended fans who refused to believe she wasn't the movie star.

Dad, meanwhile, boasted the largest medical practice in the East Bay. Back when family doctors did a little of everything, in 1962—the year I was born—he was recognized by Mercy

Medical Center as the doctor who delivered more babies than any other physician in its eighty-year history. The local medical society repeatedly elected him president, regularly utilizing him as their poster boy and political manipulator. His patients included the mayor's family and most of the City Council, as well as half the judges in Alameda County.

From the outside, our home oozed prestige, flash, and money. Yet all the wealth and glitz on the outside shrouded maniacal violence on the inside. Fear and emptiness ruled in the Connor home. Love, peace, and family comfort did not exist there.

Except when there was Liz. In my whole life, she never missed a scheduled workday. Every Tuesday, Thursday, and alternate Wednesday, she was there, letting herself in the back door through our laundry room as the day began.

Chrissy always awoke early. That was my name for her because Christine had been far too much articulation for me as a toddler. Plus, I wanted my own name for my sister, whom I loved as much as life itself. A year apart, we were inextricably bonded. Mark was several years older, and Chrissy and I needed each other desperately. On non-Liz days, our conjoined duo was all we had to rely on for survival.

Virtually every day, Chrissy woke me up and we'd sneak out of our beds before anyone else stirred, then slip downstairs to watch cartoons in the lower-level family room we called the basement. It often served as a hideout for us when Mom went crazy-eyed at unpredictable times. Always hoping it was a Liz day, we periodically turned down the volume to listen for her morning greeting. We loved the sound of her voice. It was like it flooded sunlight into the whole house, even the dark basement. "Hello, Mizzuz Connor," she chimed in her high-pitched Arkansas accent. "How are you?"

Hearing those words, Chrissy and I ran upstairs to greet our heroine. As soon as she saw us, her voice rose gleefully. "Well, hi! How you two doin'?" Even then I realized how differently she spoke to us, and to her husband, than she did to Mom and Dad. With them, she was crisp and proper. With us, the sounds of the South rolled over us like the syrup she poured on our pancakes. The excited change in her voice, switching from careful conversation with Mom, was like a fix to an addict. So deprived, so starved for affection, the simple delight in her voice was intoxicating for us. We were giddy with smiles and laughter. We knew she loved us. We knew she delighted in seeing us and we drank up every ounce of it.

Liz's morning greeting was usually Mom's signal to disappear. I don't remember seeing Mom much on Liz days. When grown, I came to know why. She had never wanted to be a mother. Mom and Dad decided not to have children when they got married. But reliable birth control did not exist then. An aunt once told me that when Mom got pregnant with Mark, Dad didn't speak to her for an entire month. He claimed it was all her fault, even though he was a doctor and knew better.

Dad was an angry man. He was a master of public appearances, with political friends, public prestige, and a social pedigree that made him feel important. He had natural charm and a highly developed sense of humor. Powerful people were his closest friends. His patients loved him and were completely impressed with his intellect and medical knowledge. He always managed to make everyone feel as if he was truly concerned and interested. But you didn't want to cross him. Anyone who tried quickly found out why. His six-foot, five-inch build and forceful personality helped ensure obligatory respect from almost anyone.

All these attributes made him an enigmatic giant in my eyes. He looked perfect for the role. I always hoped he would turn into the fairy-tale kind of giant—a benevolent hero saving the imprisoned children from their wicked stepmother. He just never wanted to play the part. The "wicked stepmother" was always played by our real mother, but the brave redeeming

Todd Connor

giant never showed up to rescue us. Dad was a giant only in physical stature and ego.

More times than can be counted, he returned home from seeing patients to find one of his children abused and bleeding, due to another psychotic break on the part of his wife. His "solution" was to pump us with aspirin, bandage our wounds, and put us to bed. Sometimes he yelled at her. Sometimes he hit her. Most times, he just sedated her and then went on as if nothing happened. In his mind, that healed everyone perfectly. At least until the next time.

He wasn't home much. His medical practice demanded most of his time. His patients loved him, and he loved being loved by them. He did house calls in those days. Many went late into the night. Mom believed those evening house calls were mostly at the house of one of his nurses, which made her even more unstable. After bedtime, Chrissy and I would often sneak to the edge of the completely darkened living room, watching the rhythmic glow of Mom's cigarette as she inhaled each puff. The scent of smoke mixed with the smell of gin in the clinking martini pitcher that served as her "husband" most nights. The liquid husband vanished by night's end and rendered Mom comatose, while the real husband snuck in before dawn and pretended he'd returned much earlier.

I always wondered if it was drinking that made her so unbalanced, or the obvious hatred she harbored for Dad. Or was it something deeply damaged inside her, something from her past? In reality, it probably was a whole lot of all of that, as I learned many years later.

But Liz days: Those were brief visits from heaven, respite from the tragic hell lived by us Connor children.

"You kids watchin' TV?" Liz would chirp like a delighted bird. "You watchin' that *Lost in Space*? Oh, I love that Dr. Smith. 'Oh the pain, the pain'," she parroted. "I love it when he say that! 'Oh the pain...'. Ooo-eee. Don't he got that right!"

Her contagious, cackling laughter, about two octaves above normal speech, followed. That laugh probably sounded funny to most people. But to us it was Mozart finally transcribing the music of the spheres, that melody that moves the deepest soul into inexpressible joy. We were completely captivated by her.

Especially on Tuesdays, her first work day each week. We instinctively clung to her as she washed, cleaned, and made beds. This surely complicated her workday. But she understood our depleted souls needed connection after the long weekend away from her. She never refused us. She turned everything into a storybook adventure.

"Now you know, babies," she instructed as we hopelessly tried helping her, "I in prison by an evil witch. An' she watchin' all my work. Now, you ma' little birds that come visit me. So you gots to help me do good, or she gonna get me! Todd, you fluff that pillow. Christine, straighten that blanket. Or she gonna get me."

When Liz got tired of correcting our flawed attempts, she borrowed from Hansel and Gretel. "You know that witch gonna eat us all up if we don't do good. An' she gonna eat me first, 'cuz I so big." She chuckled. "That ol' witch, she knows I've got lotsa meat on me. But you're gonna be next. So you kids go on outside now an' hide yo'self from that witch. Go on now." She tickled our bellies as if her fingers were taking bites out of them. She continued tickling us all the way out the back door. "She gonna eat you too. You go on out and find me a secret potion to free me from that witch. I'll call you when yo' lunch is ready."

The back yard felt huge to us. More than two acres, it seemed like a hundred square miles to play in. We continued Liz's imaginings as we played throughout the forested expanse. There were fig trees with canopy shade that had magical fruit to cure anything—even bringing us "back from the dead" more than once. There was the enormous cottonwood tree

Todd Connor

for climbing, as if we were scaling Jack's beanstalk, with just enough danger to keep it interesting. For the occasional injury, Liz was just inside with her own magical cures, like Band-Aids, Bactine, or the most powerful of all: a good cry on her lap.

As morning gave way to noontime, Liz called us in for peanut butter sandwiches at lunch, after which was naptime. Chrissy always had trouble going down for hers. As Liz served our plates, Liz played. "Now, Chrissy, I put somethin' special in yo' jelly. An' if you eat it all up and take yo' nap real good, you're gonna be a princess in yo' dreams. So eat that up real good now."

But with me, the effort was much simpler. Liz cradled me in her arms and told me made-up stories of princes and adventure. Mysteriously, all the stories ended with the good prince obediently falling into a long nap. When she held me, it was like resting on a cloud of cotton. If she ran out of stories and I didn't want to sleep, she would make silly faces. Then, as laughter rumbled up from deep within her, my little body bounced on her enormous flesh and I'd giggle, "Jell-O!" That made both of us laugh harder and she'd sing-song, "Liz done put the jiggle in the Jell-O bowl!"

Liz days seemed never-ending as we drank in every molecule of her love, savoring as much as we possibly could before the dreaded end of her workday.

"Good night, Mizzuz Connor," Liz called as she put on her coat and picked up her purse. If we were not still following her around the house, when we heard those words we ran from wherever we were to the back door, for one final connection before she left. "Liz, don't go! We love you, Liz-ee-beth!" came our repeated cries.

"I've gotta go be with my family now. My husband, he's hungry by this time. Who's gonna feed him? He be waitin' fo' me to fix his dinner." She spoke gently, understanding what her leaving meant to us.

"Take us with you! We want to go with you and ..." Before we could finish our eager appeal, Liz glanced at Mom in the kitchen and her look turned serious. We instinctively knew what this meant and stopped our pleading. We followed the direction of Liz's gaze, and there it was, Mom's eyes flaring, hearing her children say they wanted to live with the maid.

Liz leaned over both of us, wrapped her arms around us, and whispered, "I love you babies. You be good now. You mind yo' momma, hear?" Then, standing up straight, she said brightly for Mom to hear, "Well, I be back soon. Look, your momma has your dinner goin'... Mm-mmm, smells awfully good. I'm gonna get me some a that if you kids don't get there first. You best be settin' down for dinner now, b'fo' I go eatin' up all a yours."

These parting words were Liz's vain attempt to calm Mom's eyes. The back door shut as Chrissy and I stared out the adjacent window, fixated on Liz's lumbering body fading into the evening's darkness. Our tears clouded our last dim images of her getting into her car and driving off. The love and laughter that had filled the day vanished with her. Each time she left, we feared the joy that had fed us would never return.

We turned around to the reality of our home. Angst came flooding back. Our constant vigilance, watching out for Mom's crazy eyes, began again. We looked for the signs, ran for our secret hiding places when the crazy eyes came back. And most importantly we tried to hold on ... just hold on ... until Liz returned.

When crazy eyes took over Mom, all three of us kids found our own personal hiding places. We each had at least one to run to. That was, of course, unless you were the one Mom's eyes fixed on that day. Mom always had one of us as the target onto whom her maniacal rage was projected. The Saturday Mrs. Wagner came in, it happened to be Christine.

One thing that never occurred to my siblings or me was the concept that Mom was even capable of stopping once her crazy eyes took control. Never once did any of us consider that she might come to her senses. It simply never happened. We knew Mom wouldn't stop until she decided she was finished, and that would only happen when enough pain was inflicted to satisfy some sadistic need deep within her. Once her demented psychosis was satiated, a semblance of calm would return. But only until the next time.

The day after the attack on Chrissy was Sunday, a particularly dark day. Chrissy was badly hurt. She refused to eat or talk, even to me. I was terrified. She was fulfilling my fears, drifting away without me with her. I could see her fading and knew her feeling of wanting not to come back to reality, to just stay in a state of nothingness. Throughout the day, I snuck into her room periodically. She did nothing more than look at me and cry more. I didn't know what Mom had done to her this time, but I knew it was really bad.

"Chrissy, you have to eat!" I pleaded. "Chrissy let's play Queen!" Queen was a game of pretend Chrissy liked to play so she could boss me around. I didn't like the game but desperately wanted to do anything I could to bring Chrissy back. She just stared at me and kept crying. I decided to play Queen anyway, only this time I would be king and she'd have to do what I said. I snuck into the kitchen, grabbed a piece of chocolate cake, and brought it to her. "I am the king and command you to eat this magic cake!" Nothing. She again just looked at me and cried.

The day dragged on as I tried everything I could think of to bring her back to reality, and especially to me. By afternoon I, too, was despondent. I went to my hiding place under my bed and decided to spend the rest of the day there. I hoped I could stay there until the next Liz day came.

As astonishing as it may seem, that night Mom threw a forty-fifth birthday party for Dad. The caterers arrived while my despair still had me cowering under my bed. The sounds of their frenzied activity briefly brought me out of hiding to peek at what was happening. People, mostly Black, were rushing everywhere. I'd never seen a brown face other than Liz's in our house and silently begged for one of them to be hers—unfortunately, no. Everyone was busy filling trays with food, setting out bottles of alcohol, filling punch bowls, and arranging chairs inside and out. A jazz band was setting up at the far end of the living room.

The scene was surreal, eclipsing the dark violence that had filled our home the day before. My overwhelming terror, still lurking within, would not be quelled by this buzz of activity. I returned to my hiding place and hoped the party would at least make Mom happier tomorrow.

The party began at seven. Irene Thomas, Mom's best friend from college, arrived early. She doted over Chrissy and me. Her kids were much older and she missed those small child years. I loved her. Like Liz, she genuinely liked us and always made some special time with each one of us when she visited. She opened my bedroom door and called in cheerfully, "Todd? Where are you, honey?" She leaned down to see me looking out from the space beneath the bed frame. "There you are! What are you doing under there?"

I crawled out to greet her. She struggled with her uncooperative full-length evening gown as she got down on her knees to hug me. Her hands and wrists were loaded with obscene amounts of jewelry that dug into my back as she squeezed me. She and Mom often joked competitively as to which of them had married more money than the other.

Tonight, Irene seemed to be winning, as my back stung with her embrace. It didn't matter. I latched onto her like a drowning victim grabbing a rescuer.

"Oh, honey!" she responded, noticing how I clutched onto her. "I've missed you too, Todd. It's been so long. I truly have missed you, sweetheart."

Without words, I drank in her warmth. It was a healing balm I was grateful for. I would have held on for the rest of the evening if I could. But the embrace ended when I could no longer endure her diamond bracelets digging into my back.

"I'm so sad I can't see Chrissy today," she said. My eyes were glued to her as she spoke. "Your mother told me she's sick and can't be disturbed. Can you tell her hi for me?"

I burst into tears.

"Oh, honey." She hugged me once more and her diamonds began their torture again. I raised no objection, needing to be held. "Are you sad to be all alone today?"

Just then Mom burst into my room and, ignoring me, said to Irene, "Oh there you are. So, what do you think?"

Irene gasped as the vision of Mom took her breath away. She was astoundingly beautiful, looking as if a life-size Glamour magazine cover stood in the doorway. Mom was wearing a red formal with a strapless left shoulder. In the evening sunlight coming through my bedroom window, a multitude of sequins glimmered. They looked like diamonds in a free-flowing shape that cascaded from her right shoulder toward the hem at her left ankle. Seemingly angelic light emanated around her. Irene stared speechless for a moment at the dazzling scene.

"You look stunning. It's breathtaking, Jane, absolutely breathtaking." Irene stood up to take it all in. She swept a hand toward the long slit on the right side of Mother's dress, revealing her shapely leg halfway up her thigh. "Oh, and look at those slits! You naughty girl. I'm keeping Phil away from you tonight," she joked. "Other wives, beware!"

They chuckled and joked as they left my room. Irene poked her head back in as she closed the door. "G'night, honey. Be sure to say hi to Chrissy for me. I hope she feels better soon."

I do too, I thought as hopelessness crashed back on me. The brief trip to somewhere happier had been a welcome relief. But reality returned. I slipped into my hiding place again.

The party was in full swing within the hour. I snuck into Chrissy's room to see if she would come with me to steal cookies from the kitchen, which we always did during Mom and Dad's big parties. She was sleeping, even through all the noise. I didn't want to see her cry again and worried that if I woke her, I might see that horribly sad face.

I found my older brother, Mark, in his room. We snuck to the edge of the living room to spy on the activity. All the women looked as if they were at a Prince's Ball, just like in the fairy tales. The men wore tuxes. Everyone was very loud and many were dancing to the jazz band's music. Mom had a group of men around her, relishing her time as the center of their attention. Dad mostly stayed at the far end of the living room with other men, smoking and drinking. Mark and I watched for some time. It was like seeing a vivid, colorized version of an old movie of very rich people all trying to impress each other.

My brother and I took breaks from our spying to occasionally creep into the kitchen to steal something sweet from filled party trays set on every available surface. On one of our thieving runs, we rounded the corner from the hallway and stopped in our tracks. In the center of the kitchen was an enormous three-layer cake, taller than both of us put together. Several men in chef's hats were putting decorative icing on the edges. Later that evening we watched the men roll that enormous dessert into the living room. Dad was ushered to it from his smoking-men's club that had moved outside. People surrounded him as he held his hands over his eyes, attempting not to look at what was happening. "C'mon, Frank. Keep those eyes closed," they cheered. Mark and I wondered where Mom was. Finally positioned in front of the massive treat, Dad was told to open his eyes. "Happy birthday to you …" the familiar song burst forth.

Suddenly, Mom popped out of the top of the cake in a blood-red bikini, yelling, "Surprise!" The party crowd erupted with hoots and whistles and wild applause.

Hours later, as the party wound down, Dad and Mayor Bob Jackson, his good friend, sat in large, overstuffed chairs at the far end of the living room. They quietly watched the remains of one of the most elaborate parties either had ever seen. The jazz band was playing ballads, as most dancers had tired out long ago and many of the guests had departed. Having slipped back into her glistening sequined dress, Mom was at the other end of the large room, still enjoying the attention of a few of the husbands she had mesmerized throughout the evening. It was difficult to tell which she enjoyed more, their attention or the collection of their abandoned wives sitting nearby, steaming.

"Jane really outdid herself, Frank," Mayor Jackson commented. As both men watched her, they couldn't help but take in her striking beauty, like a bejeweled Cleopatra holding court. Referring to the men surrounding her, the mayor teased, "Looks like the hound dogs are hunting in your backyard, Frank."

Frank said nothing. He had consumed far too much alcohol to care.

"You have what every man wants, Connor," the mayor added. "You are the American Dream."

Frank barely smiled in response. He was exhausted from the party, but especially by his efforts to forget what he was more frequently coming home to discover. The alcohol had done little to erase the memory of bandaging his daughter the day before and redressing her wounds just before the guests had arrived. He knew his wife's mental state was deteriorating.

He wondered how to keep it hidden. His anger flared at the thought that she threatened everything he'd worked for. Worried that his mounting anger would show, he turned to the mayor, speaking as he stood. "Well, I'm afraid this American Dream better do some dreaming of his own if he's going to see patients in the morning."

Soon the last of the guests were gone. Dad and Mom didn't speak after everyone left. I wondered if I'd wake up in the morning to find Mom with a black eye. Without incident, however, both found their bed and sleep.

In the morning, Dad was already gone when I slipped downstairs without Chrissy to watch cartoons. Mark was practicing his piano lesson. I could tell he was trying to play softly so Mom wouldn't get mad. When the music stopped abruptly, I knew it was because Mom was up. After a while she came to the top of the steps and called us. "Get up here. Your breakfast is ready."

Silently, we did as we were told. Mark and I sat down to our bowls of cereal. As soon as he was done, Mark slipped out the back door to ride his bike to school. Mom slapped a plate with two pieces of toast in front of me. "Tell your sister to eat this. I'm going back to bed. And you, you stay out of trouble." She left the room.

Chrissy didn't eat the toast. She didn't eat the sandwich Mom made me take her at lunch. I spent most of the day downstairs or in Chrissy's bedroom, playing pretend games and being as quiet as I could.

Chapter 3

Tuesday finally came. As usual, I rose early and took my position watching cartoons in the basement, again without Chrissy. Then the back door made its familiar creaking and I heard Liz's cheerful voice. "Hi, Mizzuz Connor. How are you today?"

Instinctively, I turned to grab Chrissy's hand so we could run upstairs together to see Liz. I jolted back to reality, frozen as grief poured over me again.

"Todd? Chrissy?" called Liz. "Where you at, babies?"

I could never resist that voice. Even in my despondence, the thrill of seeing Liz transformed me and I began to run up the stairs. Halfway up, I halted. Mom was walking past. She paused to glare down at me, then spoke sternly to Liz again as she continued toward her bedroom. "I have bridge club here today. I need the living room and kitchen spotless by noon, Elizabeth."

I didn't move until Mom was well out of sight. We all kept our distance from Mom after one of her crazy-eyed episodes. She always seemed susceptible to relapse during those first few days. Further, I was happy to let Mom finish her instructions so I could have Liz to myself. Once their dialogue was over, Liz walked towards the basement stairs. "Todd? Chrissy? Where you at? You hidin' from ol' Liz?"

"I'm here," I answered softly, sensing it was safe to reveal myself. She was waiting for me at the top of the stairs by then. I was so relieved to see her, but none of my usual excitement was present. I looked up at her and burst into tears. Running to grab her legs, I buried my face into them as if burrowing a hole. I wanted to bury my whole self into the one place I felt safe: with Liz.

Liz was far too heavy to be able to pick me up from the ground. She wrapped her arm around me and walked me to her utility stool in the laundry room. It was the sturdiest place for Liz to sit when we kids needed to climb up on her for comfort, or when she invited us to crawl onto her lap and be engulfed by her pillowy frame. I immediately buried my face into the side of her soft neck and sobbed. I couldn't stop. It was the first time I had cried since Chrissy was hurt. My deep reservoir of grief washed onto Liz's shoulder.

"Now, now, baby, you tell 'Lizabeth what's wrong." Her soft words made me cry more and much, much deeper. The ocean of intense sadness, dammed up over the past days, poured out. Liz made no attempt to stop me. She never had a timetable when it came to caring for us. Whatever Chrissy or I needed to get out of our lonely souls, we released onto her, snuggled in her lap. She seemed to have an eternity to let us do that. This time, even I wondered if I would ever stop crying. It felt so good to feel safe again, at last.

Liz hummed "His Eyes Are on the Sparrow" as she slowly rocked me back and forth. This was interrupted only by an occasional, "It's all right, baby. You just let it out. Liz here now." A kiss on my forehead followed her words, as she continued humming and rocking.

Finally I managed to whimper out the words. "Chrissy. Chrissy's hurt. Chrissy's hurt real bad."

Liz's padded frame stiffened. "Chrissy's hurt?" Clearly, she was worried. There was one thing I could spot instantly: fear.

Liz was afraid. She kept her tone sweet as she said, "C'mon, let's go find her. She'll be okay, Todd. Liz here now. Chrissy'll be okay." She quickly put me down, took my hand, and hurried me to Chrissy's room.

We entered. Chrissy was still in bed, seemingly immobile during the last two days—same place in the bed, same position. Just as I had done at the sight of Liz, Chrissy started crying uncontrollably. "Lizabeth. Lizabeth," she murmured through her sobs.

Liz seemed relieved once she saw Chrissy. Usually there were facial bruises and cuts after one of Mom's attacks. This time, Chrissy's head, peering just over her blankets, exhibited none of that.

"What's wrong, child?" Liz spoke gently as she walked across the room. "You tell Liz what's wrong. You know Liz'll make it better. C'mon, child." She sat on the edge of the bed and stroked Chrissy's disheveled hair as my sister continued to cry wordlessly. "All right, baby. You just let it out now. Can you tell Liz what's wrong, baby? I bet I can help if you just tell me. Did you get hurt, child? C'mon, Liz gonna make it better."

Chrissy pulled back her blankets, revealing multiple lacerations on the front of her right thigh. It was bruised and swollen, oozing blood through the bandages administered by Dad. Sitting at the foot of the bed, I could not see the wounds. I was afraid to. All I saw was Liz recoiling.

"Oh Lord, what she done now? Lord have mercy!" She abruptly stood and started pacing at the side of the bed. "Oh, no, Lord! What we gonna do, Lord? That woman, she crazy, Lord! Look what she done now! Oh, Lord, what we gonna do?"

For the moment, she seemed completely unaware of Chrissy and me. Then she stopped pacing and her demeanor quickly shifted from fear into compassion. Her own tears started falling. Settling on the bed again, she wrapped us both in her marshmallowy arms. We folded into them as close as we could.

We all cried. Liz kept murmuring, "No, Lord, she can't hurt ma' babies no mo'. Oh, no, Lord, she can't hurt ma' babies. No. No, Lord, no Lord."

After a while, all of us were cried out. Composing herself, Liz cupped Chrissy's face in her hand and placed her face almost nose to nose with Chrissy's. "Liz gonna make this right, baby. You see. Liz here now. Liz gonna make this all right."

She stood up and opened the bedroom door. Looking determined, she paused, smoothed her apron and dress, patted her hair, and held her head up, as if preparing for an important meeting. She looked back and came close to both of us once more. "Liz here now," she whispered with a steely resolve. With her eyes fixed on both of us, we felt as if she was revealing a secret weapon with extreme power. "Liz is here now, and Liz is gonna fix this. That's right, babies, Liz here now."

Marching to the door, not talking to us anymore but more to herself, she repeated, "It's gonna be all right now. Liz here now." Even stronger and more forceful came those words again. "And Liz is gonna *fix* this."

As she left of the room she whispered what sounded like a coach strengthening a prize fighter, "Ain't *nobody* gonna hurt ma babies like that. Liz here now."

Chrissy's room shared a common wall with our parents' bedroom. Mom had an office and dressing area on that side of the room, where she spent much of her time. Liz blazed her way in without knocking. Chrissy and I listened intently to their muffled words. We couldn't make out what they were saying, but the tone was clearly nothing we had heard between them before. The previously subservient Liz was raising her voice as the conversation undulated between whispered, angry sounds from Mom and then sharp words from Liz that quieted it all down again. Mom didn't say much. It was clear that Liz did most of the talking.

Liz spent the entire day in Chrissy's room sitting next to the bed, resting a hand on Chrissy while she slept. I would come in and out, to climb on Liz's lap and talk about important things, like the lizard I'd caught outside. "Do you like lizards, Liz? Hey, that's like your name—Liz-ard."

"Oh, Todd, you funny." She laughed and spoke in hushed tones so as not to awaken my sister. Quickly, however, her worried face returned, and I knew it was time to play elsewhere. She never left Chrissy's room all day. I don't know what happened to Liz's work that day—the washing, cleaning, and bed-making, or preparing for Mom's bridge party.

One thing was clear to me at some point that day, however. Mom was now scared. Late in the morning she came into Chrissy's room, appearing annoyed, saying something about the dirty dishes and the laundry.

Liz calmly looked at her and responded with resolved determination. "I'm gonna stay right here, Mizzuz Connor. We talked about this. I'm stayin' right here."

I had never heard Liz talk to Mom that way before. Mom certainly never heard the help speak to her like that. Her eyes darted about as if searching for a way to hide her rage. Then I saw her countenance change as she realized Liz gave her no options. She left more scared than when she came in.

Chrissy and I didn't know what to expect when Liz had to leave at the end of the day. With Liz gone, there was no telling what Mom might do. Liz sensed this too. She took extra time with all three of us kids that evening. She called Mark and me to Chrissy's room, kissed each of us on the forehead and warned, with extreme seriousness in her eyes, "You be good now, hear? I love you babies, but you *gotta* be good fo' yo' momma. You undastand?"

She had said those words before but they delivered a more critical message that day. Mark, Chrissy, and I knew that anything could set Mom off. Liz clearly understood that. So, today, this was not a platitude about obedience. We knew these were survival instructions when she drew close and whispered, "Promise me, babies, you be good fo' yo' momma." We simply nodded, unable to speak due to overwhelming fear and grief. As she pulled away, we saw tears well in her eyes. We could see she felt as scared and powerless as we did.

Liz's drive home took only about twenty minutes, but her house on 94th Street in "The Flats" of East Oakland was light-years away from the plush neighborhood of Woodland Estates in the Oakland Hills. Geographical separation underscored the social and racial divide. The Hills were mostly white. The Flats were mostly Black.

In The Flats, small bungalows crowded side by side. The houses had been hurriedly constructed at the start of World War II. They were quickly filled by the mostly Black workers who took part in the Great Migration, lured from the South to the more racially tolerant environment of California by good paying wartime jobs in shipbuilding and industry. But after the war, the flow of government cash ended. Factories either shut down or converted to domestic production and gave precedence to white GIs returning home. Black unemployment skyrocketed, which left those in The Flats even more marginalized by American society. Unemployment and racism remained endemic problems and, by the 1960s, The Flats became one of the crime capitals of the country. To deal with the burgeoning problem, the Oakland Police Department recruited white officers from Southern towns, who were believed to know how to handle Black unrest. The recruits were generally disgruntled and brutal. By the mid 1960s, their tactics earned Oakland a claim to fame as the birthplace of the term "police brutality."

The Flats had another stark social contrast. In 1965, the area boasted more than five hundred churches. These, however, dwelt side-by-side with more than twice that number of liquor stores—more than in any similar-sized city on the West Coast. The contrast mirrored the struggle of a largely unemployed Black population that was increasingly abused by local police. Some found God. Many more found alcohol and, as the decade proceeded, illegal drugs.

Liz had little choice but to live in The Flats. She did have a choice as to how to deal with it. She and her husband steered clear of both the troublemakers and the police, and taught their children to do the same. They had succeeded, and both their sons were now attending college at Berkeley. After she pulled into the driveway of their two-bedroom bungalow, Liz hurried up the front steps calling, "Claman? Claman?" Closing the front door behind her, she called again, louder this time. "Claman, where you at?"

From the back of the house strode a tall man, slightly balding, slightly graying, but still slender and strong. "Now what's wrong that you go on hollerin' at me like that?" Claman asked, half teasing and half annoyed. With a courtly bow, he added, "An' good evenin' to you too, Mizzuz Baxter."

"Oh, I'm sorry, honey," Liz continued with frantic energy. "But Claman you won't believe what happened today. Oh, she's crazy, Claman. She's crazy!"

Disappointed his little joke had been deflected, he grew serious. "C'mon now. You sit down and tell me what on earth you talkin' 'bout. Who's crazy? Mizzuz Connor? She's always crazy, from what you say. That ain't nothin' new."

"Claman, she's really done it this time. Oh, that poor child.

That poor, poor child. She's crazy, Claman, just plain crazy," Liz ranted.

"Now, Bert." Claman tried to calm her with his special nickname for her. He had called her that from the first time he'd kissed her, more than twenty years earlier. He wanted his own special name for her. "I know folks call you Lizzie, and Liz, and even some folks call you Beth," he had told her, "but that one sounds like rich white folk. I'm gonna call you Bert. That's gonna be my name fo' you. Sometimes when I really take a likin' to ya, I might even call you Bertie." "Oh, Claman, you awful," she had chided him with a grin of delight. From then on, hearing her special name usually lightened her spirit, but not this time.

"Oh, she's done really hurt ma' baby this time," Liz said, gasping for breath.

Claman just looked at her questioningly. "Who this time?"

"Ma' baby girl, Christine! She hurt her real bad this time. She's gettin' worse, Claman. That woman is gettin' crazier." She then paused for a moment, almost holding her breath. She looked into Claman's eyes. "She's started cuttin'. That's what she done to Christine, Claman."

"She done what now?" He was incredulous. Liz had told him before about seeing bruises on the children, and sometimes burns, which horrified him. However, he never imagined it might get worse than that. He stood motionless as he processed this new information.

"She cut up ma' little girl's legs, Claman. Oh, Lord, what am I gonna do? What am I gonna do?"

Liz sat down on the couch, rocking and crying. Claman sat down beside her and stroked her shoulders. He knew something should be done. But what? "What can you do, Bert? You love them babies like they was yo' own, but they ain't yo' own. What can you do?" Claman reasoned softly.

"But they *are* ma' babies!" Liz protested. "Their momma

Todd Connor

doesn't love them. She's too crazy. Oh, Lord, what am I gonna do?"

Liz stood and bolted toward the phone on the wall in the kitchen. "No, she ain't gonna hurt ma' babies. No, no, no. She ain't gonna hurt ma' babies no more." Liz dialed the operator. "I need the police, please."

"Oh, no you ain't, Bert! You ain't callin' the police." Claman raised his voice as he rushed to grab the phone from Liz and hang it up. "Now *you* bein' crazy. You can't report that white doctor's family. Who's gonna believe you? You gonna tell the police that the rich doctor's wife, that you is maid fo', is hurtin' her children? An' they gonna believe *you*? Oh no, Bert, you the crazy one now."

"Well, what am I supposed to do?" Liz pleaded. "I can't let that lady keep hurtin' them like that. I can't, Claman. I just can't." She rested her head against the kitchen wall and began to sob. "I just can't let her hurt ma' babies no more."

Claman stood by quietly, his mind racing as to how to help without creating a mess for his wife or himself.

She snapped her head up and looked up at him, wide-eyed. "They could live here, Claman. We could adopt 'em. Mizzuz Connor don't want them babies. We could raise 'em. We could make room ...."

"Oh, Lord," Claman exclaimed, "now I know you're crazy. We can't take them kids. How you gonna get them kids here? You think that doctor is just gonna give up his kids 'cuz you say his wife is crazy? He ain't never gonna admit his wife is crazy. He know it, you know it, but he ain't never gonna admit that."

"Well, I gots to do *something*," Liz shouted as she paced to and from the living room.

"What we've got to do is talk sense here, Bert," Claman reasoned. "You ain't gonna help them babies by runnin' to the police. The police ain't never gonna believe you over that doctor and his mizzuz. They ain't gonna believe a colored maid sayin' things like that against some rich white family."

Realizing her pacing was delivering no answers, Liz sat down on the couch again. Tears rolled down her round face. She stared straight ahead, exhausted.

Claman sat beside her and took her hand. "Do you remember what they done to that colored boy in Jackson, Mississippi, when we was still down south? They killed that po' boy just for whistlin' at a white girl. Now, this ain't Jackson, but it ain't all that much different, neither. Ain't no colored maid ever gonna be accusin' no white doctor's family of nothin'.'"

Turning to him, Liz said with defeat, "But I've gotta help ma' babies, Claman. I've just got to."

"You are helpin' them, Bert. You're lovin' them like they momma never can and never will. Now, what's gonna happen if you go off and report that doctor's wife to the police? You gonna lose that fight, Bert. You know you will." His tone turned tender. "Then you're gonna lose yo' job, Bert, or worse. And who's gonna love them babies then? Then all they've got is they crazy momma. No, no, Bertie. You just gotta keep goin' up there every week and lovin' them babies as best you can. There ain't no other way. Those babies need you, Bertie. They got no one else to love 'em."

His words drifted off as she cried. She raised her eyes to the small wooden cross hanging above Claman's favorite easy chair. In a faded voice she asked, "Oh, Lord, what are we gonna do, Lord? What am I gonna do?"

Following his wife's gaze, Claman rose and lifted the cross from its hook. Her great-grandmother had whittled it after running away from her slave master. She had outlived both Liz's mother, grandmother, and most of the rest of her family, dying just before her hundred-and-third birthday when Liz was a young woman. Claman hadn't known her well, but knew everyone in Liz's family called her grandma because she was the revered matriarch of the clan. "You remember yo' grandma's stories, Bert? She found strength. She found strength to keep on goin' with God's help. And she gave you the cross 'cuz she knew you're strong enough, to keep goin' an' to fight yo' way through anything in life. You remember? She told you that before she died, when she gave you this."

Liz, heartened by his words, stopped crying and reached up to receive the family icon he held out for her.

"Bert, you take this cross with you up to that doctor's house. And you keep remindin' yo'self, with this ol' cross, that you can do this, Bert. With God's help, I know you can. Yo' grandma knew you can too. Those babies need you, Bert. You've got to keep goin'."

Liz cradled the cross on her lap, sniffling back her remaining tears. As she stared at it, she thought of her grandma's journey as a young slave girl and the stories she'd told until her death at one hundred and three. Liz murmured her plea again. "Oh, Lord, Grandma, what are we gonna do? What am I gonna do?"

Things were calm at home that night, after Liz and Mom had their little chat. We never knew what went on between them, but Mark and I were glad Mom was quiet and demure through the rest of the night.

The next day was an every-other-Wednesday, a Liz day that week. She slipped in so quietly I didn't hear her arrive. Taking Claman's words to heart, she'd come early to find a place for her grandmother's cross. She propped it up inside the laundry cupboard above the washing machine. She knew she would see it there but, most likely, it wouldn't be spotted by Mom. "Every time I come in here, Lord," she whispered, "I'm gonna see that cross and remember what Grandma done.

If she could keep runnin' to freedom, I can keep comin' here and lovin' them babies. But just like Grandma did, I'm gonna need your help."

That day, Chrissy was still not well enough to move from bed. Worse, she was so traumatized that she wasn't even willing to recover. She still refused to eat. I was terrified that Chrissy would starve and die, or that her despondency would never leave her, and I would be alone forever.

Liz, however, would have none of that. She simply would never let any of us stay in a funk. She didn't push us. She never needed to. Whenever she wanted us to do something very important, she brought her round brown face down to ours and looked us straight in the eyes. When she had our full attention, she spoke to us in the kindest voice we had ever heard. We followed her words as if some mystical power charged each request, working within us so that we simply wanted to do whatever she wanted.

When Liz went into Chrissy's bedroom, I followed close behind. Chrissy was still in bed, eyes worn-out red from continual crying. Her face was ashen. Fear gripped me again. Chrissy looked as if she was getting worse. I gasped and burst into tears. Liz pulled me to her side so I could hide my face in her skirt.

She sat on the edge of the bed, leaned over to kiss Chrissy's forehead, and started stroking her hair. Then began her hypnotic coaxing. "C'mon Chrissy, you know you've got to eat, child." Her sweet voice drifted through the air like angels carried every word on their wings. The gentle kindness was mesmerizing. Feeling the power of her love, I lifted my head. I almost wished I was hurt too so Liz would send those words my way.

She continued her persuasion. "I know you're hurtin', baby. You know, me and Todd miss you playin' with us. Won't you c'mon and walk fo' me? C'mon an' walk to the kitchen and let me fix yo' favorite breakfast. I'm makin' waffles. C'mon baby, let's go."

Liz stood up, holding Chrissy's hand. Chrissy slowly nodded and tried to comply, but winced in pain as she started to move. That caused her to burst into tears again and cave back onto the bed.

Liz immediately sat on the bed again. "It's okay, baby. Liz here now. It's gonna be all right. We'll take it slow. Now, c'mon, let's try again, baby, real slow. I'll help ya'."

Then I saw something I hadn't seen in Chrissy for days: resolve. Liz's coaxing got Chrissy back on her feet that morning. This seemed nothing short of miraculous to me. Gradually, she seemed better and better. Her color came back. Even her smile came back.

"What happened to you, Chrissy?" I asked innocently later as Liz straightened her bedroom. Chrissy looked at me and began to cry.

Liz quickly said, "Now, Todd, why don't you go get me ma' broom?" As I left to do so, I heard her encourage Chrissy again, "It's all right, baby girl. We're gonna move on and get you better real quick."

We all seemed to—needed to—forget what had happened. Liz knew that and kept close to Chrissy all day long. Chrissy still needed bed rest, but I followed Liz on her every activity. We made frequent stops at Chrissy's room for a few moments, to play a game or try to get her to laugh.

That night, when it was near quitting time, Liz did something that was strictly taboo in the Connor home: she brought Chrissy a huge piece of chocolate cake just before she left. "Now, I know I ain't suppose' to do this. And I know yo' momma gonna be mad at me." She paused, then continued in a whisper. "But we just gonna take that risk today. C'mon, Chrissy, you sit up b'fo' me and Todd eat this cake all by ourselves," she teased, and burst into laughter.

Chrissy struggled, but sat up beaming. As she eagerly dug into the cake, we both heard the words we dreaded each night on Liz days.

"I've got to go home now, babies. You kids got to behave. I'm comin' back tomorrow mornin'. You think ...."

Our little trio was abruptly interrupted as the door swung open. Mom burst in, eyes blazing when she saw the cake on Chrissy's bed. "What's going on?" she shouted, looking at Liz. "What are you doing? You know the children aren't supposed to have sweets before dinner. What the hell are you ..."

Liz stood to face Mom. She said nothing but moved about a foot in front of her, presenting herself an opposing force. Liz's face said it all. She stared at Mom with a look that even I knew clearly said, "You'd better not go there." Her large, round frame created a wall in front of Mom, shielding Chrissy and me. Her immovable presence spoke loudly enough for even crazy-eyed Mom to hear.

Mom's rage quickly evaporated, replaced by the fear we had seen the day before. "Wuh. Huh," she sputtered. Then, in a vain attempt to maintain an appearance of control, she warned, "Well, you make sure those kids don't make a mess."

"Now, Mizzuz Connor." Liz spoke slowly and deliberately, carefully holding her anger behind polite but forceful words. "You know Chrissy's still hurt. Now, I know you've got yo' rules. But I've been takin' care a her today, just like yesterday. An' I think she needs cheerin' up. An' we both know why she needs cheerin' up, don't we, Mizzuz Connor?"

Liz paused and waited a few seconds to watch Mom's fear grow, assuring a rebalance of power for the moment. "So, we're gonna let her have that cake, 'cuz she needs it now. We're just gonna have to break some a yo' rules today. 'Cuz Liz here now. You undastand, Mizzuz Connor?"

Mom's eyes watered as a mixture of fear and powerlessness consumed her. She huffed a small, "Well ...." Then, not being able to form more words and too intimidated to say anything else, she vanished from the room, closing the door behind her.

Liz turned back to us and said, "It's gonna be all right now, babies. I'm goin' to my home now but I'll be back in the mornin'. You be good 'til then, okay?"

We nodded obediently, feeling as if we had just been covered in a protective force field of love.

Turning toward the doorway, Liz mumbled under her breath, "I think yo' momma gonna be good fo' now too. At least 'til next time."

Chapter 4

Liz's interactions that week with Mom seemed to keep her in check for some time. Chrissy gradually recovered and we all, thankfully, let the memory of those events fade.

Summer faded away as well. Chrissy began kindergarten that fall, leaving every morning with Mark when he went to school. I was jealous of her because she got to play with friends every morning while I had to stay home without her. But she was jealous of me too, because now on Liz days I had Liz all to myself until Chrissy came home at lunchtime. The hard days, for me, were non-Liz days when I was home alone with Mom. I withdrew, playing as silently as possible in my room or downstairs out of her sight, or slipping out to get lost in our backyard or visit Mrs. Wagner as often as I dared.

Mom's rages resurfaced occasionally, subjecting Mark, Chrissy, and me to regular screaming and irregular beatings. She got better at hurting us where Liz wouldn't see our bruises. As sad as it sounds, over the next months we were just grateful she did nothing more than hit us.

Soon—but never soon enough for us kids, Christmas was coming. We loved that time of year. Of course all children love

Christmas. But for us, it wasn't just about a mythical Santa who loved children and brought them presents. Christmas was a time when Mom seemed almost happy.

Every year we kids tussled over the Sears & Roebuck "Wish Book" catalog that arrived around Thanksgiving. We pored over it. Mark and Chrissy were old enough to write letters to Santa telling him everything they wanted. I cut out pictures and glued them to paper as my "letter." That year, at the top of Mark's wish list was to get a pair of "moon shoes." The space program fascinated everyone in the '60s and everything "outer space" was the rage as America focused on putting a man on the moon. He showed us a picture of the "moon shoes." They were plastic, with large springs on the bottom of the soles. He told Chrissy and me that he had a note from the President of the United States that said if he got those shoes from Santa, he'd get to go on the moon trip.

Chrissy and I, of course, bought the story, as we did every one of his tall tales. We loved Mark because he was so much fun, and always looked up to him. Even when we found out he had been pulling our legs with one of his made-up stories, we never took it that he was being mean to us.

Mark also brought life to our darkened world in another, very different way. He was a prodigy at the piano. Chrissy and I were too young to start lessons. We had to wait until we each turned six. Mark had been playing since Chrissy was born, and played the piano more than one could imagine for a kid his age. But to us, it seemed normal. We didn't know how amazing he was until we were much older. By eight, Mark was mastering Chopin. I always thought Chopin was some sort of baker because his name was pronounced "show-pan." I wondered what a baker had to do with a piano. Every morning the sweet melodies of Chopin's beautiful ballads serenaded us from the family room piano, resounding through the house like caressing waves that gently awakened the new day.

"What's that one called, Mark?" Liz would call downstairs with interest. Liz didn't know much about music, but she knew Mark was special. She invited us all into the joy she breathed into everyday life. "Don't you just love yo' brother playin' that beautiful music, Christine? You must be somethin' special to have that music playin' fo' ya. Like God saying you a queen or somethin', playing beautiful music fo' ya all the time. Oh, yo' majesty, you come on and set a while so's I can fetch yo' breakfast." Liz pointed to the chair and bowed as Christine curtseyed before taking her seat at the table. This was followed by Liz's infectious laugh, which had us all laughing in no time.

"Royalty" were regular visitors at the Connor home for Chrissy and me, a common element in our play times. Chrissy, especially, had an amazingly vibrant imagination. Looking back, I realize survival required it, because of our desperate need to escape the fear and dread inflicted on us by Mom's instability.

At lunch that day, Chrissy insisted we play her favorite game, "Queen," as Liz served us peanut butter sandwiches. Before long, Queen Chrissy declared, "Look! My skin is brown!" She had peeled back the bread and spread the peanut butter along her forearms. "Everyone in my kingdom has brown skin," she haughtily declared to Mark and me, before smiling toward Liz, as if she and Liz were now the only two members in her kingdom.

Mark, who always ate fast, just gulped his last bite and laughed at Chrissy as he went back downstairs to the piano. Liz's back was to us as she worked at the kitchen counter, baking that night's dessert. I was now the only person in the room without brown skin. Queen Chrissy quickly proclaimed I was excluded from the kingdom. So naturally, I opened my sandwich and copied her. Soon I too was covered with brown peanut butter.

"Look, Liz!" Chrissy declared. "We're all brown like you!"

Liz turned and shrieked, "Oh, no! What are you kids doin'? Now, look what a mess you made." She grabbed a wet washcloth and, clearly annoyed, started wiping Chrissy's arms.

Chrissy's eyes filled with tears as she looked up at Liz. "But we wanted to be just like you."

Liz's stern look softened. "Oh, child, peanut butter ain't gonna do that. Sweet child." She kissed Chrissy's forehead, put the cloth in the sink, and turned back to her work at the counter. All of a sudden we saw a puff of white fill the air. Then she turned around, revealing her arms and face covered with baking flour.

"Now, my skin turned white," she teased Chrissy. "Are you sure only brown folks can be a part a yo' kingdom? Please, Queen Chrissy, can I be part a yo' kingdom, even though I am white now?"

Chrissy and I laughed uproariously.

"Child, don't matter what color yo' skin is," Liz continued, moving in close to Chrissy with the washcloth again. "You is part a me, an' I is part a you. Ain't nothin' gonna change that. Now, we need to get you cleaned up b'fo' yo' momma comes out and sees us like this. She ain't gonna be happy with us. What's Queen Christine gonna say then?"

After cleaning the peanut butter off us and the flour off herself, Liz leaned down and put her arms around both of us. She whispered, "Don't make no difference 'bout yo' white skin, or mine bein' brown. We are the same inside. You undastand? I loves you babies. You are my little white babies and I am yo' momma, even though I is big and brown. Ain't nothin' gonna change that, not ever. Okay?"

Later that day as Liz was leaving, Chrissy and I went through our usual tearful goodbyes.

"G'night, Mizzuz Connor." Liz raised her voice from the laundry room back door, hoping Mom would acknowledge. No response. Mom was holed up in her office at the back of the house.

Mom's lack of response was not unusual. It had become more frequent since Liz asserted herself after Mom's attack on Chrissy. Liz was gaining a certain amount of power over Mom, having made it clear she knew what was going on and would not stay neutral about it any longer. On Liz days, Mom just went about her business as if we did not exist, a welcome relief for Chrissy and me.

Every December, our home was decorated like something out of a Norman Rockwell painting. Mom and Dad threw numerous parties during the month, and Christmas Eve always heralded a big bash at the Connor house.

This Christmas Eve was no different. Chrissy and I were playing downstairs as the first guests arrived. We could hear the partiers' cheers from the moment their footsteps clattered on the floor above us. Soon Mark came downstairs with a bulge under his shirt. He looked back carefully to ensure he wasn't seen. Then he revealed his prize for all of us to share—a pilfered pound cake, still wrapped in its tin and paper packaging. Soon the stolen treasure disappeared, leaving only crumbs as we all sat on the couch watching the latest television episode of *Get Smart*.

About halfway through the show, Mom came downstairs to check on us. When we heard her steps on the stairs, Mark jumped up and turned off the TV. Chrissy shoved the cake tin under the sofa. Then we all sat frozen.

"Where are you, kids?" Mom called. Her voice was sweet. Our shoulders relaxed. When she appeared, we were unable to remove our frozen position—this time not from fear but more from awe. She was radiantly beautiful. She wore a long green gown, with a black velour top. With her dark hair and red lipstick, she looked like a china doll dressed as a Christmas queen.

"There you are, darlings," she chimed as she came over to pat us all on the heads. Behind her were several well-dressed women, apparently on a tour of the house and the reason Mom was pretending affection toward us.

I let out a wail. For a split moment, I had believed in the sweet tones and radiant glow of the benevolent Christmas queen. My breath had been taken away by my mother's beauty and charm. But as soon as the other ladies appeared, I knew. The sweetness and radiant beauty of the Christmas queen was only an apparition, an act to impress her guests. Mom pretended my outburst was that of a small child who had passed his bedtime, and scooted us off to bed with false playfulness.

As with most of their parties, Mom and Dad didn't get to bed until hours after midnight. As with most children on Christmas morning, we were awake and up before the crack of dawn. I don't know how Mom did it, with her obvious mental condition, but she was always cheerful on Christmas morning, regardless of the lack of sleep or the hangover she inevitably endured after the party.

All three of us kids got lots of great presents, but Mark was wild about getting what he wanted most—the coveted "moon shoes." When he wore them, whether walking or jumping, his feet sprung up and down, supposedly simulating the weightlessness of an astronaut. Mark was over-the-moon excited.

The holiday fantasy of ours being the ideal family always cheered Mom. Her Christmas glow usually took some time to wear off, probably because of all the parties and the beautiful clothes and jewelry Dad showered on her. This year the partying and gifts were no different, but there was no lingering cheer.

The Monday after Christmas I woke in the dark to Chrissy

crawling into my bed. "Shhh. Listen," she whispered. Angry voices rose from the other end of the house. Mom and Dad were yelling at each other in the kitchen. A door slammed. Footsteps stomped down the hall, followed by the slamming of the door to our parents' room. Chrissy and I huddled under the covers until we knew it was safe before slipping quietly into the basement family room. It was a long time before Mark got up. He helped us fix cereal for breakfast. He also made sandwiches for us at lunchtime. We barely saw Mom. When we did, her eyes were flaring. When she wasn't in her room, we stayed out of her way until we were forced to come for dinner. I don't know if Dad even came home that night. He wasn't there when I went to bed, and he wasn't there when I got up in the morning.

Liz felt the tension too when she arrived on Tuesday. Worry grew on her face through the morning but she tried to shield us children from her concern. That afternoon, I was slow in finishing my lunch. Liz had moved on from the kitchen and Chrissy and Mark, who had finished eating, found other things to do. I was not hungry but knew I needed to clean my plate before I left the table.

I was bored. I noticed Mom's purse on the kitchen counter. I slipped out of my chair and began rummaging through it—a forbidden activity.

Before I knew it, Mom was behind me. She yanked me by my arm and began rhythmically slapping me across my face, all the while screaming, "What are you doing in my things?"

Mom had clearly forgotten it was a Liz day. She began dragging me back to her room. As we rounded the final corner of the hallway, Liz came rushing from the back of the house. She and Mom nearly collided.

Mom halted and let out a startled, "What the hell?" She unleashed a tirade on Liz. But Liz stood her ground firmly, blocking the hallway from where Mom was dragging me.

"What goin' on here, Mizzuz Connor?" Liz spoke levelly. Her countenance was grave, seemingly as unmovable as her frame, still blocking the way.

Mom tried to collect herself but rage prevented her. "He needs to be punished," she growled.

Liz said nothing. She didn't move.

Mom barely flinched as she segued from her intended path. She pulled me toward my room, tossed me past the threshold, and slammed the door shut. She then clicked the hook-and-eye lock installed high on the outside, so I couldn't get out. This was a typical punishment for my siblings and me: to lock us in our rooms as if we were caged animals.

For a moment, I heard only silence. Then Mom called out, "Mark? Where are you? Time to leave for your dentist appointment. Christine, you're coming too. Everybody get to the car. Now!"

There was silence again.

From farther away I heard Mom snap at Liz. "He better still be in that room when I get back."

A few moments later I heard the front door slam and the car drive down Shady Hills Lane.

After the sound of the car faded, Liz opened my door. "Hey little man," she said. "What'd you do to get yo' momma so upset with you?"

I lowered my head in shame. "I was going through her purse."

"An' you know you're not s'posed to, right? Ladies don't like it when folks go through they purses without permission." Her voice shifted from gentle to teasing. "So what was you lookin' fo' in there? You think you gonna find some candy or somethin'? You know she ain't carryin' nothin' you int'rested in, child."

I didn't respond.

"C'mon, Todd. I got a purse and you got permission to look

in it. Let's go see if we can't find somethin' interestin' in that ol' thang."

Liz's purse was enormous compared to the small clutch my mother carried. Rummaging through it, we pulled out everything from wadded tissues to shoelaces. "Why, there's the button from my Sunday coat," she exclaimed. "Now I can sew that back on. Ooo-wee, I've been lookin' everywhere for that."

Then Liz pulled out a folded wallet, so thick it strained the strap that latched it closed.

"Wow, you must be rich," I said.

"Yes, I am rich, little man. Here, I'm gonna show you all my riches." She unsnapped the wallet and out fell dozens of pictures, mostly of children—some older than me, some younger. She told me stories about each of them. The kids came alive as I learned about the children Liz had taken care of over the years. Some were relatives, but mostly they were children of white families she had worked for. She kept the pictures as memorials of all the kids she had loved over the years. I was lost in the moment and found a deep sense of comfort, feeling that somehow I had lots of brothers and sisters who, like me, were deeply loved by Liz.

The delight of our time together shattered as Dad came bustling through the front door. "Hello, Elizabeth. Don't mind me. I came home early to get some paperwork done."

He looked down at me and then glared at Liz. "Jane told me Todd was being punished and needed to stay in his room."

She got his meaning. "Yes, sir. C'mon, Todd. Let's get you back there."

After she returned me to my room, I heard her lobbying for my early release as Dad poured himself a drink at the living room wet bar. I couldn't make out the words, but surmised the negotiations were unsuccessful.

Sometime later, Liz whispered through the door where I was still sitting, listening for anything interesting. "Bye, Todd.

I loves you, baby. Sorry I had to put you back in there. But I'm sure yo' daddy gonna let you out soon."

I heard her quietly lift the lock hook. She opened the door and knelt down to where I was sitting. "C'mon baby. Let me hold you b'fo' I go."

I clung to her as long as I could, not wanting to let go. She finally unwrapped my arms from around her neck and pushed herself to her feet. "Be good now, baby," she said as she quietly closed the door and replaced the hook.

I heard her call goodbye to my father, then the sound of the back door closing as she left. My heart sank. I didn't have any way of knowing how long I would be stuck in my room. I was afraid to call out to Dad, because that might anger him. He would probably ignore me anyway, but when he drank, he could get mean. So I just sat.

Soon after, I heard him head for the front door, his keys jingling. I heard his car pull out and drive away. I tried not to panic. I sat, huddled against the door, as night came on. When it got dark, I was too afraid to get up and turn on a light.

It was late—I don't know how late, before I heard Mom come home with Chrissy and Mark. As she came down the hallway past my room, she stopped. "Oh." The sound of the word was unusually concerned.

She unlatched the door and, in the glow of the hall light, saw me still curled up near the door, waiting for my release. "Oh honey, did your father leave you in here all this time?"

I looked behind her to see if anyone else was with her, to whom she was playing the part of attentive parent. Surprisingly, no one was there. That made me even more cautious.

She picked me up, sat on the edge of my bed, and held me as if I were a two-year-old. She attempted to rock me as she sang "Rockabye Baby."

I tried to trust the moment but simply could not do so. She was not Liz.

Soon, she either noticed my distrust or simply emptied her limited tank of affection. She slid me from her lap onto my bed. "It's time for you to go to sleep."

Starving for dinner, I began to protest but thought better of it, not wanting Mom's rare kindness to explode into something more common.

When Liz returned Thursday morning, she asked me if I'd been a good boy since she'd left. I understood the real question she was asking. I nodded, but told her nothing about being locked home by myself.

Mom went out in the morning, then stayed in her room after returning from a luncheon with a few of her friends. The day passed quietly, and all too quickly. Chrissy and I were even more clingy with Liz when it was time for her to leave. Tuesday and her return felt like a lifetime away. After giving us as many hugs as she could, she finally told us it was time to go. She called her goodbye to our mother. No response. She called goodbye again. Still no answer. Liz tried one last time, almost yelling now. "Good night, Mizzuz Connor."

"Good night," Mom acknowledged vaguely her from her distant location.

Turning back to us, Liz warned firmly, "Now, you kids be good, hear? You mind yo' momma, undastand?"

Liz looked worried. She undoubtedly had noticed Mom's eyes flashing in frenzied instability again. Chrissy and I nodded compliantly, barely holding back tears. We all knew something was coming but hoped things would not end badly, as they had so many times before.

Liz's furrowed brow betrayed her comforting words as she spoke. "Well, yo' momma must be tired from her day. So I'm gonna get you some cereal and make that yo' dinna tonight. You like that?"

We were elated, as sugary cereals for dinner were almost never allowed. Without taking off her coat, Liz filled three

Todd Connor

bowls with heaping amounts of cereal and milk. "Now, you kids take yo' food downstairs and stay quiet tonight, ya hear? Tell yo' brother to make himself some cereal when he's hungry. And ask Mark to tell you when yo' bedtime is. Then just be good and go to bed then, okay?"

We knew she was trying to keep us safe after she left. There was no objection on our part. We all had felt the heightened sense of danger over the past few days, as Mom was clearly slipping. Liz kissed the top of our heads and handed us our bowls. We took them downstairs to the family room as we heard her leave through the laundry room door. Mark's beautiful piano music continued. Chrissy pulled out a board game for the two of us to play.

Before my sister and I ate even half our dinner, Mom raced down the stairs, her eyes ablaze with the crazed look we all feared. Chrissy and I froze. Mark abruptly stopped playing, his fingers resting on the keys.

With long strides she quickly covered the distance to the piano. She slammed the cover down, hard, on Mark's hands. He screeched and wrenched his torso as he tried to pull his hands from their pinned position.

Pressing down on the piano key cover with one hand, Mom raised her other. She was holding her tan camelhair coat. The coat usually hung in the closet near the front door, under a shelf where Mark's model paints were stored out of Chrissy's and my reach. There was a large blue stain dripped down the front.

"What did you do to my coat?" she yelled. Her voice rose even louder and she leaned harder on the piano cover. "Tell me!"

Mark was now screaming in pain. Chrissy and I instinctively moved towards the stairs to escape to our hiding places. Mom took a side step, blocking our way and letting Mark free his injured fingers.

"I'm sorry," Mark wailed. "I … was getting my airplane paint and …"

With her eyes flaring into full crazy mode, Mom wheeled back on him. She grabbed his arm, yanking him from the piano bench to the floor. She reached down, grabbed his leg, and began to drag him. One of his prized moon shoes fell off. She snapped it up by the spring on the heel. As if the spring were a whip handle, she lashed his head with the hard, plastic shoe and screamed, "You brat, you need to be punished!"

Mom yanked Mark by his hair and pulled him to the stairwell. Dazed by the blow to his head, he struggled to get back on his feet. The look on his face was mixed terror and pain as she dragged him along backwards. He slipped and almost took her down with him. As he fell, Mom pulled a handful of hair out of his head. He screamed again.

Oh, Mark, I thought, you're next. Chrissy and I exploded in tears. It was the only relief we had available. It was also all we could offer our brother, whose horrified eyes stared back at us as he scrambled to keep up with Mom's march upstairs.

We heard muffled sounds above us as she dragged him into her room. The door slammed behind them.

Our hiding places were upstairs, but we were not about to go up there now. We briefly looked at each other. We instinctively knew what to do, like people in war movies—run for whatever cover was available. Chrissy scrambled in one direction and I in another. She tried to hide under the TV console. I squeezed between the freezer and the wall at the utility end of the basement. I pushed myself so far between the two that it was hard to breathe. Somehow this made me feel safe—if I barely fit in the space, maybe no one bigger could get me. I covered my ears as best I could, trying to not hear, trying to pretend it wasn't happening. The next minutes, which felt like hours, were filled with the familiar, nightmarish sounds so common in the Connor house: Mom's condemning screams about needing punishment, pleading cries of "No, Mommy. Please, Mommy."

Then, silence. I am not sure when I noticed it. The silence was barely broken by the sound of Mom's footsteps overhead, going down the hallway to Mark's room. Frozen in my hiding place, I listened for any sign that Mark was okay, even though I knew he wasn't. I heard Mark's door slam, then the sound of Mom walking back to her room and shutting the door.

Was it over, I wondered. Chrissy and I remained in hiding for several more minutes, until we were sure it was safe to come out. We crept upstairs. We were as quiet as possible. We didn't talk. We didn't even look at each other. Even though it couldn't have been later than six o'clock, we put on our pajamas and crawled into our beds.

Waiting for sleep to take me away from the horror, I kept telling myself maybe tomorrow would be better. Maybe tomorrow would somehow be another Liz Day.

Both Chrissy and I woke up early the next morning, before Mom. Dad was long gone, as usual, to see hospital patients.

"Let's go see Mark, Todd." Chrissy whispered so as to not wake Mom.

I didn't say anything, but fear shot through me. Chrissy always seemed braver than I. I don't know if it was because she was older or if she was just made like that. Either way, I usually followed what she said and did. We snuck down the hallway to Mark's room. As we slowly turned the doorknob, we heard his labored breathing and faint moans. We crawled into the barely lit room until we saw "it": a huge black eye. There was also something on his arms, something white. Something I had never seen before. It looked like white towels with tape holding them onto his arms.

When he saw us, he didn't say anything. He just looked at us with a sadness I had never seen on his face before. With difficulty, he held up his arms. His face grimaced with the pain of that movement. Both his arms, from wrist to upper arms, were covered with white material that had faint red streaks on it.

Chrissy immediately knew what had happened because of what had happened to her. She recoiled and backed into me as if she had seen a ghost. With one single motion, she was out the door. Not really knowing what had happened to Chrissy or why she was so afraid, I slipped closer toward Mark.

"Mark, what are those things on your arms?" I asked innocently. "Did Mommy put those on you? What are they for?"

He just lowered his arms and cried. Turning his head away, he refused to look at me.

"Mark. Mark, what are those things?"

"Todd, get outta there! She's coming!" Chrissy hovered at the doorway and urged me, too loud for a whisper but still trying to not be overheard. It was obvious she wasn't coming into the room again. "I hear her. She's coming! C'mon Todd."

I scurried out. Chrissy and I rushed back to our beds, pulled the covers up, and lay motionless.

Mom was moving around in her room. Thankfully, she seemed to be completely unaware of our venturing out to see Mark. When I felt it was safe, I got out of my bed and went in to sit on Chrissy's.

"What are those things on Mark's arms?" I asked.

"They're bandages," she whispered back.

"What's that?" I asked.

"They're like great big Band-Aids."

"What are they for?"

Chrissy stopped answering my questions and just looked off into space.

Todd Connor

"What are they for?" I insisted.

"Dad puts 'em on when you get hurt." Chrissy's voice was soft. She paused, then said, "Like getting cut."

That was enough information for me. Mom hurt Mark bad enough to require Dad to patch him up more than I'd ever seen before. I didn't know anything about being cut. I didn't want to know any more.

Chrissy and I stayed in her room a while longer. We didn't know what day it was. We just hoped it was a Liz day. Then we heard it—the sound of the key in the back door, the opening of that door, and Liz rustling herself inside.

We both immediately ran toward her. Rounding the last corner, we halted abruptly. Mom was standing in the hallway. She had been walking back to the bedroom wing after grabbing her morning coffee. She jostled the cup as we almost whirled into her. Chrissy and I looked at her eyes to gauge her countenance. Mom glanced back over her shoulder at the sound of Liz's arrival. Then she registered what we were up to: running to see Liz. Her eyes narrowed and her gaze flared. She hated that we loved Liz so much.

We didn't wait for what might happen next. We instinctively changed course and ran back to our rooms.

Liz saw Mom in the hallway and said, "Good mornin', Mizzuz Connor." We heard them talk for a few minutes. Then we heard Mom walk back to her office and close the door. Both Chrissy and I ran to Liz.

"Well, hi!" came her cheerful voice as soon as she saw us. Her greeting came with her usual bright smile. Her teeth always looked whiter than ours. Maybe they were. Maybe they looked that way against her dark skin. Or maybe we just saw them that way because everything about her brightened our world.

"What you two up to? You watchin' cartoons?" she asked, her voice as bright as her smile. "No, you two just got up, I can tell. My, my, you is lazy bones today. You be layin' 'round all day if ol' Liz didn't show up. Ain't that right? Sho' enough, you two be layin' 'round all day like two big ol' lazy bones." Her teasing was followed by her usual laugh.

We were so thrilled to see her we couldn't speak. The terror of the last twelve hours was gone, and our guardian angel had stepped out of heaven again to greet us. We just stared at her for a moment and then both of us leapt forward and planted our faces against her soft thighs.

"We love you, Liz," Chrissy exclaimed.

"Yeah, we love you Liz-e-beth," I joined in, trying to hold back my tears of sheer relief.

"Well, I loves you both too. So much. C'mon, let's set awhile." With our small bodies cemented to both of her legs she struggled to maneuver backwards to the sturdy stool in the laundry room. Finally, she made it there and rested her large frame on it. Chrissy climbed on one pillowy leg and I on the other. With our heads resting on her shoulders and chest, she hummed. We listened to the sound murmuring inside her chest. Every once in a while, she stopped to kiss our foreheads. Then we heard her breathing and her heart beating softly. To this day, I don't think I've known a sweeter sound. We would have gladly stayed there our whole lives.

But at some point, even her well-cushioned legs couldn't take us anymore. "You two must be gettin' hungry. How 'bout Liz make you some breakfast?" She stood as she spoke, and started toward the kitchen. Chrissy and I trailed behind her. "Where's Mark at? He a lazy bones today, too?"

We stopped, as if rooted in place, while she continued walking. The peace we had felt shattered as reality came back and images of Mark crashed their way into our minds again.

Finally Liz noticed we had not moved or responded. "What you two doin'? Ain't you hungry? Oh, are we playin' that 'Simon Says' game like we played the otha day?" She turned from the cupboard where she had pulled out cereal boxes, glanced at us, and began gathering bowls and spoons. She shuffled over to the refrigerator for the milk. "Okay, Simon says c'mon over and set yo'self down fo' yo' breakfast."

Locked in our fear, we still didn't move.

"What's wrong w'ich you two?" Her voice became slightly annoyed, as if we were being defiant. "C'mon, we can't be playin' games all day. Now c'mon, it's time to sit down fo' yo' breakfast."

We remained frozen in the doorway, staring at her, not knowing what we could possibly say.

Her face suddenly turned from annoyance to alarm. She stopped in place too. With grave seriousness, she asked, "Where Mark at?"

That was apparently the cue we needed. It was the first hole punctured into the dam to let all the pressure out. We both exploded with tears and ran to bury our faces against her legs again.

"Oh, now babies, it's gonna be all right. Liz here now." Her murmured words were comforting but her voice sounded worried. She rubbed our backs in silence for a moment. When she spoke again, she spoke with more resolve, as if strengthening herself for what she would find. "Gonna be all right. Liz here now. It'll be all right now. Liz is gonna see what's goin' on with yo' brotha. An' whateva it is, Liz is gonna make it betta."

We clung to her legs until she managed to squirm away and sit us down at the kitchen table. Then she moved faster than we thought possible. She grabbed two cups, filled them with orange juice, and set them in front of us with so much speed they nearly spilled. Before we knew what was happening she darted for the hallway to the bedrooms. "You two drink yo' juice. I'll be back in a minute," she called out as she vanished from sight.

We waited a long time for Liz to come back. When she

finally did, her forehead was furrowed. Trying to hold back tears, she looked around the kitchen frantically. She found a small towel, moistened it in the sink, wrung it out, and folded into a compress. Turning from the sink, she noticed us again. Instantly, her worried look vanished, replaced by compassion and concern. "Oh babies, you've been brave, huh?"

The dam of tears broke again as we stared at her, knowing she knew what had happened to Mark. She squeezed her marshmallowy arms around us and whispered, "Now, babies, you've got to be very good today. You've got to play quietly downstairs and not fuss. Liz is gonna help Mark today. You undastand? Liz got to be with Mark today. So you got to play by yo'selves and ..." She broke off as tears welled in her eyes. Pulling herself together, she continued, "You've got to stay outta yo' momma's way today. You just play by yo'selves, downstairs, outta her way. You undastand, babies?" She kept on to get acknowledgement. "You undastand, Chrissy?"

Chrissy nodded.

"You undastand, Todd?"

I also nodded, as neither of us could speak through our tight throats. She released us from her enveloping hold and, without a word, Chrissy and I silently proceeded to the downstairs family room where we stayed, doing exactly as Liz said—keeping as quiet as we could.

We heard Liz make breakfast for Mark. "Oh, Lord, what am I gonna do? What am I gonna do?" she murmured repeatedly as she worked.

Midmorning, Mom emerged for more coffee, only to find no hot coffee and our dirty breakfast dishes still on the table. We heard her huff in disgust and go to the laundry room, where dirty clothes from the previous night were still in the hamper. Angry now, we heard her footsteps headed toward the bedrooms. "Elizabeth?" she hollered. "Are you here? How come my coffee isn't made? And you haven't done a thing ...."

As she opened Mark's bedroom door, she found Liz sitting next to Mark's bed, softly whispering to him, "It's gonna be all right Mark. Liz here now."

"What the hell are you doing in here? I need my coffee and this house is a mess! What the hell are you doing with my son in here?"

Liz stood, controlled temper visible on her face, and spoke carefully. "Now, Mizzuz Connor, you've got to calm down. Mark needs his rest and quiet."

Mom, not calming down at all, yelled, "I don't need to calm down! This is *my* house! Who the hell are you to tell me to calm down?"

Liz rushed to the door and kept on moving, her body's heavy momentum pushing Mom to the side and into the hallway. Liz closed Mark's door behind her.

"Now, Mizzuz Connor, we're gonna talk about this, but you best calm down." Sensing her attempt to diffuse the situation was not working, Liz turned her back on Mom and proceeded down the hallway. Mom, still raging, followed, two steps behind Liz all the way. Once in the kitchen, Liz went straight to the desk where the family telephone sat.

Mom was still yelling. "Who the hell do you think you are to talk to me in my house like that?"

Liz, focused on controlling her anger, didn't respond. She calmly sat down at the desk, picked up the telephone, and dialed the operator. After a moment she said, "Yes, I need the hospital, please." She paused, then spoke politely. "Is it an emergency? Well, I think it is, but ..." She paused again. "Does that mean you're gonna send an ambulance? Okay. Then yes, it is an emergency. The address? Yes, it's ..."

Mom lunged for the phone and slammed her hand on the base to disconnect the call. "What the hell are you doing?" she screamed, staring at Liz with pure hatred.

Liz's face was without emotion as she responded politely

but matter-of-factly. "Mizzuz Connor, Mark is hurt bad. He needs a doctor. So I'm callin' a doctor." She reached for the phone again.

This time, Mom yanked it from Liz's hands. "His father is his doctor!" Her rage was moving into fear.

Liz's face remained emotionless. "Well, Dr. Connor ain't here, Mizzuz Connor. So I'm callin' anotha doctor."

"No," Mom shouted, sheer terror in her voice. "You can't do that!"

"Well, why not?" Liz asked plainly. "Mark's hurt bad. He needs a doctor and his father ain't here. So why can't I call anotha doctor?"

There was no answer from Mom. She stared at Liz, speechless, her lower lip quivering as fear fully gripped her.

Liz had her just where she wanted her. "Well, Mizzuz Connor, if you ain't gonna let me call a doctor, then I guess I'm gonna be Mark's doctor today. You undastand? I'm gonna be Mark's doctor." She paused to make sure Mom understood. "Which means I ain't gonna be yo' maid today. Ain't nobody cleanin' yo' house today unless you do it yo'self. You undastand, Mizzuz Connor?"

Mom nodded in paralyzed silence.

"All right then," Liz continued, even more calmly, relieved that her plan had worked. She knew she couldn't call the hospital for the same reason she couldn't call the police. She reflected back on Claman's words: "They ain't never gonna believe no colored maid over that rich white doctor and his mizzuz." She knew it was true and was glad she didn't have to go through with the phone call.

"Now, Mizzuz Connor," Liz continued instructing Mom, "you just go run yo' errands and do what you gotta do today. I'm gonna be busy doctorin' Mark and takin' care of Chrissy and Todd."

Mom disappeared back to her room and didn't come out

at all. Liz spent the rest of the day sitting with Mark, singing to him, stroking his hair, and quietly waiting while he slept. Every time he woke, she got up from her chair and kissed him on the forehead. "I loves you, Mark. It's gonna be all right. Liz here now. It's gonna be all right."

Mark didn't talk that day. But Liz got him eating. Regularly, she checked in on Chrissy and me. We followed her instructions carefully and stayed downstairs, making very little noise.

When it came time for Liz to leave, she had our dinner ready and brought it to us to eat in front of the TV. "Now, you kids eat yo' dinner, then just go right to bed, you hear?"

We followed her to the back door, doing our best to hold back tears as we watched her disappear into the darkness again.

It was too early for bedtime, and we knew we weren't in trouble. But we also knew there was safety in what she said. We went to bed as soon as we finished dinner. As I went to sleep that night, tears came again as I silently begged, "Please, God, make Mommy better tomorrow."

Chapter 5

What Chrissy and I didn't know was that Mom had cut Mark's arms using the blade of the same scissors she had used on Chrissy in the summer. On the days Liz came during Mark's recovery, she spent a lot of time with him and eventually got him back to normal.

In a way, however, Mark was never really normal after that. He missed the first week of school after the Christmas break, just enough time for the black eye to look better and for the bandages to come off. Dad wrote him an excuse, saying Mark had been very sick with the flu and injured himself during a delirium. He wore long-sleeved shirts until the scabs healed. Once again, the dark Connor secret was safely shielded from the world around us. Mark's demeanor was much sadder now. He became more distant than he had been before, and more preoccupied. He buried himself in his piano practicing, as if the ugliness we were immersed in could be drowned out, somehow, by the beauty of Chopin. For Chrissy and me, it worked. Mark never knew how much the beauty of his music helped us all to forget.

Liz now tried to find ways to get Dad involved. She knew he knew. Who else had put those bandages on? Liz didn't believe that Mom was capable of stopping her rages.

"What woman could ever do that to her babies? She gotta be terrible sick," Liz theorized to her husband one night after dinner. "That poor woman don't know better. I've gotta get through to that Dr. Connor. I know he knows. I know he must care somethin' fo' them. He keeps bandagin' them. But I don't understand why he ain't gettin' her help. I'm gonna have to talk to him about it."

"Say what, now? He a respected doctor," Claman told her again. "How's he gonna take that kinda talk from his maid? He ain't listnin' to you, Bert."

"But he's got to listen," Liz pressed, as Claman shook his head. "I can't let her go on hurtin' ma' babies no' mo'. I know she's crazy. She can't help herself. But he knows better. He's just weak." Seeing Claman's disapproval, she stopped, then announced, "Well, I'm gonna tell him and ain't nothin' gonna stop me." She left the room, continuing to speak as she resolved within herself that she had to do something to save her babies.

Claman shook his head again, picked up his paper, and pushed back in his easy chair. "Lord, ain't no way fo' me to stop that woman, once her mind made up."

She came in extra early the following Tuesday, to catch Dad before he left for his hospital rounds. Her ritual now was to arrive before Chrissy and I were up. First thing, she went to the cross she had hidden in the laundry cupboard. Putting her hand on it, she prayed. "Lord, give me Grandma's strength today. You know I need it, Lord."

"Hi, Elizabeth. What are you doing here so early?" Dad greeted her as he made his way into the kitchen. In the adjacent laundry room, she scrambled to put the cross away.

"Uh, Dr. Connor, I really need to speak with you, sir." She spoke in a nervous, hushed tone.

"Well, Elizabeth, I'm on my way out the door." He grabbed an apple from the basket on the counter and scooped up his medical bag. "I'm sure Jane can take care of whatever you need. Is it about the refrigerator not working right again? I told Jane to stop repairing that old thing and just go buy a new one."

"No, Dr. Connor, it's somethin' else, sir. Somethin' private." Liz looked around to assure herself Mom was not nearby.

Impatient now, he said, "Liz, if this is medical, you should see your own doctor. I mean I am not really ... I mean it wouldn't be right." Not wanting to be so blatant as to say he wouldn't treat a Black person, he stumbled on his words.

She laughed. "Oh, no, Dr. Connor, I'm fine. Ain't nothin' gonna hold me back. No, sir!" Then, more hushed, she said, "No, Dr. Connor, it's somethin' else I really need to speak to you about."

By this time, he had lost his patience and Liz had lost his attention. He strode toward the front door. "Sorry, Elizabeth, I really have to go."

Liz turned away from the closing door and moaned, "Oh, Lord, you got to wake up that fool doctor."

A few weeks went by without another major incident from Mom. We saw her crazy eyes from time to time. However, we were all well trained and anytime we saw her crazy eyes flash, we made ourselves scarce. That, combined with Mom's awareness that Liz was watching, seemed to help.

Liz never knew what she was walking into on Tuesday mornings. She knew the biggest risk of Mom having one of her psychotic breaks was between Friday and Monday, the four straight days she was not around. So on Tuesdays especially, she followed her ritual—go to the laundry cupboard, touch Grandma's cross, and pray that prayer: "Lord, give me Grandma's strength today."

Chrissy and I moved with this weekly rhythm too. We learned to hold ourselves together from Thursday evenings, after Liz left, until Tuesday mornings, when she came back. Conversely, Thursday afternoons were a special time with Liz. She always finished her work early to spend extra time with us before she left. These moments were essential for our surviving the next few days without her.

Todd Connor

"C'mon, you two. Let's set a while befo' I go," she said each Thursday around four o'clock. We, of course, complied eagerly. "Now, let me tell you two a story. Once upon a time, there was a queen and a king. But they wasn't growed up. They was just kids. And they had a lady workin' fo' them. But this lady, she wasn't just a maid or a cook or somethin'. This lady, she was the luckiest lady in the whole land. You know why?"

Mesmerized, we shook our heads as we listened.

"'Cuz she got to play all day with the little queen and king. And she loved them babies. She loved 'em so much she couldn't even tell 'em how much she loved 'em. But this lady, she couldn't be with them kids all the time like she wanted. She had so much to do around the castle. And she had her own little castle to take care of too. So she had to leave from time to time. But, because she loved the king and queen so much, she always came back to them. No matter what, she always came back. But it always was sad when she had to leave. They all cried when she left. The queen cried. And the king cried."

Chrissy and I always had tears in our eyes by the time we got to this part of the story.

"And the lady cried too. 'Cept she couldn't show that 'cuz she was workin'. But the lady was always sad about goin'. And the lady couldn't wait to come back to see the cute little king and queen again."

Various renditions of that story, told to us over and over on Thursday afternoons, deeply sealed the memory of Liz's love and comfort as we prepared to face the next four days without her. Then, if something happened and crazy-eyed Mom raged over those Liz-less days, Chrissy and I held onto those bonding moments. Whenever Mom's crazy eyes appeared, her goal was to inflict pain. The more we cried, the more she continued. So we held back as much as we could through the days until Liz returned us to the safety of her pillowy lap, soft neck, and spiritual humming.

That meant, for Liz, many Tuesday mornings were filled with a flood of tears from Chrissy and me. If the previous four days had been violent, as they often were, quite some time was required on Liz's lap for her to soothe us.

Knowing this, Liz prayed her prayer first thing every Tuesday morning before anyone knew she was there. This was especially true on another Tuesday when she saw Dad's car in the garage and knew he had not gone to work. Maybe today would be the time when she could to talk to him. So Liz came in, touched her grandma's cross and prayed her prayer, then turned and was startled to find me standing, waiting.

"Well, hi, Todd," she chimed. She quickly closed the cupboard, then leaned down to tickle my belly. "Hey, you sneakin' up on ol' Liz?"

As I giggled and squirmed away, I pointed up at the laundry cupboard. "Whatchya got up there?"

"Oh, this?" Liz opened the cupboard and took out the brown wooden object. "This here's my grandma's cross." Liz pulled up her stool and I climbed onto her lap to re-connect the bond that had tattered since Thursday. "You see, child, my grandma was a slave."

"What's a slave?"

"Well, slaves is what my kinfolk used to be in my grandma's day. They had to work fo' people and do whatever the people told 'em to do, even if they didn't want to."

"Oh. Like when Chrissy plays Queen?"

Liz smiled and said softly, "Yeah, that's right, Todd. When Chrissy's playin' Queen, we gots to do whatever she say." Then her voice became more serious as she struggled to explain in words I would understand. "'Cept, when we're playin' with Chrissy, we just playin'. The people my grandma worked fo', they wasn't playin'. In fact, they was real mean, Todd. Real mean."

My brown eyes widened in fear as I processed this new information. I knew all too well what "real mean" felt like. I couldn't imagine anybody would ever be mean to Liz or anyone in her family. "Why were they mean to your grandma?"

"Oh, Todd, I loves you, baby. Look at you cryin' fo' my grandma." Squeezing me closer, she rocked, to comfort me and herself, as she thought about her grandmother's struggle. "Grandma's fine now," she said reassuringly. "She's with God, and she be singin' with the angels now. Yeah, she's real happy now and nobody's mean to her no mo'."

Satisfied, I leaned my head on her chest again. That way I could hear the rest of the story in one ear and Liz's heartbeat in the other.

"No, Todd, my grandma had the biggest smile and the sweetest laugh you ever did hear. Why, I think she was the happiest person I ever met."

I listened intently as I pictured an older version of Liz, who had the biggest smile I'd ever seen and the best laugh I'd ever heard.

"But my grandma had to run away from her master. Uh ... a master is like Chrissy bein' Queen. You undastand?"

I nodded, not wanting to interrupt the story or the sound of her heartbeat.

"You see, my grandma's master hurt my grandma with all his meanness." Liz spoke carefully, trying to be honest but keep the story from its darkest elements. "So she decided to run away one night in the middle of the night, when no one was awake. You see, fo' my grandma, she couldn't just quit playin', like we do with Chrissy. No, she couldn't just walk away when her master was bein' mean."

I knew exactly what it felt like to not be able to get away when Mom was "bein' mean." I stiffened on Liz's lap, waiting and hoping for a happy end to this story.

"Now, she was real scared of runnin' away, 'cuz her master was gonna be real mad and come after her. And if he caught her he was gonna hurt her worse for tryin' to get away."

My heart pounded from intimate knowledge of that feeling.

"And where was she gonna go? Who was gonna feed her? And where was she gonna run to? So she prayed every night. And to help her pray, she whittled this here cross. You know what a cross is, Todd?"

"Yes," I said. "I've seen it at church."

"That's right, child. People who believe in God use it as a symbol of God lovin' them back. My grandma knew how much God loved her. So she made this cross and used it to help her pray to God every day. She prayed that God would give her the strength to do what she needed to do—to run away from them mean people. And she knew if God loved her that much, He was gonna someday give her a way to run away from that mean master."

Knowing she was treading on risky ground, Liz rushed to end the story. "So my grandma made this cross to remind her that God was gonna give her a way to run away and be safe. An' she did. Then when she got real old, she gave her cross to me. She tol' me it'd help me remember that God loves me, and that He's always gonna help me."

"Are you gonna run away, Liz?"

"Oh, no, child!" Liz exclaimed. "I ain't never gonna run away from you, baby. No, Todd, you're stuck with me. I ain't never leavin' you." Her arms enveloped me as she laughed and rocked me until I smiled up at her. "Now, c'mon, little man, we need to get fixin' yo' breakfast."

I squirmed to hold on and buried my face on her chest.

"Now, c'mon, I've got to get workin'." She pulled my face up to look at her in the eye. "I ain't never gonna leave you, Todd. Never, ever," she whispered and kissed my forehead.

I continued to stare at her, not wanting the moment to end.

"What you lookin' at?" she questioned as she contorted her face just to make me laugh. When I burst into cackling laughter, so did she and her lap started the Jell-O bounce. I was in heaven.

When Liz cut my Jell-O bounce short, it was obvious she had something on her mind. As she put me down disappointingly early, I would have protested but I saw the seriousness on her face. I knew not to get in her way when she had something she needed to do.

"Now, you go on downstairs an' watch yo' cartoons fo' a bit," she instructed. "I'll fix yo' breakfast in a little while." Noticing my dejected look, her serious face melted back into a caring smile. "Don't worry, baby, I ain't gonna leave you and I sure ain't gonna let you starve."

Satisfied with one more moment of her intoxicating love, I complied without protest and scurried downstairs.

As Liz moved from the laundry room haven into the kitchen, she heard a newspaper rustle in the living room. Looking in, she saw Dad reading the paper in his overstuffed easy chair.

"Hello, Liz." He greeted her cheerfully but somewhat weakly. Dad was usually cheerful to adults he liked, and he did like Liz.

"'Mornin', Dr. Connor. You not feelin' so good?"

"Better than I did when we got home from church Sunday." He glanced through pages of the newspaper as he talked. "Nasty bout with a stomach bug. Today's the first day I've felt well enough to be up. I'm afraid the master bath needs an extra cleaning, and please see the bed sheets are changed."

"I'm sorry to hear that. You feelin' well enough to eat if I fix you a nice breakfast? You want some a my grits? You know they're good fo' yo' stomach, Dr. Connor."

"How about those thick pancakes of yours?" he asked.

"All right, comin' right up," she responded, turning back to the kitchen.

"What I really want is that world-famous fried chicken of yours, Liz," he hollered at her back.

Her laugh resounded from the kitchen. "Oh, Dr. Connor, you gonna need yo' own doctor if I fix you food like that right now. You just set there and I'll make you pancakes." Another high-pitched laugh followed. "Fried chicken when you're sick. Dr. Connor, you crack me up."

After she bustled around for a while, I came upstairs and must have looked dejected.

"Oh, Todd, I almost forgot about you! I'm sorry, baby. Here, you set right there." She pointed to my chair at the kitchen table. "I'm gonna get you some pancakes like yo' daddy 'll be eatin' today."

Soon I was stuffing my face with her pancakes and loads of syrup. She put Dad's plate together and took it on a tray into the living room where he was still reading. She closed the door to the living room with the back of her foot. That was unusual because Liz never closed doors to the rooms. But I was preoccupied, feasting on her pancakes, and didn't think much of it as I stuffed my face with more and more of her delicious delicacy.

"Here you go, Dr. Connor," she proclaimed proudly. "One big ol' plate a pancakes with lotsa butter and syrup, just the way you like it."

"Oh, that looks good enough to heal any disease, Liz." He laid his newspaper aside. "Can you come to the hospital and feed all my patients? I'm sure they'd all be well in no time. Who wouldn't?"

"Oh, Dr. Connor, you're funny. You crack me up."

"Hey, wait a minute." He continued his joking. "Maybe we should keep this under wraps. Your good cooking might put me out of a job."

"That's right, Dr. Connor." Liz played along. "You'd best be scared a ma' pancakes!"

Liz and he usually enjoyed each other whenever they spoke for a few minutes. He knew she was good to us children, and kept the house clean. Liz respected him. But she couldn't get over why he didn't do anything to help his wife or his kids. He was rarely home, which Liz knew was a factor. Usually, after joking with him like this, Liz would head right back to the kitchen. She liked him but knew to keep her place. This time, she lingered, awkwardly standing next to his chair, searching for words.

Dr. Connor noticed, and his smile morphed into puzzlement. He spoke more formally now. "Was there something you wanted to say, Elizabeth?"

"Dr. Connor?" Liz started, not really knowing how this was going to go. She had been rehearsing for weeks, but now her mind went blank. After a brief pause she repeated, "Dr. Connor, is Mizzuz Connor feelin' okay?"

His puzzlement vanished, replaced by guarded suspicion. He turned his focus back to cutting his pancakes and responded nonchalantly. "Oh, she's fine. I think I'm the only one who got this crud. But I'll bet she could use some of your pancakes anyway, just to keep her healthy, right?" He tried to resume their previous jovial banter.

"No, I know she's feelin' okay, but I've been wonderin'." Liz paused, again searching for a way to ask her question. "I mean ... is she really *feelin' okay?*" Liz emphasized the last two words to imply she knew something was obviously wrong.

Dr. Connor put his knife and fork down and looked up at her, completely serious and very guarded. Emotionlessly, he said, "I don't know what you mean. Do you think she doesn't look well?"

"I mean ... do you think she's feelin' *well?* I mean, you're the doctor." Liz rambled nervously. "You think she's doin' okay? 'Cuz I ain't so sure, Dr. Connor, and I'm worried about things around here."

Inside, Liz could here Claman's cautioning voice, "Girl, stop yo' fool talkin'!"

Dr. Connor looked at her, silent.

Liz took a deep breath and her next words rushed out. "Dr. Connor, I'm worried about yo' kids. Chrissy and Mark have been hurt real bad lately and—well, I'm not sure what's happenin' and I don't know what to do. An' yo' wife seems fine when I come here on my days, but I ain't so sure about her when I ain't, and ..." Her voice trailed off into silence. Her heart pounded and her breathing felt panicked. Liz refused to hear Claman's voice, yelling inside her head now, "Shut yo' fool mouth, girl!"

Dr. Connor sat looking up at her, stone-faced. During her rambling, she hadn't noticed his face. He was angry and it showed. But, internally, alarms were sounding at the possibility that the family secret might be revealed. He was not presently concerned about Liz. What power did she have in this situation? What voice could any Negro have, that would pose a threat to him? Further, the thought that his Negro maid would have any opinion about his wife's condition or his home life simply had not occurred to him. He didn't consider himself a bigot, at least for the times. In fact, he thought of himself as quite progressive. But Liz was, after all, the help, and it was not her place to have an opinion.

Now, however, it was obvious she did have one. His mind was jumbled. Internally, he felt a resounding cacophony of anger and fear, as if Mozart and rock 'n' roll were both playing at once, competing for an audience. Each was demanding resolute attention. He was torn between the two. On the one hand, how dare this Black maid question what went on in his home? How dare she imply he was not doing his job as a good father and, more insultingly, as the children's doctor? She absolutely had no right to question him. On the other hand, she *was* questioning him, making it clear she was not satisfied with his handling of the problem of his wife. The notion that this would be discovered by anyone other than this insignificant Negro maid was unthinkable. Or was it? Could she tell someone who would care? Would anyone actually listen to her, over his reputation, stature, and, yes, his race?

Liz pressed further, "Dr. Connor, you think yo' wife is doin' okay? I mean, really?"

"What I think is that you'd better be keeping your place." He rose, towering over her with imposing dominance. Shoving his tray at her, he said, "I'm finished with my breakfast. And *we* are finished with this conversation."

Stunned, she took the tray and obediently started toward the kitchen. Claman's warning came ringing back again: "Ain't nobody gonna believe no colored maid over that rich white doctor an' his mizzuz." But standing in direct opposition to his warning was the deep pain that pounded inside her from seeing the abuse of her little white babies. She desperately needed to find an ally who was willing to fight for them. How could their own father not be that person?

Ignoring her first thought, and strengthened by her second, she stopped in her tracks and turned to try a different approach. "You know, Dr. Connor, I think there was some other doctor 'round here a while back."

"What?" he snapped back. "What are you talking about? I'm my family's doctor. There wasn't any other doctor here."

Liz proceeded, watching his countenance, hoping his anger would wane long enough to let her play out her new plan. "Well, when I come in the otha week, Mark was all bandaged up. He was hurt real bad. So some doctor musta bandaged him up. I know it wasn't Mizzuz Connor, 'cuz she don't know doctorin' like that. Now, I know how hard you're workin', and I know you ain't around much. So I just figured some otha doctor came by and bandaged him up."

Liz waited a moment. He stared at her speechlessly, enraged. Clearly, however, growing fear was bubbling to the surface. She saw it in his eyes.

"Now, I looked at his arms, Dr. Connor," she continued, "and I saw how bad he was cut. And I know Mizzuz Connor is takin' care a yo' kids when I'm not here and you're workin' so much. So I started wonderin' if she's feelin' okay. You know, 'cuz Mark got hurt so bad when she was takin' care a him. So maybe she called anotha doctor to fix him up and you didn't know? Ain't that right?"

Liz paused again, still gauging the reaction to her words.

His anger, now evaporating, faded into a depressed, worried look. Dr. Connor took his seat again and stared despondently through the picture windows into the sprawling, wooded backyard. He felt numb. Here he was, sitting in a house he had thought he could never afford, in a neighborhood he thought would never accept him, with prestige and money he never dreamed possible to achieve. And now the beautiful reality projected to the outside world was rotting from within, as his mentally ill wife threatened to bring down all he had scraped for his whole life. Furthermore, this Negro maid knew the Connor secret and was forcing him to deal with the messy realities he had no desire to face.

"Dr. Connor." Liz raised her voice briefly to regain his attention. "Like I was sayin', there musta been some otha doctor here 'cuz Mizzuz Connor can't bandage up like Mark was bandaged up. So you may not be aware a things around here like I am." She paused again, watching to see if her strategy was working.

All anger vanished now. Dr. Connor stared despondently out the picture window, motionless, expressionless. Not understanding the reality exploding inside him, she grew impatient with his silence. She pushed one step further. "Do you know who that doctor was, Doctor? Maybe you should leave me his number, just in case you ain't around and the kids get hurt again. Don't you think that'd be a good idea, Dr. Connor?"

Slowly, he came out of his daze and looked up at her, tears in his eyes. He had sunk into the soft pillows of his easy chair, as if buried under an avalanche that had hit him with its crushing weight. A childlike weakness appeared on his face, making him look as if he were too small and too young to know what to do or say.

Oh, he is one pitiful fool of a man—he's supposed to be protectin' them babies, Liz thought as she moved closer to the easy chair. Looking down at him, she spoke directly but gently, as if to a fragile child. "Dr. Connor, she's gettin' worse. I think you know that. She's gettin' much worse. Now she cuttin' yo' babies, Dr. Connor. We've got to do somethin'."

He remained unresponsive. Liz swam in an ocean of her own feelings, as complex as they were impassioned. She was enraged at the man, who just kept bandaging up his children and did nothing to help or to restrain his mentally ill wife. His biggest response so far was this crumbling display, collapsing right in front of her. Liz wasn't sure whom to pity more, him or his sick wife. But for Liz, the bottom line was to find safety for her babies.

Why don't he show some reaction, she wondered. Liz knew sometimes the doctor had "reactions" to what was going on in the Connor home. Occasionally, when he came home to another abused kid, he raged and beat up Mom. Liz reflected back to those Tuesday mornings when she tended both bruised children and wife. Liz could see, at those times, what made Mrs. Connor hate her husband. She wondered if that was a driving force behind the woman's more frequent and more serious rages.

Liz couldn't hold back any longer. The dam finally broke. "Dr. Connor, I know I am just yo' colored maid and I got no place to question a fine man like you. But I love yo' babies. You *know* I love yo' babies, Dr. Connor, like they was my own. You undastand me, Dr. Connor?" With her lips quivering, she went on. "So as far as I know, it's *my* babies gettin' hurt. And they ain't no way I can go on seeing *my* babies get hurt like that. Ain't no way, Dr. Connor. Ain't no way at all."

She took a deep breath and continued, in a more scolding voice. "An' you can't keep bandagin' 'em up and hope it's gonna be all right. I can't believe you think that's really makin' it all right. It *ain't* all right around here, Dr. Connor. It ain't never gonna be all right if you don't do somethin'. This keeps goin' on like this and she's gonna kill those children. You've got to do somethin', Dr. Connor."

He sat silent through her whole speech. Once she finished, she expected an explosive reaction. Instead, he simply turned away, hunched his shoulders, and buried his face in his hands.

"I don't know what to do, Liz. I don't know what to do."

With this surprising admission, Liz had to redirect her own thoughts. She was still frustrated and angry at this weak man. She suspected most of his tears were over his problem of exposure and not over his kids or his wife. But it was a start, she thought. In spite of what she thought of him, she reached into her ocean of compassion and spoke kindly. "All right now, it gonna be all right. Liz here now. We gonna figure a way through it."

He composed himself in a moment and looked up to stare out the big picture window. When he spoke, he revealed himself in a voice as vacant as his gaze through the glass. "You know Liz, I grew up poor. Really poor. So poor that my mom lost her mind, and my dad deserted us kids. I had to look after my younger siblings. I was so scared as a kid. Do you know that kind of scared, Elizabeth?"

"I know what scared is, Dr. Connor." Liz responded softly, thinking "and so do yo' kids."

"I saw what being poor did to us," he continued. "I was terrified of living that way my whole life. I thought if I just made enough money, if I just did something important, like become a doctor, all that fear would go away and I would have a great life. But I look out on all this ..." He swept his arms out, indicating the beautiful yard and large house. "I built all this up. *I* did it. I earn a lot of money. I see the prestige and respect I get in this town. But I'm still scared. What do I have to do so that I'm not scared anymore?"

He turned to look at Liz as if she had the answer. Realizing he had asked the unanswerable, he turned his gaze back to the picture window. "So, when Jane started hurting the kids ... well, that just made me more scared. I guess I thought I needed to work harder, make more money. Because I always thought money could fix anything."

He then looked back at Liz. His eyes were again tear-filled, but his face angry. "Yes, she's getting worse. I know it. But I don't know what the hell to do about it."

Liz responded calmly but firmly. "Dr. Connor, your wife is sick. She's not sick like the kind you can fix. She's sick in her mind. She needs a doctor who can fix her mind."

Calmed by her steady words, he said, "I know. She needs a psychiatrist. But where can I take her? Everyone in this town knows me. Hell, everyone in this town expects me to *be* the doctor, not the one who needs a doctor. I'd have to take her out of the state for treatment. Then what would people say if we just took off like that? Oh, damn it, I don't know what the hell to do."

Liz did her best to hold her anger. What is wrong with this man, she thought, that he cared about his neighbors more than he cared about his own kids? Liz had never struck anyone, but she surely did want to smack some sense into this man. Instead, she calmly said, "Dr. Connor, that don't matter when it comes to yo' kids. They're gettin' hurt. You've got to stop that. And you've got to help yo' wife. There must be someplace that'll help her."

Just then, there was a crash in the kitchen and a loud

outburst from me. Liz rushed for the kitchen. "Todd? You okay? What happened, baby?"

Liz found me standing by the stove, with the skillet and several pancakes strewn across the floor. She panicked as she hurried over to me. "You hurt, baby? That skillet burn you?"

Liz, of course, hadn't left the stove on, and the skillet with the extra pancakes had been moved off the burner. Still, she checked my fingers and toes to see if I was hurt. Relieved that I wasn't, she held me and said, "It's all right, baby. You ain't hurt. You're just scared, that's all. Were you tryin' to get mo' pancakes? Oh, I'm sorry I been talkin' to yo' daddy so long, baby. C'mon, let's set you down and I'll make you a new batch a pancakes."

Dad burst into the kitchen. "I've got just the fix, Liz," he announced as if he had just had an angelic visitation answering the deepest mysteries of life. "I'll take Jane to Mexico. She could use the rest, and God knows I could use a vacation."

Before Liz could argue with him about that not being the right "fix," he started for the bedroom to find his wife. Calling back, he said, "Liz, can you stay with the kids next week? I really need you to. Can you square it with your husband and the other families you work for?"

Dumbfounded by his sudden exuberance, she answered tentatively. "Well, I'm sure I can, Dr. Connor. But are you sure that's the fix we been talkin' about?"

Out of sight, he didn't answer.

Chapter 6

Liz showed up the following Tuesday carrying a big suitcase. She came in extra early so Mom and Dad could catch their plane to Mexico. I heard her open the back door while I was still in bed. I jumped up and ran to her, wearing just my underwear.

"Look at you, little half naked man, comin' out to greet me befo' you get dressed," her chipper voice remarked.

Unthinkingly, I flung myself at her with full-running force and wrapped my arms around one of her legs.

"Oh, child! You gonna knock ol' Liz down like that," she yelped, then laughed as she took a step back. "Now, you go put some clothes on b'fo' you catch cold. Go on now. I be here when you get back."

"No." I looked up at her from my grip on her lower leg with a big grin on my face.

"Oh, please, sir," she begged in her high-pitched playtime voice. "I'm gonna need my leg to get my work done today. How am I gonna take care a ma' babies without ma' leg?"

She tickled my ribs until I let go, then spoke in a gentle command. "Now go on, little man. You get dressed so I can get to helpin' yo' momma and daddy befo' they go."

Reluctantly, I obeyed. Liz was relieved, as she wanted a minute to touch her grandma's cross and pray again before the day began.

"Elizabeth." Mom's businesslike, rushed voice startled Liz as she closed the cupboard to conceal the cross. "I have a list of things the kids have going on this week. And here is cash for groceries." She placed the money envelope and schedule on the washing machine and moved into the kitchen to avoid further discussion.

Mom had been cool and distant with Liz since being challenged when Mark was hurt. She knew that Liz knew. That kept a sort of armistice between them. This was just fine with Liz as long as Mom didn't hurt us anymore. And even though it was less than comfortable for Liz, she wanted to keep that pressure on Mom.

Liz was not hopeful, however, that this would keep us safe for long. She was also not hopeful that Mom and Dad's vacation would change anything, either. It enraged her how Mom kept hurting us. It was doubly enraging that Dad never seriously addressed the issue. She cried for us. She prayed for us. But beyond that, she felt no ability to truly fix anything.

For Liz, our situation created feelings in her that were more complex than just our situation. This complexity ran deep. Deep because she loved us, and the notion of anyone hurting us was intolerable. But those feelings also ran deep because of what she wore on the outside: brown skin that rendered her as weak, powerless, and, in many ways, as abused as we were. Liz shook her head as the enormity of the situation overwhelmed her. She looked down at her hands resting on the washing machine. One hand rubbed the skin of the other. "Really Lord? The color a my skin is gonna keep ma' babies from bein' safe? Gimme Grandma's strength, Lord." She then took a deep breath and refocused on Mom's instructions.

"I'll take care of everything, Mizzuz Connor," Liz responded subserviently as she followed into the kitchen. "You go on and have a good time with yo' husband. Rest up. I'm sure you could use it, Mizzuz Connor."

Mom turned away nervously. "Well. All right then. Everything seems to be set. We will be home next Sunday evening."

Liz lowered her eyes. "Okay, Mizzuz Connor."

Dad came in just then. "Hi, Elizabeth. I think we are all set." He paused as he sensed the tension between Liz and Mom. "Are we all set?"

"Oh, sure." Liz spoke brightly, lightening the mood. "Everything's fine, Dr. Connor. Just fine."

Mom said nothing, but walked back to her room. Dad and Liz watched her go. The quiet moment felt strained for both of them. Liz, not shying from the tension, asked, "You sure this is gonna be the fix she's needin', Dr. Connor?"

"This is perfect. Just what the doctor ordered. For both of us!" Answering cheerfully, he ignored her meaning. Exiting quickly, he added, "I just need to load the car and we'll be off."

Liz came to help me finish getting dressed. She also got Chrissy and Mark out of bed. "All right, you kids," Liz urged, "you've got to say goodbye to yo' momma and daddy. C'mon, they'll be goin' soon."

Within a few minutes she had us lined up by the door, almost like a reception line, waiting for our parents.

"Oh my. Well, I feel like the queen." Mom seemed compelled to show some sort of warmth as she said goodbye to us in front of Liz. She reached her cupped hands to our faces, as if to hold them with affection, but pulled back quickly, as if repulsed. "Oh, I just did my nails."

We each got a quick smooching sound of her lips just above our heads as she moved toward the door, where she stopped at the mirror to check her lipstick. Dad, now rushing because they were late, walked past us and ushered Mom out, saying only, "Bye, everyone."

This lack of affection was standard for the Connor home. But it was irrelevant now. After the door shut behind them,

Chrissy, Mark, and I all breathed a sigh of relief. Uninterrupted smiles were soon plastered onto our faces as sustained time with Liz began.

"You kids want pancakes fo' breakfast?" Liz asked with joy in her voice. For the first time, I fully realized how she truly enjoyed us as much as we did her. Her love was so intoxicating and such a desperately needed commodity for me, I never really considered if she was having an equally good time. That week I would see it. It was clear.

"We're gonna have lots a fun, ain't we? I'm gonna cook real good fo' you kids, with my pancakes and fried chicken and whatnot. Why, I think I'm gonna get you kids fat this week! That's it. You're gonna be as fat as ol' Liz when yo' momma come back. She ain't even gonna recognize you. We'll just be lookin' like four fat children: three little white ones, and one big ol' brown one!" Her teasing was followed by our uproar of delighted joy.

She did her best to follow through with that promise, too. Mornings were packed with pancakes, grits with butter on top, bacon, sausage. No eggs were allowed, however, because none of us liked them. Each afternoon she baked cookies after school while Chrissy and I watched TV or played outside. Dinners were everything fried—fried chicken, fried pork chops, chicken-fried steak.

She even got me to eat fish, which I had always hated. But no one had ever made me fried catfish before. And I didn't know it was fish because it sure didn't taste like fish. I liked it so much I asked for seconds.

"Can I have some more cat?"

Liz, Chrissy, and Mark all laughed at me. "Baby, that ain't really a cat," Liz said. "This is fish. Folks say it just looks like a cat when it's still in water, 'cuz it got whiskers." She kissed my cheek to make sure I didn't feel picked on as my brother and sister continued to giggle. "I love you, baby. You crack us up."

The first night Liz stayed with us, Chrissy and I argued over who got to have her lie down with us at bedtime. We both wanted to fall asleep in her arms.

"Now, Chrissy," Liz whispered to her as we watched our last TV show before bedtime, "I'm gonna lay down with Todd first, 'cuz you know he falls asleep fast. Then I'll be in to lay down with you. So don't fight with yo' brother. Undastand?" Chrissy nodded, feeling honored that she was let in on this secret while still being promised her own time with Liz.

Of course, each night I thought I had died and gone to heaven as we cuddled on my bed and Liz told me bedtime stories. Her stories were different than the ones I had heard before. She told stories that sounded almost real. Her stories weren't about princes and witches and potions, like the ones I was familiar with. Hers were about freeing slaves, and about people who learned to be strong in all kinds of scary situations. They had an authenticity to them, unlike fairy tales. Later in life, when I thought back on those stories, I came to believe she was telling us stories that had been passed down to her from her grandmother and others.

As hard as I fought to stay awake, to let these moments go on and on, my fight was futile. I did fall asleep pretty fast.

Each day she drove Chrissy and Mark to and from school in her 1951 Chevrolet station wagon. It was an old car, especially in our neighborhood. People stared at the heavy Black woman behind the wheel. Chrissy and I didn't notice the frowning faces. We noticed the staring, but just figured they were jealous of us being with Liz. We pretended we were in a procession with a queen, where people naturally stared. Mark, though, was a little embarrassed.

The second day, after we picked up Mark and Chrissy from school, she didn't take us home. She had packed an overnight bag for all of us, and we went to stay at her house in The Flats. We were thrilled. We spent the afternoon playing games in her back yard. She didn't let us go beyond her fence. At the time, we didn't understand that her neighborhood was dangerous. Ironically, we felt completely safe at her house, which we never felt in our own. The crime we endured at our home, nestled in Woodland Estates, was nonexistent at hers.

Late that night, long after bedtime, loud screams and flashing lights came through the bedroom window. Chrissy heard it first and woke Mark and me. We rushed to the front window to see what was happening. Three police cars and several white officers were on the front lawn of the house next door. One was holding a Black man's face down on the ground. The officer was yelling, with his gun drawn and pointed at the back of the man's head. Another shouting policeman kicked the man in the side. The other two officers were on the front porch holding a woman, who was trying to break free to help the man on the lawn.

Liz awoke after the three of us had already perched for some time at the front window, watching the whole scene. Claman continued snoring in the back bedroom.

"What you kids doin'?" Her hushed voice carried alarm as she rushed to pull us away from the window and close the curtains. Just as she did, we were seen by one of the officers.

Within seconds there was a knock on Liz's front door. She ushered us back to the bedroom before she answered. "Hush, and stay here," she said as she closed the bedroom door. We complied with her request for silence, but after we heard her open the front door, we snuck to the hallway where we could watch what was happening.

"I done tol' you, Officer." Liz sounded annoyed but controlled. "I am babysittin' these little white children fo' the whole week while they momma and daddy on vacation."

The officer towered over her as she spoke. His shoulders seemed as broad as he was tall. Apparently, he was not satisfied with her answer because the next minute, he was inside the house.

"What are you doin', comin' into ma house?" Liz's voice had an edge of fear.

The officer ignored her as he pushed her aside. He spotted us crowded at the edge of the hallway, peering around the corner. Looking back at her, as if he had discovered something she was hiding, he said, "So I guess these are the children?"

"You can't just come into ma' house without askin'," Liz protested feebly.

The officer ignored her. He looked at us. "What are you kids doing here?"

"You kids keep quiet," Liz instructed. She then moved between the officer and us. "Who do you think you are? You can't come into my house without askin'."

She'd barely finished her sentence when his beefy arm flashed out and his hand struck her cheek. Liz's head snapped back and she yelped in pain.

We all froze. The officer turned and asked his question again. "What are you kids doing here?"

None of us spoke. There was no way we were going to respond. This was feeling as scary as our own home.

Liz pressed a palm against her bruised cheek. "Mark, tell this officer who yo' best friend is." Her voice was fearful now.

Mark, nervous at being singled out, spoke sheepishly. "Mikey."

"Speak up, child," Liz said.

"His name is Mikey," he said louder.

"What's his last name, Mark?" Liz asked.

"Jackson."

"An' what's his daddy do?"

"He's the mayor."

Liz paused and looked up at the gigantic officer in the hallway. His forceful countenance shifted as a frown of worry crossed his face.

"The mayor ever come over to yo' house?"

"Uh-huh," responded Mark.

"Yeah, and he likes my cookin', don't he?" she said.

Mark nodded.

"Do you know Mikey's phone number at his daddy's house?" Liz asked.

"Yes," answered Mark, and rattled it off from memory.

Liz looked at all of us and said, "All right, children, now you go on back to bed. Ain't nothin' mo' to see out here."

She turned to the officer, still standing as an immovable roadblock in the hallway. She took a step closer to him, shifting her head upward so he would see her anger. She pointed her finger up at his face as she spoke. "So, now, am I gonna call the mayor's house? Or are you gonna get outta *ma* house?"

Saying nothing, he looked at Liz, then at us, and back at her through narrowed eyes, as if pondering whether to believe anything he'd just heard. After a moment, he turned to the door. He stopped and looked back on last time. "Ma'am you best keep those kids out of sight."

Liz crossed her arms over her chest and glowered.

The next day after school, we begged Liz to take us to her house again. She was not going to repeat the events of the previous night, but we did go there to play. She made us dinner and then took us to her church's Wednesday night "celebration."

"How come they call your church a celebration?" Mark asked as we piled into her car to go the few blocks to the Christian Tabernacle Church of God in Christ.

"That's what we call it when we worship God," she responded. "We are celebratin' His love."

Her version of church was nothing like the Latin Mass we were accustomed to. People sang loudly, clapped their hands, and swayed with the music. A group in long robes stood up front, dancing and singing. Mark, Chrissy, and I were mesmerized. We had never seen anything like it. These people lived in one of the poorest, most crime-ridden neighborhoods in the country, in circumstances further complicated by the brutality of the Oakland Police Department. Yet they were the most joyful people I had ever seen. Everyone in the church seemed so happy—happy with life, and very happy with God. I didn't understand, but I knew one thing: whatever they had, I wanted.

The end of the week came all too soon for my siblings and me. After dinner on Saturday night, none of us, including Liz talked much. A foreboding sadness had settled in, knowing our parents were returning the next day. They'd been gone only a few days but the week had felt like an eternity of bliss and we didn't want it to end.

"Yo' momma and daddy are comin' back soon," Liz reminded us as we all sat down to watch reruns of I Love Lucy after dinner Saturday night. Chrissy was on one side of Liz and I sat on the other as she snuggled us close like a mother hen protecting her young. "And Chrissy, we need to make sure yo' room is all cleaned up befo' they get back," Liz warned. Chrissy and I had been making forts that day with virtually every blanket and towel in the house. "You know how yo' momma don't like no messes. We best clean that room first thing tomorrow."

Mark was lying on the floor watching the TV and listening to Liz's warnings. We all were silent, contemplating the impending return of our parents. None of us laughed much at the antics of Lucy and Ethel.

"Now "I get to come back after only one day a bein' gone," Liz comforted us. "You undastand? There's gonna be one day without me bein' here. Then I'm comin' back. Can you kids be good 'til then? I'll be back befo' you..."

Three loud tones from the TV stopped her before she could finish. Lucy disappeared and a man's face filled the screen. "We interrupt this program with a special bulletin," the announcer's voice blared. "Another sinkhole has opened in the East Bay hills. No injuries have been reported but nearby residents are being urged to take precautions. We have a helicopter over the scene now." As the announcer continued, the helicopter camera showed a large home that had partially collapsed into a gaping crevasse. I'd never seen anything like it before.

"Wow, cool!" Mark yelled. "Can we go see it tomorrow?"

"No, we cannot," Liz said.

"What's a sinkhole?" I asked.

"It's when there's a big hole hiding in the ground," Mark said excitedly. "And all of a sudden what's on top goes whoosh and falls in! Wow! This is neat!"

"No, it is not," Liz said. "Those poor people just lost they house. Thank the Lord they didn't lose they lives."

It was scary to think the ground under me could disappear. "Is a sinkhole going to get us, Liz?"

"Oh, baby, we're safe. Don't you worry none. Ain't no shortage of trouble in this world, but you know Liz will always keep you safe." Liz pulled me closer for a quick hug and then got up and turned off the TV. "Now enough of this scary stuff or you'll all be havin' nightmares. Mark, you can stay up but you two young'uns get ready for bed and I'll read you some stories. Off you go now. Scoot!"

Sunday afternoon came too soon. We all stayed in our rooms as we heard our parents enter through the front door. Liz came down the hallway, collecting each of us and ushering us out to greet them. The first thing we noticed was that Mom looked different. She was tan, and smiling like she did at parties. For the first time in a long time, she really looked happy. There was no trace of her crazy eyes.

"Hello, darlings," Mom chimed as she came up and kissed

each one of us on our cheeks. We all cautiously kissed her cheek in return, as was expected. But none of us trusted the moment.

She then turned to Liz and asked, "So how were they?"

"Oh, they was fine, just fine," Liz answered cautiously. She knew she had a tightrope to walk with Mom. On one hand, she knew Mom wanted her to take care of us and free her from her duties. On the other hand, Mom never wanted Liz to have too much fun with us because that made her insecure and ultimately jealous, which usually lead to something dreadful. Knowing this dynamic, Liz was always careful how she described our time together.

"Yes, Mizzuz Connor," she continued politely. "The children behaved real good while you was gone. They got they homework done and never gave me no problems. They did just fine." Liz carefully omitted the experience at her house. Mark, Chrissy, and I were never going to tell either.

"Well, how nice. Would you make sure they have their dinner before you go?" With that, Mom went to her room to unpack. We all breathed a cautious sigh of relief.

After giving us a knowing smile for our silent omission about the detail of sleeping at her house, Liz went outside to help Dad with the luggage. "Well, Dr. Connor," she said, "sho' look like whatever doctor you took yo' wife to sho' did help her. I don't think I've seen her that happy in a long time."

Taking luggage out of his Cadillac's trunk, he stopped briefly to look at her curiously. "Why Liz, I didn't take her to any doctor. We went to Mexico, remember?"

"Well, yes, sir. But I thought you was goin' there to see a doctor that could find a way to help Mizzuz Connor get better."

Pulling out the last bag, Dad paused again to look straight at Liz. "She is better. I'm the doctor here, remember? And I say she's better. I hope that's clear to you now, Elizabeth."

Liz understood his not-so-subtle meaning and stepped out

of his way as he carried bags past her to the house. When he was out of earshot she muttered to herself, "That man is some kinda fool. Yes, Lord, he is some kinda fool." She closed the garage door and headed back to the house.

It was especially hard to see her leave that night because our week with her was so amazingly refreshing. She went through her same ritual of drawing in close to me and Chrissy, reminding us, "You mind yo' momma now, hear?" This time she added, "Now she's all relaxed and happy from her trip. Don't you do nothin' to upset her, ya' hear?"

All three of us nodded obediently. As she walked out the door, we proceeded to the window to watch her drive away. Then we went downstairs, Mark to the piano and Chrissy and me to watch TV, being as quiet possible so as to not upset Mom. We knew nothing had changed.

Todd Connor

Chapter 7

After their Mexico trip Mom was actually a little better, at least for a brief time. We were by no means abuse-free. Nor was this a time when we never saw crazy eyes. Occasionally she would stick us with pins or slap us across the face. We considered that fairly tame. We just did our best to stay out of her way and to drink up every moment we could with Liz when she was there.

The week after Mom and Dad returned from their vacation, I suddenly found myself in Chrissy's kindergarten class at Blessed Child Academy. It was all so confusing. I didn't like losing my time with Liz. I didn't like not knowing the other kids. Chrissy had her friends but they were girls and didn't want to play with me. The boys took a long time to become friendly toward me. The nuns never did. The first time Sister Stephen rapped my knuckles I burst into shocked tears. The second time it happened I thought that compared to Mom's beatings it was nothing. I got used to staying as silent in school as I was at home. It was years before I learned that Dad had insisted I be accepted into the class, thinking it would cut down on the violence at home. He had threatened to withdraw his ample financial support from the school, as well as Chrissy and Mark, if the Mother Superior didn't acquiesce to his demand.

Things were at least somewhat quieter at home. For a while.

In the spring, Mom began slipping back into more crazy-eyed days. There was more yelling, and more quick-tempered snaps at all of us. And, of course, there were more slaps across the face and sticking us with sharp objects.

We all knew what was growing in her, but were unable to control it or stop its inevitable explosion. Her volcano of madness would erupt one day, and one of us would lie wounded in the aftermath. We knew it. As her internal fury grew, our fear and despair grew with equivalent force.

One beautiful April Sunday day, unfortunately for me, I became the final catalyst sending her over the edge. After we sat through a boring Latin Mass in the morning, the rest of the day was ours to play. Right after church Dad went conspicuously absent again. It was a hot day, and Chrissy and I begged Mom to turn on the front lawn sprinklers for us to run through.

Mom, still slipping, surprisingly complied. However, one of the ways we knew she was drifting away from reality was that she didn't notice obvious things. So the sprinklers, which probably should not have run for more than ten minutes, were left on for well over an hour. Chrissy and I were in heaven as the lawn became a soggy mess. We slid farther with each run. The pooling water splashed like a wake behind a ski boat. We shrieked with laughter as each of us took another turn. What we failed to notice was that we were tearing up the beautifully manicured grass. Continuous sliding not only turned the lawn to mud, but also transformed our skin from pale white to dark brown.

"Look, Chrissy!" I called, noticing the metamorphosis. "We look like Liz! She's our mommy now!" We both shrieked with delight as we scooped up mud and wiped it onto ourselves, to turn as brown as possible.

Our childlike joy abruptly shattered with shrill terror as Mom lunged out the front door. She rushed to turn the water

Todd Connor

off. Then she whirled around with snapping energy to glare at Chrissy and me. It looked as if she could have kept spinning and drilled right into the ground. And there they were: her crazy eyes, in full terrorizing force.

"What are you kids doing?" she screamed.

Chrissy took off running, all the way around the house to get out of sight and hide. Fear rendered me motionless.

"You horrible kids! Look what you did to my lawn!" She grabbed my arm and yanked me around raging and shaking me like a ragdoll. Then, for one brief, hopeful moment, she snapped out of her insanity to look up, scanning the street for attentive neighbors. Her eyes darted back at me again, regained their wrath, but now her voice was a menacing growl. "You need to be punished."

She kept up her near-demonic rumble as she dragged me into the house, snarling, "You need to be punished."

My arm seemed to separate from my shoulder as it dragged my body behind it. As she worked her way through the long hallways of the house, jolts of pain seared through my arm, eclipsed only by the fear of what was coming. I knew this was my turn. She had been getting worse; even at my young age, I knew it. I didn't know what was ahead. But I knew I was in for far worse than I'd ever endured before. So I started in with the familiar but completely futile pleadings that she couldn't hear over the sound of her own voice: "No, Mommy! Please, Mommy! I won't do it again, Mommy!"

Still screaming, she dragged me into her room and threw me on the bed as if I were an old coat. I was completely covered in mud and already making a worse mess on her white carpet and light green bedspread. Her crazed eyes saw none of that.

She slammed the door behind her and locked it. She was completely unaware when Chrissy began kicking it from the outside and yelling, "No, Mommy! Todd! No, Mommy!

Don't! Todd!" Mom went to Dad's closet and grabbed a belt. She wrapped it around my ankles and secured my legs to the bottom leg of her bed.

She stopped screaming then. Her eyes watered and bulged with rage. Her lips formed into a sadistic smile, and her whole face seemed engrossed in concentrated thought. Her breathing quickened and her nostrils flared with every breath. It was as if everything human evaporated and something else, something not human at all, replaced her. Through clenched jaw, her words repeated, "You need to be punished."

She went to a drawer in the master bathroom and pulled out the long scissors, the ones I found on Chrissy's floor when Mrs. Wagner interrupted.

She had never cut me before. But after having seen what she'd done to Chrissy's legs and to Mark's arms, I knew what was coming. I squirmed and tried to free my legs from their noose. By the time I really started trying to escape, she was on me, shoving me down, holding my chest with her left hand as she opened the scissors with her right, exposing the sharp edge of the single long blade, which she soon began scraping against my upper thighs.

"No, Mommy, No, Mommy. I'll be good, Mommy! I promise, Mommy! No, Mommy! Please, Mommy!" I shrieked to a vacant, insane face, eyes aglow with demented fury.

The following moments were far more methodical than any previous chaos I had endured. Clearly, she had done this before. Maybe she had even had this done to her before. She seemed to be repeating some abusive pattern previously experienced in her own history. Also, now there was a horrifying satisfaction in her countenance. She was no longer screaming, just continually growling, "You need to be punished."

She was completely deaf to my cries. It was almost as if she was no longer aware I was there anymore. She was acting out some sadistic ritual on any flesh she could find. It didn't really matter whose. Satisfaction was growing in her face as she repeatedly slashed my young, squirming legs. She was enjoying this.

The pain was unbearable. She cut slowly across my skin, deep enough to draw blood but probably not so deep that Dad could not stitch me up without leaving scars. She was watching the slashes and the blood, occasionally looking up to assure the full amount of pain was being inflicted, evidenced by my pleading face.

My voice, rasping from my continued screams, grew fainter as I gasped for air, struggling to breathe as her left hand bore down harder on my chest, attempting to immobilize my squirming body.

Then slowly, and most thankfully, the room started to close in … and then to spin … and then all sounds faded … and I stopped even trying to breathe. I passed from consciousness into a most welcome state of peace.

Chrissy eventually told me that she had stayed outside the locked bedroom door, kicking at it and yelling. She said that when my screaming stopped, the house became deafeningly quiet. A few minutes later, the bedroom door opened and Mom carried my bloody body, as limp as if dead, into the hallway. She never even noticed Chrissy, although she almost tripped over her.

Mom carried my lifeless body to my room, dropped me on my bed, and walked out in a daze, still not seeing Chrissy standing there, motionless. Silently and robotically, she walked into her room, shut the door, and locked it as before.

The house was still as a tomb.

Chrissy said she rushed to my room, her mind racing with thoughts that I was dead. When she saw me, the mud caked on my corpse-like body glistened with blood.

Frantically, she ran to our shared bathroom, grabbed two large bath towels, and ran back to my room. Her panic was now manifesting in a combination of dread, action, and tears. Even at six years old, she knew how to focus her fear and hurt. She went to work cleaning the mud and blood off of my still unmoving body, doing her best to control her panic and grief. "Todd!" she told me she kept whispering while she worked, "Don't die, Todd. I need you."

Then she heard Mom's bedroom door open and she dropped to the floor, scrambling under the bed.

Chrissy said Mom didn't see her there when she came into my room. She stared over my motionless body. Then she pulled back her arm and slapped my unconscious face, hard, as she again growled, "You needed to be punished!"

Panicking, Chrissy gasped, then put her hand over her mouth to stifle the cry she'd made. But Mom didn't even hear it. She turned and left.

Chrissy crawled out of hiding and stood staring at the red mark on my face from Mom's new assault. I moaned and turned on the bed.

"Todd! Come back, Todd! You've got to live. Please." She pulled my blankets up around me, as if lovingly tucking me into bed for the night. Then she tiptoed out, to seek safety in her own room.

When I came to, it was getting dark. My first thought was total confusion, not from what Mom had done to me, but in disappointment that I was still alive. Regretfully, I'd returned to the Connor home.

As consciousness grew and I skimmed past my death wish, I heard Dad yelling at Mom and her screaming back at him. I couldn't make out words. Through my pain-induced haze, fear reflexes and the need to run and hide kicked in. My legs instinctively jerked into movement. Searing pain from my wounds made me scream. The room began to spin again. I fell back, drifting in and out of consciousness.

Dad, still yelling, stormed in and picked me up, not in a

loving or tender way, but as if he was carrying an inanimate object. He kept yelling at Mom. "What the hell is wrong with you? Why do I have to keep coming home to this? Now look what I have to do! Stupid bitch! You *crazy*, stupid bitch!"

He carried me, rolled up in the blanket Chrissy put over me, into the bathroom and laid me on the floor. Then, as he rolled open the blanket, his face turned from annoyance to shock. "My God, Jane! What have you done this time? My God!"

My heart lightened slightly—he seemed to care about what had happened to me. Maybe my Dad was the good giant who'd save us after all.

Then Mom was in the bathroom doorway, shouting, "He needed to be punished! You weren't *here*. You don't *know*. These kids are out of control. He needed to be *punished*."

He shot back, "Look what I have to clean up for you now. You crazy, stupid bitch."

My heart sank. Dad didn't care about me. He was angry because of the complications this caused for him.

The next few minutes were a blur as they both kept arguing. Dad put me into the bathtub, turned on the faucets, and scooped running water over my wounds. The room spun in and out. Their shouting continued. All I could do was sit numbly and watch blood and mud spiral down the drain as Dad washed the lacerations on my body. The mud that had made me feel like part of Liz was almost completely gone now. I continued staring at the blood and mud mingling with the water until my mind lost its grip again.

I woke up in my bed the next morning. For a brief moment, I thought it had all been a horrible nightmare. A spark of hope flashed as I considered that. Then I tried to move my legs. I realized the nightmare was, unfortunately, very, very real.

After Chrissy and Mark went to school, I was left home, alone, with Mom. She came into the room sometime midmorning and informed me that the bandages needed to be changed. I squirmed to pull away from her, but the pain was too much. Tears came as I tried to utter the familiar, feeble plea, "No, Mommy. Please Mommy." But my voice was gone, spent from my screaming the day before.

She pulled back the covers, exposing my bandaged legs. "You know the best way to take off bandages is fast and all at once." Her crazy-eyes flared with the impending satisfaction of causing me more pain. She yanked one bandage off the first leg. With a piercing explosion of pain, the room immediately began spinning. And then came the same treatment to the second leg. "No, Mommy. No, Mommy …" I once again faded into the precious peace of unconsciousness.

I slept on and off throughout the day, hoping she would not come back. She never even bothered to see if I was hungry. Still, I was grateful for her absence.

The following morning, I again awoke uncertain of what had happened. The piercing pain of trying to move brought it all crashing back. I lay motionless. I wanted to cry, to release the enormous pain and grief of the last few days. But my mind was drained. I was numb.

Then the rustling at the back door met my ears. The mere hope that Liz might be there to save me burst open the floodgates of more tears.

"Liz! Liz!" I called, hoping she could hear me from so many rooms away. I found my voice and called out louder, "Liz-a-beth! Liz, I need you, Liz."

"I'm comin'." Maybe she thought I was home sick with a cold or the flu. Her bright-eyed face peeked through as she opened the bedroom door. "Who's that callin' me this early? That my sweet boy Todd?"

She struggled to see into my room, still darkened by the closed curtains. Her voice turned serious as she noted that I wasn't moving in my bed. "What's wrong, Todd? You hurt?"

Gasping for breath through my sobbing, I tried to talk, but couldn't gain enough control to form words.

"Baby? What's wrong?" She sat down on the side of my bed, her eyes searching my face for injuries. She reached above me to open the curtain and let the sunlight in. "What's wrong, Todd? C'mon, baby. You tell Liz what's ailin' you."

I continued to struggle for words.

"What's wrong, child? Whatever it is, Liz is gonna make it better. You'll see. Liz here now."

As she cautiously pulled back the blankets, she recoiled at the sight of my bandaged legs, fresh blood still seeping. "Oh, baby! My sweet baby boy!" Liz frantically pulled me into her arms. When I yelped in pain from the movement, she released me and stood up. "Oh, baby, I'm sorry."

Through my tears I squinted up at her brown face. Horrified, she stared into space as tears streamed down her cheeks. I heard her murmur, "Oh, Lord, what are we gonna do now? Lord, you've got to help me here."

Taking a deep breath, she looked at me. She kissed my forehead and whispered, "I'm gonna fix this, Todd. You'll see. Liz here now. It's gonna be all right, now. Liz here now."

She knew she couldn't rock me to comfort me. Instead, she stroked my cheek as she hummed one of her familiar spirituals. She never took her worried eyes off me, interspersing her humming with the words, "Gonna be all right, baby. You'll see. Liz here now."

She stayed this way as I continued to cry. I cried for a long time. I am not sure how long. At some point, the exhaustion from my tears wore me out. As I was falling asleep, Liz kissed my forehead again and stood up. "I'm gonna make it all right, baby. Liz here now."

Chapter 8

It was clear to everyone except our parents that Dad's Mexican vacation remedy was no remedy at all.

"That fool doctor. Look what she's done to my baby now," Liz whispered angrily to herself as she tiptoed out of the room.

Liz made her way to the laundry room window that Chrissy and I looked out every night as we sadly watched her vanish into darkness. She reflected on all those nights when she left us looking out at her. We never saw her beyond the shroud of darkness, but each night she walked far enough from the house so as to not to be seen by Chrissy and me. Once darkness shadowed her from our view, she would gaze back at our tearful faces, backlit by the cozy-seeming house lights, to see the pitiful faces that moments earlier had begged her to take us home with her. Once fully concealed, she invariably let her own tears fall. Chrissy and I never saw that. Nor did we hear her prayer each night as she drove away from our home: "Lord, why you put me in that house and make me love them babies when you don't let me keep 'em safe?"

Liz stared out the window, again beseeching God. "Lord, you made me the momma they ain't got. Then why ain't you givin' me a way to save ma babies? You've got to give me a way to help 'em. You've got to."

Conscious that she needed to pull herself together, she wiped her tears and turned to the laundry cupboard. Opening it, she saw her grandma's cross and took a deep breath. She said out loud, "Well, Lord, you got Grandma outta her mess with slavery. I guess you can get me an' ma babies outta this mess too."

Liz started a load of laundry and made breakfast for Chrissy and Mark. As they ate, she heard Mom coming down the hallway.

"Oh!" Mom's voice was startled as she rushed into the kitchen, then she continued nervously. "I didn't know you were here already, Elizabeth. Uh, I am off to run errands and then to bridge club today. I won't be back until late."

Liz didn't turn around to acknowledge her. "Uh huh." She responded with the most disinterest she could deliver, while inside, her anger seethed.

"Dr. Connor is home," Mom continued in businesslike tone. "He is doing paperwork. So, I need you to take the kids to school."

Liz turned to stare at Mom. Anger flashed on her face as she responded, "I can take Chrissy and Mark to school, Mizzuz Connor. But what about Todd?"

Fear flared in Mom's eyes. "He's sick. Dr. Connor will check on him later."

"Uh-huh. He sick, is he?" Liz said tonelessly, and turned back to Chrissy and Mark.

Again, I slept much of the day. But whenever I did wake up that morning, Liz was sitting next to my bed. Every time my eyes opened she leaned over and kissed my forehead.

She fried chicken for lunch, partly hoping it would cheer me up, but also to get Dad out of hiding in his home office so she could talk to him.

"Oh, boy!" he exclaimed as the smell predictably drew him into the kitchen. "Is that Liz's famous fried chicken I smell? Liz, I swear, you're trying to make this whole family fat."

"No, Dr. Connor," she responded flatly, "I just thought

Todd oughta have somethin' special today." She turned from washing dishes and dried her hands as she looked at him. He sat down at the kitchen table and grabbed a chicken leg from the platter. He ignored her mention of me.

When he said nothing, Liz pulled out a chair and sat down. "Dr. Connor, we've got to do somethin' about what's goin' on around here."

He abruptly stopped chewing and looked at Liz. His eyes narrowed in anger. "What the hell are you doing, sitting at my table?"

She slowly stood, backing away from the table as he continued his tirade.

"I don't know what you're talking about that *we* need to do something. This is my house. My wife. And my kids. You are nothing but the maid. So unless you don't want a job in this house, I suggest you get that nigger ass of yours back to work and keep your mouth shut."

Backed against the kitchen sink now, she turned away from him in shock. "Yes, sir," she responded dutifully. In the decade she'd been with the Connors, he'd never called her that vile word before. Her hands gripped the edge of the sink. It was the only thing she could think to do to barely control the rage and sorrow detonating inside herself.

She paused for some time, trying to calm down and formulate a plan. Dr. Connor continued his lunch, assuming he'd ended any threat she posed to him.

"All right then." Liz walked to the phone and lifted it from its hook. "If you ain't gonna solve this problem, I guess I'm gonna have to call someone who will."

He sprung from his chair and lunged for the phone. Ripping the cord out of the wall, he flung it. It slammed into the tile backsplash above the stove. Pieces of plastic and metal shattered into the skillet of chicken grease and across the stove and counter. "What the hell are you doing?" he screamed.

Liz flinched at the enormous, violent figure towering over her. Though terrified, his intimidating stance also helped. She smelled gin on his breath. Now she understood. He knew he was powerless to fix the mess in his own home. His youngest was lying in bed, debilitated by his wife's latest mental fracture. He hadn't fixed her with the vacation in Mexico. He hadn't stopped her beating the children by beating her. So now he was just going to drink the problem away. She regained the resolve to stand her ground.

"Who the hell do you think you are?" he raged, pressing himself threateningly close.

"Dr. Connor, I ain't scared a you." She lied to herself as much as to him. Looking straight up at him, she raised her hands as if in compliance, but also to push him back if she needed to. "I am *not* scared a you. No, sir. I ain't. You need to calm down now, Dr. Connor. Todd is hurt bad and Mizzuz Connor needs help. This ain't about me. It ain't about you. It's about keepin' yo' kids safe."

He grabbed a paperweight off the desk near the phone and sent it flying. Almost instantly it exploded in shards that merged with phone parts. "You come into my house acting like my kids are *your* kids. What I do in my house with my kids is my business. You stay the hell out of it."

"Dr. Connor, that don't make sense if you love them kids. Now you just calm down and ..."

His fist crashed into her cheek. Her mind reeled as her body did too. The force of the blow knocked her to the floor.

"You stupid nigger!" he shouted, stumbling to regain his own balance. "Get the hell out of my house. You hear me? You're fired!"

Struggling to stand, she pleaded, "Dr. Connor, you know you don't mean that. You know yo' wife needs help."

"Well, that's not going to be from you! Now, get out before I hit you again!"

Cringing, she moved toward the back door, but still trying to reason with him. "Dr. Connor, what about yo' children? What are they gonna do?"

He raised his arm as if to strike again. She scuttled backwards. He came after her, his fist clenched. Stumbling over the kitchen chairs, backing into the laundry room, she grabbed her purse from the laundry room counter. On the threshold of the back door, she turned back and protested one last time. "Dr. Connor, you can't make me not see yo' children no more. They're like my own. You know that. I've got to see ma babies."

Charging to the back door, he pushed her the rest of the way out. "You stay away from my kids. You hear me? Get your ass out of my house and away from my kids!"

The door slammed.

She saw him appear at the laundry room window. He glared at her and drew the curtains, shutting her out of the Connor home and out of her babies' lives forever.

She stared at the window, stunned, then sank down on the back step and sobbed.

Liz sat there for some time, dazed, trying to sort out what had happened.

Everything was quiet. She heard birds chirping and the leaves of the big cottonwood tree just outside the door rustling in the wind. She felt the sun warming her skin. The peace was therapeutic. It took some time. It took some self-rebuke. It took some prayer. But she was not going to be stopped. As sure as that sun would be shining tomorrow, Liz told herself, she was not going to give up. Not now, not ever. "We're gonna find a way, Lord," she said aloud. "I know we're gonna find a way to help ma babies."

Todd Connor

Thoughts of just how that was going to happen whirled as she finally made her way to her car. Keys in hand, ready to open the door, her mind flashed as if a bolt of lightning jolted her. "Todd!" she cried out loud. "What's he gonna do now?" Her mind raced. What would he think of her not being with him when he needed her? For leaving without even saying goodbye? She knew he'd never understand.

She quietly followed the walkway through meandering trees and shrubs around the sprawling ranch house to the window above my bed. She lightly tapped on the glass and spoke softly. "Todd. Can you hear me?"

I had been sleeping until Dad's yelling woke me. I never before heard Dad yell at Liz. So this was a frightening turn of events that kept me in hyper-vigilance as I strained to listen. Groggy, I was alarmed enough to fight sleep. I lay immobile, hoping the mayhem in the kitchen would stay there, far away from me. Then everything got quiet for a long time before I heard Liz's muffled voice.

"Liz?" I responded weakly. Thinking she was in my room, darkened by the drawn curtains, I asked, "Liz? Where are you?"

Then the tapping came again at the window. The head of my bed was close enough to the curtains that I was able to reach up and pull them back without moving my legs.

"Liz? Why are you outside?" I saw her face, puffy on the left side, with what looked like a black eye forming. I was used to seeing Mom with black eyes but I had never seen Liz's skin show the bruised bluing of blood under the surface.

"Hey, little man." She tried to sound cheerful, though her tears gave away her true feelings. "I'm gonna be away fo' a while."

Panic shot through me like a knife. "Why?" I cried before stopping myself. Remembering Dad's yelling just moments ago, I reverted to scratchy whispering. "You can't go. I need you."

"I know, baby, but I've done made yo' daddy mad. So he's

sendin' me away. But I love you, Todd. You know that, don't you baby?"

I nodded, unable to speak. What would life be like without Liz? The thought gripped me with palpable fear.

"I'm so sorry, Todd. I love you, baby. And Chrissy and Mark too. You all have to remember that. I'm gonna try to come back. Maybe yo' daddy gonna change his mind."

She held her brown hand up against the window glass in a vain attempt to touch me. I stretched my body to reach my hand to the window, even though it required enduring the piercing pain. I pressed my small white hand against the spot where her large brown palm was. Staring at her, feeling her warmth through the cool window, I couldn't speak. Neither of us could. Here there was no color, no race, just love emanating through the glass barrier between us. We both lingered as long as I could before the pain became too much. I let go and fell back onto my bed. I strained to reach for the window again. But the pain sent the room spinning.

I heard another window open nearby. Then Dad's voice, yelling, "I told you to get the hell out of here! You hear me? You want me to hit you again? I'll do it, you stupid bitch." I heard the window slam. Then nothing else.

Startled, Liz recoiled, pulled away from the window, and rushed to her car.

Claman was home when she arrived. The factory where he worked had closed temporarily due to rumors of possible race riots in the area. The plant owner, Sol Weisman, a Jewish immigrant who had barely escaped the violence of Adolf Hitler and Nazi Germany in the late '30s, had no interest in exposing his factory or his workers to any kind of unrest.

Claman looked up from reading the newspaper as Liz shuffled in the door. "What you doin' home, Bert?"

She collapsed on the couch across from him and buried her face in the pillows, hiding the swelling bruise around her eye and muffling her tears.

Alarmed, Claman rose and asked, "What's the matter, Bert?" He knelt on the floor beside the couch and rubbed her back. "Why ain't you at the Connor house like you supposed to be?"

When Liz didn't respond, Claman simply waited. Finally, she regained enough composure to sit up. Liz saw shock register on her husband's face.

"What happened to you? That woman throw somethin' at you?" He rose and rushed to the kitchen. Grabbing ice from the freezer and wrapping it inside a dishtowel, he ranted, "What the *hell* she think she's doing? Hurtin' her kids ain't enough? Now she's goin' after you?"

"It's not her," Liz interrupted. Claman froze in his steps. She took in a deep breath and let it out. "It was the doctor that done it. I was tryin' to get him to do somethin' about savin' his kids. But he wouldn't hear none of it. He got real mad. He busted the phone. Then he hit me. He fired me. An' he threw me outta the house." She sobbed and buried her face in the pillow again. "She hurt Todd this time. Real bad."

"The *doctor* hit you?" Claman's low words hissed with anger, then rose in volume. "Who the hell does he think he is? Why, I have a mind to go on up there and ...."

"Now, Claman, you calm down b'fo' you go off doin' somethin' you're gonna regret," she warned, though appreciating the fight he had in him, especially for her. "You know we ain't got no rights in this. You said it yo'self. Dr. King ain't movin' fast enough fo' us. Or ma babies. Nobody's fightin' fo' them neither."

The phone rang, startling them both. Claman stepped into the kitchen to answer it. Liz heard him say, "Yes, she here."

He came back into the living room. "Mizzuz Rinetti wants to speak with you."

They exchanged a nervous look as Liz moved towards the phone. The Rinetti family represented the other half of her workweek and her income.

"Hello Mizzuz Rinetti. How are you?" Liz's voice was somber. Claman waited as Liz stared silently forward, emotionless, listening.

"Yes ma'am, I undastand. I'm sorry to hear that. You were a good lady to work for. Please, Mizzuz Rinetti, say goodbye to the children fo' me ... All right. Bye now." Liz hung up the phone and rested her head against the kitchen wall. Claman looked on, not knowing what to say. After a moment she said, "I don't feel good, Claman. I'm goin' to bed."

Claman said nothing as he watched his defeated wife make her way to the back of the small house and close the bedroom door. He knew what had happened. Dr. Connor had made one phone call and done his dirty work.

Liz stayed in her room for a number of days. She spent most of her time in bed, rising only occasionally to feed the dog or make dinner for Claman. She barely ate. When she missed Wednesday choir practice at church for the second time, people started pestering him about her. At first it had been easy to tell folks she was sick. The second week, after her enormous black eye had healed, Claman knew he had to help his wife re-enter normal life.

"You gettin' up today?" he asked as he got ready for work on Thursday morning. "Maybe you oughta start lookin' fo' work again. You know we can't make it on just what they pay me."

"You know I won't find work in this town after what Dr. Connor's done." She rolled over in the bed and turned her back to him.

"Now, that man doesn't know everybody," he gently argued.

"An' what about goin' to that agency in Castro Valley? You've got a car. That nasty doctor don't know anyone out there."

She didn't respond. He thought of emphasizing how they were going through their small savings and wouldn't make next month's power bill if she didn't find something. But he knew his wife's fragile condition. So he said nothing more.

As he finished his coffee in the kitchen, he was surprised to see her come in and offer to make his breakfast. She was fully dressed for the first time in two weeks. A hopeful sign of recovery, he thought.

The phone rang before they could resume their conversation about her finding work.

"Hello?" Liz answered.

Claman heard a child's voice on the other end of the line.

"Well hey there!" For the first time in two weeks, there was brightness in Liz's voice. "What're you doin' callin' me like you a grown-up young lady? How'd you get ma number? ... You took it from yo' momma's purse? Well, ain't you the smart thang."

"Who is it?" Claman whispered.

Liz put her hand over the receiver. "It's Christine."

Claman's nerves jangled. He was certain Mrs. Connor would not want her daughter talking to Liz.

"An' how yo' baby dolls doin'? You bein' a good momma? That Chatty Cathy that Santa gave you still talkin' up a powerful storm?" Liz's smile beamed as she reentered the child world of one of her "babies."

After several minutes, Liz asked, "And what about Todd? You two been playin' Queen lately?"

Then her countenance changed. "Christine, you cryin'?"

She looked at Claman grimly as she listened. "Say what? He ain't talkin'? What do you mean?"

Liz's brow furrowed as she listened again. "He ain't got outta bed yet? Lord, it's been two weeks ... An' what? Somethin's wrong with yo' hand?"

Fear flashed on Liz's face. "What happened to yo' hand, child? Christine, darlin', I need you to try to calm down so you can tell me what happened. Did yo' momma do somethin' to yo' hand? ... Hello? Christine? You still there child? Darlin', try to tell me what happened."

Liz stiffened. Her voice became almost submissive. "No ma'am, we was just talkin' ... No ma'am, I'm not tryin' to cause trouble ... No ma'am, there's no need to call nobody ... No ma'am, I ain't gonna call again."

Liz hung up the phone and put her head against the wall. Neither she nor Claman spoke.

"Claman," she finally said, still leaning her head against the wall as if it was necessary to hold up her heavy thoughts. "I just can't do anythin' fo' ma babies. Their momma's gettin' worse. It sounds like she now done somethin' to Christine's hand. An' I can't do a thing about it."

She lifted her head from the wall as her mind began to clear. "Somebody's got to do somethin'. Nobody else but me knows about all this. I've got to figure out somethin'."

She looked at Claman and her eyes spoke before her voice did. "You know I'm never gonna give up tryin'. Not now. Not ever."

A second later her eyes brightened. She straightened her back and stared off. "That's it! That's what I've got to do!"

Before Claman could form words of warning, she rushed to the bedroom, grabbed her purse, and headed out the door.

"Now where are you goin'? Now, don't you go—" Claman complained as he watched her leave. He knew better than to try to stop her, but he worried for her safety. He knew that when it came to taking care of children, there was no reasoning with her.

Chapter 9

Liz definitely had a plan. It might not have been a good one. But at least she had one. She left the house without explaining it to Claman because he would, of course, argue against it. If she allowed herself to stop and think, she probably would too. She decided she had to do something to save her babies, but that's pretty much where her strategy stopped.

"I've gotta tell the police what's been goin' on," she muttered to herself as she started her car. She imagined Claman sitting next to her in the passenger seat, saying "That's yo' plan? Bert, you as crazy as that Connor woman." She chuckled, thinking it was much easier to hear from an imaginary Claman than from the real one. She knew it wasn't a good idea. But she didn't have a better one.

Oakland was then gaining national attention for its racial tension and police brutality. Blacks never turned to the police for any crimes in their neighborhoods, *ever*. Many Blacks had experienced the bigotry of police officers when they lived in the South. As far as law enforcement was concerned, to them, Oakland was the South. Distinct lines were drawn between the Black community and the Oakland Police Department. And those lines were never breached.

Huey Newton and Bobby Seal were consolidating their power base with Oakland's newly formed Black Panther Party.

Initially intended to peacefully support the Black community, as police violence against Blacks increased so did the Panthers' response tactics. As Blacks began gaining more of a political voice nationally, the Oakland officers seemed to believe cruelty was the way to keep that voice muted locally. As a result, the surge in police violence only led to greater anger and fear throughout the Black community.

Driving through The Flats, Liz witnessed the mounting public display of this unrest, passing more and more bold graffiti that declared "Kill Whitey" and "Kill the Pigs." The growth of Dr. Martin Luther King's Civil Rights actions, the burgeoning free speech movement that had begun on campus in Berkeley, and the expanding protests against the Vietnam War, were reaching a tipping point of dynamics on the verge of boiling over as Liz drove down Highway 580. Though it went against every grain of her being, she knew the only choice she had was to appeal to the only authority that might have the power to save the Connor children: the Oakland Police Department.

It took some time for Liz to make her way downtown to the central police station. She had never been there before. No one wearing brown skin had, at least not in the last decade, unless in handcuffs.

Oh, Lord, what am I doin' here, she wondered. Fear shot through her, causing her to reconsider the line she was crossing. A plaque next to the door was emblazoned with the police logo and the words, "The Oakland Police Dept. Here To Assist, Guard, and Protect." Liz bit down on her tongue as scorn boiled inside her. "Girl, you watch yo' mouth now," she scolded herself in a whisper. Her heart raced and her mouth went dry as she opened the large glass doors and entered the stately government building. Out of reflexive habit of her life in the South, she immediately looked for "whites only" signs on the bathroom doors and drinking fountain as she passed those near the entryway. She didn't see any, but she knew she'd best use neither. Lordy, she thought, I'm glad I didn't have but one cup of coffee this morning.

A middle-aged, white, balding officer stood behind the long front counter, leaning on his elbows and reading a newspaper. He glanced up as Liz entered but quickly turned his eyes back to the paper.

Liz stood quietly, her fingers nervously working the top of her purse as she waited for him to acknowledge her. She felt herself blush as other officers in the area glanced up, glared, and looked away. Finally, just as she was losing her resolve, the officer looked up.

He tilted his head from side to side like a puzzled dog. Then came a caustic smile revealing his yellow teeth. Disdain snarled in his voice as he spoke. "Are you lost? Or are you here to turn yourself in?"

His contempt so startled Liz that she was unable to speak. She doubted he'd ever seen anyone in brown skin enter who wasn't in handcuffs.

"I said, are you lost?" He spread his arms wide against the desk and leaned across it, belligerent and intimidating. "'Cuz you sure as hell look like you're lost."

"No sir, I'm not lost." Liz answered politely, her voice barely above a whisper. "I need to speak to a police officer. Sir."

"You want to talk to a police officer? What about?"

"Yes, sir." Liz ignored his tone. Craning her neck, she looked around for any face that might look at all helpful. "I want to make a report."

"Oh you do, huh? Well, just what kind of a report do you want to make?"

Only then did it hit her. She actually hadn't thought any farther than walking through the police department doors. Claman's warnings came crashing back: "Ain't *nobody* gonna believe no colored maid over that rich white doctor and his mizzuz." Trying to control her mounting fear, she continued, "Well, uh ... I, uh ... I want to make a report about some kids bein' hurt."

"Kids being hurt?" the officer snapped back. "What the hell are you talking about? Does this look like a schoolyard where we care about some of your kind being hurt? "

Liz continued to look beyond him, trying to find someone else to appeal to. Seeing no one, she looked at him and said, a bit less politely now, "I'm not talkin' 'bout schoolyard fights. I need to speak to someone—"

The officer cut her off, raising his voice now. "Look, we don't have time for whatever is happening to your little monkey kids. Frankly, we're too busy fighting off the dead-beat dads that made those little monkeys." Several cops behind him snickered and one even applauded.

The room went silent as another man came into view. Liz noticed he was not in uniform, but knew by the way the other officers acted that he had to be someone important.

The man stopped, looked at Liz, and then glared at the desk officer. "Is there a problem, Smeagel?"

"No problem here, Captain." The officer's response showed the required respect for the man's rank, but an equal amount of contempt and disdain. Turning to look at Liz, Officer Smeagel said, with a sneer, "This *lady* was just leaving."

Liz shook her head in protest, responding more forcefully now, "No sir, I am not leaving. I am lookin' to make a report."

"What kind of report?" The captain walked up to the front desk.

Sensing she finally had someone's sincere interest, Liz moved away from the offensive officer to where the captain was standing. "I need to make a report about some kids gettin' hurt. Can you please tell me who I should be talkin' to?"

"I'm Captain Thomas Whitmore. And you are?"

Liz was surprised when the man extended his hand to

shake hers. "My name's Liz Baxter. Elizabeth Baxter. Uh, Mrs. Claman Baxter."

"Now, what's this about children being hurt? If it's a schoolyard situation, you should talk to the principal."

Liz leaned in and spoke in more private tones. "No, sir. It ain't no schoolyard thing. Is there an officer I can talk to ... privately ... that handles this kind of thing?"

"Well, I am still not sure what kind of 'thing' you mean. Maybe you should talk to your pastor."

Liz could tell Whitmore was growing impatient but she had come too far to leave now. "No. I need to make a report."

Grudgingly, but also with some curiosity fleeting across his face, Whitmore opened the gate at the counter. "Okay, step this way, ma'am. We'll talk in my office."

He walked ahead of her, without conversation, and led her down the hallway to his office. It was a small, cluttered space. Books were opened and papers strewn across them as if some mighty wind had blown through the room just before they arrived. As she waited for him to move books and papers off the one chair across from his desk, Liz almost chuckled, thinking, this was a man who certainly needed a maid. She noticed a nameplate on the desk. It read "Capt. Thomas Whitmore. Interracial Relations Specialist."

Whitmore paused for a moment, holding the armful of jumbled papers he'd collected, and nodded for her to sit. As he scanned the room for a suitable resting place for his bundle, Liz wondered why he didn't just throw it in the trash where it looked like it belonged. She smiled again.

Captain Whitmore noticed. "Something funny, ma'am?"

Startled into seriousness, Liz responded, "Oh, no, sir. I'm sorry. I was just thinkin' of somethin'."

"You were laughing at me and my mess, weren't you?" He gave up finding a clean place for the pile and dumped it onto another pile on the credenza behind his desk.

Liz didn't know what to say, but sat motionless, worried she had offended the one person who might listen to her.

As he sat down, he said, "Oh, it's all right. I know I'm a slob."

Relieved, Liz said with conciliation, "I'm sure you is very busy, Captain."

"That's right. There's no shortage of crime in this town."

"Um, sir, it says you is interracial relations." Liz nodded toward the nameplate on his desk. "Uh, what does that mean?"

"It means I'm here to try to make things better. You don't need me to tell you this city's a tinderbox. It's a new position. Mayor insisted on it. I'm the lucky man, you could say, to get it. Transferred in a few months ago from Chicago's South Side, where I was the unofficial specialist. Now, why are you here?"

Liz started talking. About halfway through her story, she realized the captain was staring off into space. She stopped talking. "Sir? I ain't here to waste my time or yours. If you can't help me I'll find someone who can."

Whitmore's attention snapped back to Liz. "Excuse me, Mrs. Baxter. I apologize. It's just that you remind me of someone I knew a long time ago. Her name was Nellie. She did laundry for us when I was a kid, and I learned a lot of good from her."

Liz looked at him puzzled, incredulous that any white police officer would have ever met anyone like her.

"I remind you a someone?" Liz chuckled. "Well, there ain't too many like me. I can assure you a that."

"No, you misunderstand Mrs. Baxter. I grew up in Tennessee. Miss Nellie was our washerwoman but she was more like an aunt to me. For some reason, you remind me of her. I miss her very much and I guess I just let my mind wander."

"Hmm." Liz huffed and mumbled, "I'll bet she made you pay better attention than you've been payin' now." Liz looked startled as she realized he heard every word.

"Yes, ma'am." Whitmore smiled, remembering similar

Todd Connor

rebukes from Miss Nellie so many years ago. "Of course she did. And then she made me apologize. Mrs. Baxter, please accept my apology."

He pulled a notebook from a desk drawer. "I really should be taking notes on all of this. So I need you to start over, from the very beginning."

Feeling more comfortable with him now, Liz gave him a very familiar and slightly disapproving "Mmm Hmm," and began again. "Well, as I was sayin', I've been workin' fo' the Connor family fo' some time now."

"The Connors?" Whitmore interrupted. "Dr. Frank Connor's family?"

"Yes, sir. That is what I had said." Liz's irritation slipped out again as she spoke. "So like I was saying, yes, I been working for Dr. Frank Connor's family fo' some time now."

His countenance abruptly changed from alarmed to gravely serious. "How long?"

Liz remembered where she was and what she was doing. Her fear bolted back but she did her best to cover it. "Right about ten years, now. Since just after the first a ma babies was born. I mean, the Connor babies. I was tellin' you, they've got three children at home now. They had just one when I started workin' there."

Liz continued with the family's details, but kept avoiding the problem that brought her there. The truth was, she didn't know how to raise the real issue. After the family particulars were over, she started telling the stories that she enjoyed. "Oh an' that Todd," she mused, "he's got the biggest brown eyes, especially fo' him bein'...." She paused.

Whitmore, looking up from his note-taking, smiled and finished her sentence for her. "You mean for a white child?"

Slightly embarrassed, Liz said, "Yes sir. Fo' a white child, he's got such big, dark brown eyes."

"Mrs. Baxter, I am sure Dr. Connor has a beautiful wife and

kids. And I am sure they live in a great big beautiful home. But something tells me you are not here to give me a catalog of the Connor amenities you enjoy." Putting his pen down and resting his arms on the desk, Whitmore asked pointedly, "So tell me, Mrs. Baxter, why are you really here?"

Liz squirmed her massive frame in the too-small chair. "Well, sir. As I said, I been workin' fo' Dr. Connor's wife mostly. She's beautiful an' all. But she's not always …"

Struggling for words, Liz paused, cautiously watching Whitmore's eyes for any hint of disapproval. Curiously, he seemed completely neutral to whatever she might say. "Well sir, she not always right. Uh, I mean, Mizzuz Connor is not always doin' right by her kids."

Whitmore's face went blank.

Liz went on, her voice low. "Sometimes, sir, she just ain't right in her head. I mean, in her own mind. You undastand?" Liz asked her familiar question to see if Whitmore would nod with some sort of understanding.

He did not nod and showed no emotion or understanding. He said, "Why don't you explain to me what you mean by that."

"Well, sir, she gets these eyes. They ain't right. I mean, she don't look right." She realized she was rambling and Whitmore's impatience was showing. Fearing she would lose him, she blurted, "She's been hurtin' her kids, Captain Whitmore. Real bad."

Liz couldn't believe she actually made the accusation. Simultaneously, however, she felt relief that she had finally said the words. The dam inside her had released its pent up pressure and now it was time to open the floodgates. She saw Whitmore's face show shock. Though he said nothing, having his full attention gave her the courage to reveal the whole story—how she came in on Tuesdays to often find the children bludgeoned or bruised. Lately, she explained, the abuse was worse, much worse. "She's been cuttin' them babies now. Cuttin' them so much they can't get outta they beds."

It felt good to just let the truth out with very little regard for how it sounded or appeared to this white man. Along with the release of truth came a flood of tears as she added, "I don't know what I can do, Captain. Every Tuesday, when I come up there, I never know what I'm gonna find. Sometimes it's Christine, the little girl, who's been hurt. Sometimes, it's one of the boys."

She paused, gulping back deep sobs for a moment before managing to hold back the full depth of her grief. "And what she done to Todd last week. Well sir, I can't keep quiet any mo'. I just can't. I've got to do somethin'."

Liz reached out and grabbed Captain Whitmore's arm resting on the desk. The racial situation in Oakland was irrelevant now. The only thing that mattered was saving the Connor children. She forgot where she was, who she was talking to, even the color of her own skin. She grasped Whitmore's wrist as if he were an absent-minded child who needed to pay attention. She stared at him dead on through tears and said, with extreme urgency and pain in her voice, "She's gonna kill them kids, Captain. She's gonna kill ma' babies. Captain, I swear. She's gonna kill 'em."

Words were no longer possible. Letting go of Captain Whitmore's arm, Liz's head and shoulders curled downward as she heaved deep sobs and buried her grieving face in her hands.

Stunned by the woman's allegations, Whitmore sat frozen in his chair. Liz's dissolution gave him a minute to think. But think what? What was he to make of what he'd just heard? Whitmore had been in Oakland long enough to know Dr. Frank Connor was one of the mayor's closest friends and family physician. In fact, Connor took care of most of the city's political enclave, including the City Council and school board members' families. He also, Whitmore thought, plays golf with my boss, the police chief. Child abuse in the Connor home? It couldn't possibly be.

As Liz continued crying, Whitmore flashed back to the first time he had met the Connors. It was at the policeman's ball a few months earlier. Dr. Connor seemed to take a personal interest in Whitmore as soon as he learned the captain was the new hire to help calm the city's racial tensions. And that wife of Connor's—wow, what a knockout, he mused at the memory. Jane Connor had worn a red sequined dress with an embarrassingly deep cleavage line. She looked like she had walked right off the Hollywood movie set of *Gentlemen Prefer Blondes*. He remembered how men surrounded her at all times throughout the evening, and how she smiled constantly and laughed loudly to ensure their eyes stayed fixed on her. Shaking his head back to the present, he looked at Liz still crying uncontrollably in front of him.

This Baxter woman has to be wrong, he told himself as he started reasoning a way to calm his troubled notions. He wondered if it was she who was the mentally unstable one. Maybe her reminding him of Miss Nellie had allowed him to drop his guard too early. Maybe she had made this whole story up. He started feeling more skeptical with each questioning thought. Then, killing the last bit of doubt in his mind, he stabbed the final, convincing dagger into his uncertainty— even if it were true, he didn't want any part of anything against Dr. Connor. It would be professional suicide. Maybe, he thought, this Baxter woman had come in to set him up and get him fired. Everyone in Oakland knew he was there to help calm the racial tensions. Not all were supportive, especially the growing vocal factions. He knew there were people, both white and Black, who wanted him to fail. That's what this is, he decided. Someone sent this woman in. If he bit on her story, it would be exposed as a lie and he'd find himself out of a job. It had to be a set-up. Once his doubts were dead, he took a deep breath and started to see this all from a different angle.

Liz raised her head to continue her statement, expecting Captain Whitmore to resume taking notes. Instead, she found the scowling frown of a skeptic staring back at her. She realized she had not really gauged how Whitmore was receiving any of what she was telling him. She held her breath and stared at him, unsure of how to proceed, no longer feeling safe enough to do so.

Whitmore resumed the interview and proceeded as if her words had no impact on him at all. "Mrs. Baxter," he said, slowly and deliberately, "do you know what you are saying here? Do you realize what you are accusing Dr. Connor and his wife of?"

"Yes sir, I undastand," Liz said meekly.

"I don't think you do." He lowered his voice. "I don't think you understand at all. Mrs. Baxter, no one in this town will believe a word of what you just said. Hell, I don't really believe you, in spite of those persuasive tears of yours."

Liz's face tightened and she responded with strong resistance. "Well, I am not lyin' Captain Whitmore. And I ain't pretendin' these tears neither. I love those children. And I've got to find someone who can help me save 'em from their momma. "

Whitmore erupted. "I mean, Christ! It's Dr. Frank Connor, for God's sake! Really, do you have any idea who you are talking about?"

Liz stared at him, not knowing how to react. Fighting down her fear again, she pressed forward. "You may not believe me, Captain. Maybe nobody's gonna believe me. But I've got to find someone to help me save those kids. Mizzuz Connor is crazy, Captain. She gets a crazy look in her eyes and when I see that, I know she's slippin'. Then when I come back the next day, or after the weekend, she's done somethin' awful to them kids."

Whitmore said nothing. They both stared at each other, Whitmore watching for some hint of pretense or acting, and Liz, biting her lip to hold back both more tears and her growing anger towards this man. She seemed completely sincere, Whitmore admitted to himself. He just didn't know how to process what he had heard. He certainly didn't want to believe it. He prayed that he didn't have to. Yet, as he stared silently at the shaking Black woman before him, he realized one thing was absolutely clear—Elizabeth Baxter was convinced that the wife of one of the most prominent men in the San Francisco Bay area was abusing her kids, and capable of killing them.

"Aw shit." The words burst out of him, giving away his internal conflict. He closed his eyes, took a deep breath, then looked at Liz and spoke slowly. "All right now. Let's just say for a minute that you are telling the truth. Let's set aside the fact that you are talking about Dr. Frank Connor. And let's set aside that believing you means professional suicide for me. You say she's been cutting them. What do you mean? She actually cuts them with kitchen knives?"

"I'm not sure what she uses. All I know is, I come in the mornin' some days and one a them's been cut on they legs or on their arms. I don' know how she does it. But there they are, all cut up. And bruised, like they've been beat up too, when I get to work."

"Well, where is Dr. Connor in all this? He must know what's going on. Are you saying he is hurting his kids too?"

"No, no. I've never seen him do nothin' like that. But …."

Whitmore leaned forward with renewed interest while he considered what he might be able to pursue if Dr. Connor was somehow unaware. But with his internal conflict still battling, he couldn't erase his continuing scowl. "But what?"

Liz lowered her head. "He knows." She kept her eyes focused on the floor, as if ashamed of the words she just uttered.

"He knows what?" Whitmore pressed, annoyed now.

Liz knew Whitmore was automatically defending Dr. Connor, and it had a deep effect on her. It tugged something loose inside her. Something she never admitted to herself before—that she was beyond angry at the man, the doctor, who saved lives outside his home while his own children's lives were threatened. He was the one who should have been reporting the horror to the authorities. He needed to be the one protecting his children. Instead, she was forced to fight his battle for him, to protect what he should have held dear, the lives of his children. She hadn't just lost respect for the prominent doctor everyone else loved. She hated him. And there it was—something she never admitted before.

She raised her head and focused that force of hatred and anger at Captain Whitmore, who was trying to defend Dr. Connor from the indefensible. She looked him straight in the eye and spoke, plainly and forcefully. "Yes, Captain Whitmore, he knows all about it. He's been knowin' about it fo' a long time. And he won't do a thing to stop it. He keeps bandagin' them up and pretendin' it ain't gonna happen again. But it does happen again. And it's been happenin' all along, again and again and again."

Whitmore leaned farther forward, and growled in a whisper, "Do you know what you are saying?"

"I know exactly what I am sayin', Captain Whitmore." Liz's voice was as full of fire as her gaze. "I know who Dr. Connor is like nobody else. I wash that man's socks. I change his dirty sheets. I fix his coffee. I'm the one takes care a him when he's sick. And he *knows* I know what's happenin' to his kids. How he's doin' nothin' to save his own babies. And how he's hidin' it from everyone. And I know his wife is gettin' worse. I tol' him, she's gonna kill them babies someday if somebody doesn't step in. I tol' him. And he hit me. And then he fired me."

Whitmore didn't move. Liz pushed back her chair,

interpreting his frozen silence to mean he was unwilling to help. She was done trying to convince him. Disgusted by his ignorant defense of the "all-powerful" Dr. Connor, she didn't even want to look at him anymore. She reached into her purse, drew out a tissue to wipe her eyes and nose, then replaced the tissue, snapped her purse closed, and stood to leave.

It was shock that had rendered Whitmore silent. He felt the burn of truth in her words. It was something he wouldn't be able to explain until much later, but Liz had the ability to burn truth into a person. Her words were as piercing as her eyes, and the impact of both was unavoidable. Two questions roiled in his mind: how could he help those kids, and how the hell would he keep his job if he did?

"Aw shit! Ho-ly shit."

Liz stopped at the door and looked back at him. "You say that word a lot, Captain. I'm pretty sure yo' Miss Nellie did not teach you to talk like that."

"I'm sorry Mrs. Baxter. I don't mean to be crude. Or disrespectful. And no, Miss Nellie definitely did not teach me that." He chortled and added, "I learned that all by myself."

Liz gave him a mildly scolding look and murmured another "Mmm-hmm" as she turned back to the door.

"Just a minute, Mrs. Baxter." He scrambled to keep her there until he could satisfy his own conscience. "Honestly, the truth is, I really don't know what to do. I mean, Christ! It's Dr. Connor we're talking about. Mrs. Baxter, please sit down. I don't think we are done here."

"Captain Whitmore, I can tell you don't believe me. And even if you did, you won't do anything about this problem. You keep sayin' 'Dr. Connor, Dr. Connor' as if he's God or somethin'. He ain't God. That's sho' 'nuff true."

She stood facing him, her wide frame in front of his desk. With weariness and disappointment in her voice, she asked, "Captain Whitmore, what if I was one a them white ladies that live up in Woodland Estates? You'd be listenin' to me then, right? Well, some a them white lady neighbors, they know. I know they know, 'cuz I can tell they know. If I was one a them tellin' you this story, you'd be listenin' then, wouldn't you? But none a them gonna come tell you. Why? 'Cuz they scared. Just like you is scared. They're scared a makin' somebody upset. Scared a makin' the neighborhood look bad. They probably scared a big ol' Dr. Connor too. Just like you."

She shifted the weight of her heavy body from one foot to the other. "Or what if somebody from my neighborhood come in here and tell you 'bout some colored kids bein' hurt by they momma? You listen then? No you wouldn't. 'Cuz none a them be talkin' to you in the first place. They're scared too. They ain't scared a they neighbors. They scared a you an' every other police officer. So here I come. Fat, little ol' Elizabeth Baxter. And I'm the only one comin' forward and tellin' you the truth. The truth nobody else is gonna tell you. An' you ain't listenin'. You ain't gonna hear it from no white lady, 'cuz she ain't comin'. An' you ain't gonna hear it from no colored lady, neither, 'cuz she ain't never gonna tell the police nothin'. An' yet, here I am. That's why you ain't listenin'. Ain't it, Captain?"

Fighting back tears again, this time of frustration, she turned to the door and opened it.

"Wait," Whitmore said. "Look, you've got it right. No one wants to go up against Dr. Connor. It's going to be impossible to get anyone else to believe this. And ..." He paused as Liz stared at him. "And how the hell am I going to make this stick, coming from a ...."

"From a Negro maid?" Liz spoke the words he'd left unsaid. "This isn't about me bein' colored, or about Dr. Connor being white an' rich an' respected. It's about those kids, Captain Whitmore."

"Aw, shi ..." He stopped himself, not wanting to draw

more disapproval from Liz. He could feel her pulling on the moral character Miss Nellie built into him. He knew he was not going to get away with doing nothing. So, like an annoyed teenager who reluctantly agreed to do his chores, he said, "All right. I'll look into it. But don't count on anything. You don't know who you're dealing with here. You really don't, Mrs. Baxter."

Liz left the police station half hopeful, half convinced that her effort had been a complete waste of time. As she made her way back to her car, she prayed, "Lord, that man's a good man, he's just scared like everybody else. He needs Grandma's strength, Lord. Give him that. Oh, and gimme that too, Lord. And please protect ma babies fo' me 'til I find out what to do."

Todd Connor

Chapter 10

After Liz's firing, Mom and Dad practically celebrated her absence. Mom especially. No longer did fear grip her that Liz would show up to discover the damage of her rampages. Dad's relief was in knowing Liz would not be able to expose the truth behind the facade of their American Dream.

Mom was only partially aware of what she had been doing. For as long as she could remember, she had encountered periods of slipping away from reality into a rage-filled altered state. She never knew exactly where the anger came from or what would trigger her descent from the rational to the out-of-control. However, she was not completely unaware of her actions. She simply no longer cared that some force inside her played out its maniacal need to injure her children. When her conscious mind eventually regained control, she retained only vague memories of what she had done.

Only later—many years later, would I learn the genesis behind her mental hell. Her early life was anything but peaceful. My mother, Jane Pierce, grew up in an upstanding, church-going family. Her mother, Violet, sang in the church choir and for many years insisted that young Jane and her little sister, Dorothy, join her. Jane decided at an early age that church was not for her. She was bored there. Her lack of religious interest was fueled by her dad, Donald. Donny, as everyone called him, was intellectual, and one of the few in the little farm community of Dixon, California, who had gone to college. After graduating from UC Berkeley in 1920 with a chemistry degree, he began a promising career with Shell Chemical. Donny and Violet were on their way to financial security when they began their family with Jane's birth in 1923. Five years later Dorothy came along. Donny and Violet both wanted more children, but when the crash hit in October 1929 and Donny lost his job, it dashed all hopes of expanding their family. Then, the ten thousand dollars they had struggled to save over the first eight years of their marriage vanished completely when their bank failed in 1930. Seemingly overnight, like so many others, they were destitute. Fortunately, the small family was supported with food from Violet's father's nearby dairy farm. Also, Donny's dad owned a rental house behind his home in Dixon, where they were able to live.

Little Jane adored her father, who told everyone she was the apple of his eye. But after the Depression hit, his eyes turned dark and distant. By the age of seven, Jane felt abandoned by him. Donny was rarely home, as he sought odd jobs to make ends meet. Violet made pies that Jane and her little sister tried to sell door-to-door. Unfortunately, those living behind neighboring doors rarely had any more money than did Jane's family.

Jane grew to hate her life after the crash of '29. She was angry but didn't really know why. All she knew was that life used to be great, and now it wasn't. Vague remembrances of a playful existence, their secure home, and her doting father rattled inside of her. Ostensibly overnight, all that had been dashed by something she could not understand. Jane's life became as unsavory as the seemingly endless meals of vegetable soup "made mostly of water," as she recalled later in life.

"My shoes would have tasted better than that soup!" she joked once at a New Year's Eve party she and her husband threw. As she spoke, she pulled up the hem of her designer gown embarrassingly high to display the red Italian pumps she wore. Her legs looked far more delicious to the men around her than any meal they could imagine.

The lavish parties she and her doctor husband hosted were an eclipsing remedy for them both, designed to erase the emotional ravages left inside of them by the Great Depression.

Like Jane, Frank Connor was six years old when the Depression hit. Their landlord was good enough to not evict his family, but they barely scraped by. His immigrant Irish parents found themselves without work and, on most days, without food. His father, a talented musician, managed to scrape together a little money teaching music lessons, but proceeded to drink it all away at the local pub. Frank recalled many times when his mother stretched the same pot of potato soup for a week or more by feeding the family of six only one meal a day. The Depression's fallout catapulted his mother into mental illness, leading to a nervous breakdown in 1933.

At age twelve, Frank became the "man" of the house, caring for his three younger siblings. Under the immense pressure put on him at such a young age, Frank vowed to never be poor again. With every bite of week-old potato soup; with every night he put his siblings to bed, cold and shivering from lack of heat and food; with every dawn when he had pulled his passed out father off the front steps; with every night he was awakened to calm his mother's night terrors, his determination strengthened. The only answer, as he saw it, was to grow up to be rich, important, and powerful. He longed for everything the American Dream promised, and vowed to do whatever it took to get it. As he achieved that goal, the dark memories of his struggle were shoved deep into a place he swore he would never again look.

For Jane, however, the poverty of the Depression did not deliver her deepest injury. The most damaging event was in

1930, not long before her ninth birthday. Her parents sent her for a weekend with her uncle and aunt in nearby Winters, California. Their son, George, was several years older but always took an interest in her. At family gatherings, her cousin always sat and talked with her. Often George invited Jane to dance around the picnic tables "like Fred Astaire and Ginger Rogers." After her father abandoned her, George became the one person Jane could turn to. He made her feel pretty, special, and important.

The weekend of this particular visit was in early October. Her uncle Alfred was out harvesting almonds from their large grove. Standing on the front steps of the farmhouse, surrounded by almond trees spreading out in all directions as far as one could see, young Jane asked, "How come you aren't helping, George?"

George looked away. Even at age eight, Jane had seen the look that passed over his face often enough to recognize it as shame, but she had never seen it in him before. "Dad doesn't want my help," he answered. "He says I'm as useless as an empty almond shell."

While George's young cousin worshiped him, he was not well regarded by his father. Jane's uncle was a burly brute of a man who did not think highly of his son's preference for the pageantry of movies, rather than the hard work and sweat of the farm. George's father didn't hesitate to express his disdain through physical abuse, as obvious from the black eye George sported on the day Jane arrived. When she asked him about it, he muttered something. All Jane understood was "I'll show him ... thinks I'm not a man."

"What?" Jane asked.

"Nothing. You wouldn't understand. You're just a girl."

For the first time, Jane heard ugliness in her cousin's voice.

Later in the afternoon, George had daily chores to do in the barn, while Jane helped her aunt Betsy with dinner. Once that was finished, she went looking for him. Entering the darkening barn as dusk settled in for the evening, she called, "George? Where are you? Can we play Fred Astaire and Ginger Rogers like we used to?"

She heard a crash deep in the building, near the milk room. Jane rushed over to find her cousin standing in the middle of half a dozen broken milk jugs, fresh milk spreading around him.

"Shit! Dad is going to kill me for this!" Cowering to the floor, George curled into himself and covered his head with his arms as he rocked and murmured over and over, "He's going to kill me."

When Jane reached out to comfort him, he shoved her. "Get the hell away from me! He thinks I'm not a man. He thinks I'm a ..." His words drifted off into sobs.

Jane asked softly, "What do you mean, George? You're a boy and you're almost grown up. That means you're a man. What else could it mean?"

George's right arm flew out and he swept Jane's legs out from under her. Before she could react he was on top of her, pinning her to the floor. Through clenched teeth he growled, "Not a man. I'll show him. I'll show that bastard."

"Ow!" Jane shrieked. "Let go of me. George, stop! You're hurting me!"

George pressed one hand over her mouth as his other hand yanked at her dress. As hard as she struggled and shrieked beneath his choking hand and smothering body, her little girl strength was no match for his teenage brutality. She gave up her futile resistance and went limp. The ordeal took only a few minutes but to Jane's mind it seemed to play out in slow motion. After George was through violating her, he stood, pulled up his pants, and looked down at her. Disgust blazed from his eyes. She felt all his hatred for his dad now focused onto her. She lay in pain and shock, unable to speak or even move.

George took one last lunge and clenched his hand over her mouth, squeezing it until tears slipped from her eyes. "You say one word of this to anyone, and I'll kill you. You hear? I'll kill you."

Astounded, Jane knew he meant his threat. She knew there was no one to turn to. What she didn't know was that such abusive cruelty that took only minutes of real time would inflict a lifetime of devastation. Her life was irreparably altered. George's brutal act stole what vitality had remained in Jane's soul. She knew she couldn't talk to her mother, who sugarcoated everything like one of her apple pies. Already deeply hurt by her distant father, her silent pain hardened into rage.

First she directed it at George, but as she grew it was unleashed against her parents and sister, then against men, then against anyone she might dare trust. There was nowhere to turn for understanding or release of what was ominously growing deep within her. Jane grew dark, not outwardly, but inwardly. Her parents noticed but were too engrossed in their own struggles to pay attention. In time, the darkness formed a life of its own, and became a force that demanded an outlet beyond her control.

By her early teens, Jane noticed she enjoyed making people cry—especially her little sister, Dorothy. There was such a sense of power in inflicting pain, and such satisfaction in releasing the anger inside her. At least for a while.

She vowed to never be poor when she grew up, no matter what she had to do. She vowed to never trust men, but she too wanted the American Dream that included marriage and a family. "I'm going to marry a rich doctor, live in a big house, and have eight kids," she bragged to girlfriends in high school. With her dark brown eyes, slender figure, and brunette hair, she knew she was turning into a beauty, and knew that was her currency to get ahead.

After graduation from high school, she was admitted to her father's alma mater, UC Berkeley. It was a financial struggle, but she knew college was where she would meet men who would get her what she wanted. The year she turned twenty, 1943, the movie *The Outlaw* came out. It's female star, Jane Russell, became the rage for her sultry performance. It was then that people began stopping Jane on the street, at restaurants, and in elevators to ask "Miss Russell" for an autograph. She responded to being catapulted into constant attention as if it were her due. Once, after signing the actress's name in front of a shocked girlfriend, Jane shrugged and said, "It's just easier." When her friend scolded her for such deception, Jane jokingly brushed her off. "Well, I can't make Miss Russell seem unfriendly now, can I? After all it's only half wrong. Jane *is* my name."

Her looks didn't hurt her when she met Frank Connor. They both worked their way through college with jobs at the Kaiser Shipyards. As World War II raged onward, Kaiser Steel built battle ships for the war effort in the Pacific, completing a ship every week at its massive Port of Richmond shipyard just north of Berkeley. The Depression was finally over, and good-paying jobs were plentiful. Jane and Frank shared the back seat of a car to and from work every day. Unbeknownst to either of them, the young married couple in the front was attempting to set them up. At first Jane disliked the young man who was always late for the ride and often slept to and from work. That fall semester, they also ended up in an economics class together. She became doubly irritated with him because he rarely showed up for class but seemed to get A's on every exam.

"He makes me so mad sometimes," she confessed to Nina, her girlfriend in the car pool's front seat. Frank was, of course, asleep. "He's always late and makes us wait for him, and then he falls asleep. It's just plain rude. He's like the walking dead. And he hardly ever shows up to class and *still* cruises. Why the heck isn't he in the army anyway? He doesn't look 4-F to me."

"Oh, he's not," Nina's husband, Al, chimed in. "Frank's got a 3-A deferment. He's the sole support of his mom and younger brothers. Working full time, going to school full time, and taking care of his brothers would make anyone tired all the time."

"Yeah, and I think Frank's cute. If I weren't married to this handsome hunk, I might just give you a run for your money in catching him," Nina teased. "You're one silly Sally if you don't snag him. Why, in ten years he'll be rich and married. Why shouldn't it be you? I bet you'll manage to keep him awake!"

"Now, don't you go trying to set me up, Nina," Jane scolded. "Didn't someone say he wants to be a mortician? Oh, my gosh! Just what I always wanted to be: a mortician's wife!"

Both girls stared at the sleeping Frank and cackled, covering their mouths with their hands so as not to wake him. When he snorted as he turned to his side but still didn't wake, they jumped and laughed hysterically. Al complained, "Hey, you two. Cut it out. That's my pal you're talking about."

Ignoring Al's rebuke, Jane added, "Maybe he should be a mortician. He'd at least have it quiet at work and could still sleep a lot." The women's laughter continued as the car turned into the shipyards and Al announced loudly enough to wake up Frank, "Okay! We're here."

"Huh? What?" Frank straightened up in his seat next to Jane. "Sorry. Guess I fell asleep."

"You guess?" joked Jane. "We thought you were dead." She and Nina giggled like schoolgirls as they hurried off to their jobs in the accounting department.

Al, getting out of the driver's seat, said, "Ignore them, Frank. They're just teasing you."

Frank straightened his six-foot, five-inch frame out of the car, towering over it, Al, and anything else nearby. He watched the two women scurry toward the office building. "I'm going to marry that girl, Al. You'll see."

"Okay, lover boy, you do that," Al said. "But right now it's time to wake up and stop dreaming, Romeo. Time for work."

After that day, Frank stayed awake on the rides. He wooed Jane into a courtship, and their eventual wedding seemed like a fairy tale on the surface. By the time they married, he had switched his major to pre-med, becoming the darling of his professors and then the doctors he worked alongside as he completed his degree. His obvious drive for wealth gained Jane's interest. She strove to prove she'd be the asset he needed to succeed.

But no one, especially Frank, knew what really was going on inside her. No one saw the nightmares and cold sweats that woke Jane on many nights, as her subconscious relived those life-altering minutes when she was just eight years old. Still, with her current life being fun and active, with an obviously bright future ahead, Jane managed to appear stable to those around her.

However, in marriage Jane realized her idea of the American Dream didn't exactly fit her own dream. She'd landed a handsome doctor as she'd predicted. But Frank buried himself in work, quickly creating an income that allowed them to purchase the home of their dreams. Being married to him was hard as she tried to fit into the expected role of a successful doctor's wife.

Jane discovered early in their marriage that Frank had never been faithful to her—not when dating, not when engaged, and certainly not after exchanging their vows. It wasn't long after she joined the Woodland Estates Bridge Club, in a step to move them up the social ladder, that she began overhearing snickers and gossip about her husband's "bedside manner." But Jane had a way of ignoring pertinent information that interfered with her ambitious goals. Still, this became the last straw, the last breaking point of hope for her. George's few minutes of brutal expression of his supposed manhood now took a new hold on her, and a psychotic inner frenzy began seeking an avenue for violent release.

Compounding matters, Jane was shocked to discover after the wedding that Frank wanted no children. But, being Catholic, he refused to use contraceptives and there was no alternative birth control. Relying on the far from perfect, Church-approved rhythm method, Jane became pregnant soon after the wedding. She was stunned when he flew into a furious rage, accusing her of purposely miscalculating her cycle so as to get pregnant. "How could you trick me like that, Jane?" he screamed when she gave him the news. He didn't speak to her for weeks.

My father's anger toward my mother for the pregnancy unleashed a rage within her greater than she'd ever known. Instead of directing it at her husband, she directed it at their first-born. As a child, I didn't even know I had another brother. Donny, obligingly named after the father my mother grew to hate, was born in 1950 and had been so damaged by my mother that he was sent to an institution long before I was born. My parents never spoke of him. Even Liz didn't know about him until much later.

When Mom later became pregnant with Mark, it was clear to Dad that she could not handle the emotional strain of motherhood. And whatever had gone on with Donny, Dad was not about to allow her to repeat it. That is when he sought out an agency to find household help.

Mom was still grasping onto her dream of raising lots of kids, even though she knew it was clearly impossible for her. Nonetheless, she vehemently opposed having help, because she believed she was supposed to do everything on her own. "Donny was sick when he was born, Frank. It wasn't me. It was him," she pleaded after Mark was born, trying to explain what happened and why she didn't need anyone's help.

Her husband stared at her in disbelief, not willing to argue but also not willing to relive the pain of something he wanted to forget. He called an agency and requested a woman to act as nanny and maid several days a week.

It was Liz who was sent to be interviewed one Saturday. When Frank opened the back door, he tried to hide his reaction to her obesity and his immediate decision to reject her.

"Hello, Dr. Connor. I'm Elizabeth Baxter." Highly skilled at gauging people's reactions to her, she read the look on his face but greeted him cheerfully. "The agency sent me over to help with yo' baby and mizzuz today. Now, I know what you're thinkin' Dr. Connor. I'm big, but I am a hard worker. You'll see. Now, you show me the laundry room and I'll get started. And I can't wait to meet yo' new baby! I love children, Dr., you'll see."

Impressed with her confidence but still skeptical of her agility, he said, "Well, the baby—Mark, is asleep, and so is his mother."

From behind him came his wife's unfriendly voice. "Who are you? And what are you doing in my house?"

Frank stood looking nervously between the two women, not knowing what to say. He hadn't told his wife he'd moved forward with hiring help. He'd known it would just lead to another fight.

Liz nodded and smiled. "Hello, Mizzuz Connor. I'm Elizabeth Baxter. I'm here to help you and yo' new baby."

Jane, her eyes flaring in anger, looked at her husband as if to burn a hole into his skin. Her voice was icily polite as she said, "Frank, I need to speak to you in the kitchen. Please." She turned and left the room, with him following reluctantly.

Liz heard their hushed argument and took the opportunity to peer around a few corners to see what she was getting into. Between the obvious tension and the household disarray, she had to chuckle. "Looks like these two could use two a 'ol Liz about now."

The Connors didn't hold down the volume for long. Soon their tempest was a full hurricane. Frank felt the urge to strike his wife, as he often did to put an end to an argument. Knowing Liz was nearby, he decided it best to just leave as quickly as possible. As he slammed the back door behind him he yelled, "Okay then, *you* fire her!"

Jane felt herself slipping, as she had so many times before. She was overwhelmed with the need to get away, immediately. But how could she run with a baby and that ... that unknown woman in the house? Her anxiety was greater than she could bear. Within seconds it screamed above all else for her full attention. She grabbed her car keys and went out the same door her husband had left through. Her racing mind completely eclipsed both the baby and the enormous Black stranger in her home.

Jane didn't remember going to a movie to escape the screeching voices in her mind. It was six in the evening when she returned home. As she walked in the door, awareness crashed back to her. She only vaguely remembered the argument with Frank, and had forgotten all about Liz. Her last clear recollection was of putting the baby down for a nap hours before. Panic washed over her as she made her way down the long hallways to Mark's nursery at the back of the house.

There Liz was, her featherbed frame of a body sitting in the rocking chair, singing as the baby in her arms stared at her and cooed.

Just then Frank walked down the hallway. "Well. I wondered if you were coming back." His voice was terse. "As you can see, Liz now works for us."

Jane had enough sense to know it had been unforgivable to leave the house as she'd done. She had left before, forgetting Donny on many occasions. But then, no one was around to know. She really did want things to be different with Mark. She really did want to be a mother, and a good one. Reluctantly, she accepted Liz as maid and nanny to our family.

It wasn't long before Liz realized Mom's instability. On the first Tuesday of her half-week schedule after the Saturday she was hired, she noticed something odd about Mrs. Connor when she arrived.

"What are you doing here?" Jane accused as she saw Liz letting herself in through the laundry room back door.

"It's Tuesday, Mizzuz Connor. Dr. Connor says I'm to work Tuesday and Thursday and every other Wednesday. Remember?" Liz responded respectfully.

Mrs. Connor continued to stare at her blankly. Liz's smile faded as she realized something about the woman wasn't right.

"Why don't you go on and do some shoppin', Mizzuz Connor?" she encouraged softly. "It'll be all right. Liz here now. You go on and do yo' shoppin' and see yo' lady friends. I'll take care of everything."

Jane still looked confused and dazed.

"You go on, Mizzuz Connor. Liz here now. Thing's gonna be all right."

The woman nodded as if she were a child receiving instructions on some overly complex task. As if in a fog, Jane turned and silently left.

By the time Christine was born, Jane's psyche had deteriorated to the point that Liz wondered if she was leaving the children at risk as she left at the end of each workday. Confirmation of her fears came one day when Christine was almost a year old. Sometime after Jane had left for the day, the doorbell rang and Liz answered it.

"Are you the help?" a well-dressed woman asked.

"Yes, ma'am."

"I'm Kay Wagner. From next door—the white house, down the hill. May I come in for a moment?"

"Mizzuz Connor isn't home, ma'am."

"Well, it's actually you I want to talk to," she said nervously.

Assuming she knew the reason for such a request, Liz quickly chimed, "Oh, Mizz Wagner, I've no mo' days to help folks. I work here half time and I work fo' another family the other half. Thank you, but I'm all full up."

"Oh, no, I don't need help." Kay Wagner chuckled, still a bit nervous. "My kids are grown and it's just my husband and me now."

"Uh huh. Well, I guess it's okay to come on in and set a while. Mizzuz Connor gonna be home soon." Liz wondered where this was all going as she moved into the living room, motioning for Mrs. Wagner to have a seat on the couch. "Can I get you somethin' to drink?"

"Oh, no thank you. I won't stay but a minute," Kay Wagner said as she sat down. "I just want to ask you something."

"You want to ask *me* somethin'?" Liz felt a heightened sense of caution now. She drew a chair from the dining table and perched on it awkwardly. Her mind raced, wondering what this white lady wanted if she didn't need a maid.

"Well, I see you've been working here for some time now. You come in the middle of the week. Is that right?" Kay asked.

Liz cocked her head in puzzlement and responded slowly. "Yes, Mizz Wagner. I come Tuesdays and Thursdays and every other Wednesday."

"Oh, I'm sorry. It's not that I mean to pry. I was wondering about the children, uh ...." Kay Wagner paused, casting glances around the room as if searching for the right words to say. Finally, she blurted out, "Are the children okay? I mean, are they being treated okay—when you're not here?"

Liz quickly assumed the blank expression she'd learned decades earlier to hide her emotions from a white person. "Mizz Wagner, I don't know what you are gettin' at. The Connor children are doin' just fine."

"Yes, they seem fine. When you're here. But I can tell you, things are very different when you are not."

"What you mean by 'dif'rent'?" Liz realized her voice had an edge, as she began judging Mrs. Wagner to be one of those meddlesome neighbors she'd encountered at other homes. She had met too many rich white ladies who loved to see what their neighbors were up to so they could gossip about it. Liz knew her place, and that meant revealing nothing.

"Mrs. Baxter, you are not here all the time. I am. I know the difference between the days you are here and those you are not. I have never met you before but I knew you were here in the middle of the week. Do you know how I knew that?"

Liz sat silently, stone faced, waiting for more details before she asked this woman to leave.

"It isn't because I watch your car come and go. I can assure you, I do not. It also isn't because I am good friends with Mrs. Connor. We are cordial, but certainly not friends." Kay Wagner paused briefly. "I know you are here during the middle of the week because I never hear the children screaming on those days. When I hear them, it's not the screaming of children at play. They sound terrified. I'm just curious—are they ever scared when you are here?"

Liz clenched her jaw in an effort to not let her reaction show. What Kay Wagner was saying confirmed the unsettled fear she had on leaving at the end of her workdays. "The babies ain't scared a me, Mizz Wagner. They've never looked scared to me."

"I'm sure that's true. But I assure you, that is not the way it is when you are not here. I know. You know the distance between this house and mine. I hear the screams from all that way. And I often see something strange in Jane Connor's eyes when I encounter her with the children."

Liz's heart pounded. She knew exactly what Kay Wagner referred to. She too had seen Mrs. Connor's eyes turn strange.

Liz didn't like that crazed look, but hadn't known what to make of it. She had never dreamed that look might mean Mrs. Connor could do harm to her children.

"And those bruises on little Mark," Kay went on. "Didn't you ever notice those?"

"Well, he just four, Mizz Wagner. Little boys, they get bruises and boo-boos all day long."

She spoke carefully, but Kay Wagner's question answered something Liz had often wondered about. Most kids got skinned knees and scraped elbows, but she now realized that Mark, and more often lately, Christine—who was just beginning to walk, did seem to experience more serious injuries when she wasn't around. Many Tuesdays, she found at least one of her babies with bruised eyes or burned hands, occasionally serious enough to require bandages administered by their doctor father.

Jane always explained away the injuries when Liz arrived. It had started when the Connor children were just babies. Sometimes she had seen what looked like cuts on their little bottoms. "Oh, the safety pin got caught in the diaper again," Jane Connor would explain blithely. "Can you show me again how to pin those diapers the way you do, Elizabeth?" Later, it was, "Oh, you know, Mark likes to reach up for things on the counter. He put his hand on the stove." Or, "Christine wasn't watching where she was going and fell down the stairs again. Children can be so clumsy sometimes." Liz never dreamed that these injuries were anything other than what Jane Connor said they were.

As memories of the strange injuries flashed through her mind, Liz had to acknowledge the nightmare she had been ignoring. An overwhelming mixture of sorrow and fear made her stomach sick. She knew Mrs. Wagner was right, something was seriously wrong in the Connor household. She wanted to cry or scream, or both. She could do neither. Nor could she let this white lady see her growing fear.

"Ma'am, I don't think I know anythin' of what you're talkin' 'bout." Liz spoke slowly and carefully. She stood. "I think it best if you be goin' now."

Kay Wagner stood too, deflecting her gaze away from Liz. "Yes, I suppose you're right. I'm sorry to have bothered you."

As Liz opened the front door Kay Wagner said, "Please don't mention any of this to Dr. and Mrs. Connor. I want to stay at least friendly with them as neighbors."

"I don't know that there is anything to say, Mizz Wagner."

Kay Wagner wore an expression of worried sadness. She nodded and said softly, "Thank you. It was nice to meet you, Mrs. Baxter. I am very glad you are here. Especially for the children's sake."

Liz nodded wordlessly. She knew if she opened her mouth she would burst into tears. Once the door was closed, she put her forehead against it and let the floodgates open.

"Oh no, Lord. Not ma' babies."

Chapter 11

Those were the memories that flooded Liz's mind as she drove out of the police station parking lot. How could she have been so blind, she asked herself as she reflected on all the years of injuries: the bruises, cuts, and burns. I been a damn fool, Liz scolded herself—how could I not see any a this? She remembered her reasoning back then, and how ridiculous it now seemed. For a moment she thought she should just pull over to let her tears roll. Something, however, rose up in her again, as it had so many times before.

Liz had an amazing way of refocusing her anger and shame. Every time Chrissy or I did something wrong, she had one thing to say to us: "Okay, Todd, now you need to tell yo' sister you're sorry," she'd say after I pushed Chrissy for not yielding to one of my wishes.

Reluctantly, I complied. "I'm sorry, Chrissy."

"Now, you tell yo' brother you forgive 'im, Chrissy," Liz instructed. Chrissy would have much rather slugged me, if not for Liz standing right there.

"I forgive you, Todd," she obeyed after a lengthy pause.

"All right now," Liz went on. "But we all know 'sorry' don't fix it. So what're you gonna do to make it better fo' yo' sister, Todd? What are you gonna do to really fix it an' make it up to her?" This would be followed by my doing some task of Chrissy's, such as making her bed or clearing her dishes after breakfast. Liz's philosophy required saying sorry with some sort of action—to make sure we really were sorry, and to let the other person know it was sincere.

As Liz drove, she found herself right in the middle of her own morality requirements. "Oh, Lord, I am so sorry fo' how blind I've been," she prayed aloud as tears slipped down her brown cheeks. "And I know, Lord, *sayin'* sorry fixes nothin'. What am I s'pose to do now to prove it?"

Liz turned off the freeway at 98th Avenue. At the end of the exit, she had a decision to make. If she turned right, she'd go down the hill to her home in The Flats. If she turned left, she would head into the hills, to the white neighborhoods, towards Woodland Estates. She felt at a loss. Her house was empty, with Claman at work. Her babies were in their classes at Blessed Child Academy. She was grateful for that—it meant they were safe for the moment.

A sudden thought struck and she impulsively turned left. The teachers at the school knew her. Maybe they'd let her see the children one more time, so she could tell them how much she loved them and how sorry she was.

Liz slowed as she passed the school. The fenced playground that stretched between the four-lane boulevard and the school building was filled with children at recess. Clusters of laughing children played basketball, dodge ball, hopscotch, and other games, creating a picture of joy. Liz smiled as she passed, soothed by seeing children play.

Then she saw one small child standing alone, clinging to the cyclone fence separating the playground from the boulevard. He was staring out, away from the other children behind him in the schoolyard. As her car slowly crept along, the child's face became clear. It was me.

Liz pulled the car to the curb and stopped right in front of me. She watched as I remained motionless, staring across the road as if in a trance.

Liz Here Now   147

She got out of her car. "Todd," she called out.

Normally, I would have brightened at the mere sight of her. But I remained still, my eyes barely reacting to her appearance.

Liz hurried up the sidewalk as fast as she could move her large body. As if through a fog I heard her call out again, "Todd baby, it's me, Liz. Liz here now, child."

What Liz didn't know was that I was still in the someplace else I had been carried away to the month before, when I'd been so badly hurt and when Liz was fired. I hadn't let go of her tear-filled eyes as she said goodbye to me through the window. I clung to the lingering image of my small white hand pressed against the warmth of her brown palm on the glass. Those images were my only lifeline, all that had held me together since. Everything else seemed a blur. I was aware of nothing, except deep depression and its compensating companion: sleep.

I had screamed so hard when Mom attacked me that for several days I couldn't speak at all. My vocal chords recovered but, with Liz banished from my life, I didn't want to speak to anyone. I barely spoke to Chrissy, and certainly did not want to speak to my parents. I felt betrayed by everyone in my world. Damaged and scarred, despair engulfed me. Since my mother didn't kill me from the outside I decided to die on the inside, and completely withdraw from the world that had so abandoned me.

My withdrawal worked to the advantage of my guilty parents, however. My silence provided them a good means of lying away what really happened to me.

Chrissy told me Mom announced one evening at dinner while I was still bedridden, "Your brother has laryngitis. He needs to stay in bed until he recovers."

"He talked to me just fine when I went to his room before dinner," Chrissy protested.

"I said, he's sick with laryngitis." Mom's eyes flared at

Chrissy. "You shouldn't be in there. You don't want to get what he's got. Do you, Chrissy?"

It wasn't a question. Both Chrissy and Mark cowered in understanding of Mom's threat. Dad said nothing.

Within a few days, the bandages on my legs were removed, leaving the lacerations to scab over and eventually heal. With no need to dress the wounds daily, Dad came into my room only in the morning to put a tongue depressor in my mouth and look at my throat, as if searching for some debilitating vocal ailment. If I had known any swear words then, I would have screamed them at him. Instead, I remained silent in growing hatred for him and his pretense.

More than a week after the attack I still refused to get out of bed or utter a word.

Mom entered the room one day as Dad finished his false throat exam. Fully pretending the throat ailment was real, she asked, "What should we give him? Should we continue to feed him soup?"

"I guess so. Just continue to give him soup until he recovers." Dad's voice sounded a bit guilty.

Even at five, I knew the truth. To them I was only 'him.' Neither my injuries nor I were important. Keeping up the pretense of their American Dream—that was all that mattered.

With Liz no longer around to coax me out of despondency, I was gradually mutating into a mix of anger and fear. My parents gave me a little brass bell to ring when I needed food or water. Whether an attempt at kindness or admission of guilt, I wasn't sure. But I soon used it as a weapon to make them jump.

Mom's facial expression moved from a look of rage to one of uneasy concern as she urged me to talk. "What will the neighbors and your teachers think of us, with a mute son?" she asked. "If you don't start talking, people will say you're stupid."

I just glared at her.

After I missed more than two weeks of school, my teacher, Mrs. Johnson, called to find out how serious the illness was. "Will Todd be joining us again for the rest of the term? I would hate to hold him back. He was doing so well before ...."

"He can't talk and can't get out of bed," Mom blurted into the phone.

"I don't think I understand," Mrs. Johnson said. "He can't talk *and* he's bedridden?"

"That's correct." Mom's voice was sharp. "He has to stay in bed. Doctor's orders."

"It sounds quite serious," Mrs. Johnson said. "Is it contagious? Should I talk with Dr. Connor about the other children in Todd's class?"

"No." Mom's voice began elevating to a high-pitched frenzy as she tried to suppress her fear and control the teacher's suspicion. "I am sure he will be better soon. I am certain he will be."

I was not. I spent an entire month, uncommunicative, in bed. Finally, knowing that there was nothing physically wrong, Dad came into my room one day and announced, "Todd, you are going to school tomorrow. You're fine."

The next day, I got up with my siblings, ate my breakfast cereal, and went to school, without saying a word to anyone except Chrissy, who had been secretly coming into my room daily to talk and play games.

When I rejoined my kindergarten class, I recognized the real damage without being able to understand it. Something psychological had shifted deep within me, from which I would not recover for decades. Before I'd been a bright-eyed, imaginative little boy who reveled in the imaginary games of his big sister and who giggled uncontrollably with the joy of the Jell-O bounce on Liz. That boy was gone. He had sunk into an ocean of confusion and fear.

Recess became a time for me to flee in search of escape and

quiet. The noise of the other children playing, which previously excited me, now made me afraid. Everything made me afraid. I was afraid of the kids on the schoolyard. I was afraid of the kids who had been my playmates. I was afraid of the tremendously kind Mrs. Johnson, who had always been so gentle with me. Other than the comfort of playing with Chrissy, I was afraid of being home. The only time I had any relief from fear was when I went to sleep at night. When all was still and quiet, rest finally arrived for me, and retreat from a world of tense daily experiences. So when Liz found me staring aimlessly out at the boulevard through the cyclone fence, she was entering into something that had become my daily ritual to cope with the inescapable, pervasive fear.

Liz, of course, saw the change in me immediately. She came up to the fence and bent down so her face was in front of mine.

"Todd. It's me, your 'Lizzie-beth.' Oh, baby, what's wrong?" With concern, she looked into my eyes through the fence. She wrapped her warm brown fingers over mine, entwined with the grid of the cyclone wall that separated us. "Can you tell Liz why you so sad, baby?"

I didn't respond. Tears that had started silently were growing into gulping but still silent sobs.

"Oh, Todd." Liz's voice was a sad whisper. "Did one a them kids hurt you? You need me to go talk to yo' teacher about that?"

I shook my head no and continued to cry.

Liz intuitively realized this had nothing to do with what might have happened that day, but with what had been done to me the month before at home.

Desperation sometimes makes people do things without any thought to where the action might lead. All we know is the next step to take, with no idea where that will lead or how to deal with the aftermath. Sometimes people are driven to those decisions from greed or anger. That always ends badly. Other times, those decisions are driven by deep love, the kind that erases common sense and rational thought. It's the kind of love that compels action. That love now became the consuming force that propelled Liz into a series of decisions that only desperate love could ever make.

"Baby, I'm gonna talk to yo' teacher and you're gonna come with me today," she said. "That sound okay with you?"

I nodded with a burst of relief. Just then, the bell rang and the children all started back to their classrooms.

"Now you go on in to yo' classroom, and I'll come getchya." She started to move back along the fence toward the gate to the school office. "You wait fo' me in yo' classroom. Okay, Todd?"

I nodded and obediently walked back inside.

As Liz entered the front glass doors of the school, Chrissy ran up, yelling her name. She slammed into Liz's legs so hard Liz was sure her round body would roll back out the door. As she regained her balance, she smiled. "Oh, Christine! How you doin', girl?"

Grinning, Chrissy looked straight up at Liz. Liz's heart stopped at the sight of an enormous black eye with small cuts around it. Liz gently pushed Chrissy back from her leg and leaned over to inspect the bruise. With grave seriousness, she asked, "What happened to you, child?"

Chrissy teared up. She started to wipe her tears with her right hand, which revealed a huge bandage around her index finger and thumb.

Liz caressed Chrissy's face. "Honey, what happened? Liz here now. You can tell me, baby."

Fighting back tears, Chrissy stared into Liz's big brown face and whispered, "Mommy says I fell. In the roses."

Liz fought to keep Chrissy from knowing the anger surging inside her. "Well, you're comin' with me now, baby. C'mon, we're gonna get Todd too. And Mark, too."

Liz took Chrissy by the left hand and walked to the principal's office. She opened the door quietly and ushered Chrissy inside. At a desk behind the counter, a woman looked up from her work.

"I'm here to get the Connor children," Liz announced. "I'm Mrs. Baxter, the Connors' maid. I've come to pick 'em up."

"Please, have a seat. Let me go get the principal." The woman spoke politely as she rose, opened the door into the office behind her, then disappeared inside and closed the door behind her.

Liz sat down on one of the vinyl office chairs, Chrissy beside her. Liz stared at Chrissy's bandaged hand and black eye, and shook her head. When Chrissy looked up at her, Liz tried to smile reassuringly.

It was not a fall into rose bushes that caused Chrissy's injuries, and Liz knew it. What she didn't know was that, the previous weekend, Mom baked an apple pie, in a vain attempt to get me talking. Chrissy and I both knew it wasn't from kindness—she was drastically afraid that she'd be discovered as my psychosomatic sickness lingered embarrassingly long. Chrissy was doing her spelling homework at the kitchen table and I was coloring in a coloring book. Mom pulled the pie out of the oven and placed it on the counter very near the table. She then reached for a sharp knife, to cut into the pie and ensure it was done. Chrissy, without thinking, eagerly leapt from her chair to the counter. She reached up for a piece of crispy crust that had broken off. The tip of the knife descended. It impaled the small bridge of flesh between her thumb and index finger. Chrissy's flesh was pinned down by the knife in Mom's hand. With her left hand, Mom backhanded a slap across Chrissy's face, delivering the black eye.

Chrissy screamed uncontrollably, unable to escape the knife holding her hand to the counter. In terror, we both saw Mom's crazed eyes and twisted grin.

Mom grinned at the blood on the knife and Chrissy's terrified screams. Taking pleasure in Chrissy's pain, she leaned down and looked straight into Chrissy's screaming face as she yanked the knife upward. Then she said, through clenched teeth, "Let that be a lesson to you. Put your hands around sharp knives, you could get hurt. *Never* do that again. Do you understand me?"

Chrissy crumpled to the floor, writhing in pain.

"Oh, shut up. It's not that bad." Mom reached for a hand towel in a nearby drawer and brusquely wrapped it around Chrissy's hand. As my terrified sister scurried away and I cowered under the table, Mom shouted, "Now go to your room! And don't get blood on *anything*, you hear?"

Dad, of course, properly bandaged the wound when he came home that night. He didn't say a word when Mom told him, "I told her not to run outside near the rose bushes. Now look what happened. It's her own fault."

But Liz wouldn't learn that truth for a long time to come. Several minutes went by as she and Chrissy sat patiently, and silently, waiting. Finally, Sister Aloysius, a tall, stately nun who was the principal, emerged with the secretary behind her. Liz stood as she approached.

"Mrs. Baxter, is it?" Sister Aloysius reached out to shake her hand.

"Yes'm. I'm Mizzuz Connor's maid. I come to pick up the children early today."

"Yes, I think I remember you from last time. When the oldest Connor boy was sick a few months ago."

"That's right, ma'am," she said politely. "I came to get Mark last March when he got sick in class. His momma was out that day, so I came to get 'im."

"I see," said Sister Aloysius. "And you're here to pick them all up today ... early?"

"Yes, that's right. They all got appointments today. So I've come to pick 'em up. Early."

"Odd, we didn't get a note from their parents." She looked from Liz to Chrissy, and back. "You know we usually require a note."

"Oh, Mizzuz Connor musta forgot." Liz glanced down at Chrissy's astonished face, hoping the child would stay silent. She had often scolded us children to always tell the truth—now she prayed Chrissy would not say anything about her lie.

"Well, we really require a note from a parent," the sister insisted mildly.

"Well, I don't know about that, ma'am. I'm sure she give you a note tomorrow to make everything right an' all."

Though Sister Aloysius said nothing, Liz realized the nun didn't fully trust her. Her next words poured out with forceful energy. "Sister, ma'am, you see this little girl's hand? She needs to see her doctor. She needs some attention right now and I'm supposed to take her there. Right now. An' Mizzuz Connor told me to get all the children, 'cuz while I'm there they all gonna see the doctor. Now, Mizzuz Connor worked hard to get this appointment with the doctor like this, all togetha. She's gonna be very upset if they can't go to they appointments now."

"I thought Dr. Connor was their doctor."

"Uh, oh ..." She panicked a bit, grasping at some way to recover. "He ... he's outta town. So Mizzuz Connor went outta her way to get another doctor to see to Christine's hand and to see all the kids at once. I'm tellin' you, ma'am. She's gonna be really upset if I can't get them to their appointments."

The stern nun studied Liz carefully. She glanced at her secretary, who shook her head slightly and shrugged. When she turned back to Liz, she said, "We called the Connor home and no one answered."

"That's right, ma'am. Mizzuz Connor ain't home and ... and, they daddy's gone on a trip somewhere." Liz was relieved that either Mom wasn't home or wasn't answering the phone.

Believing she now had convinced the sister, she poured on just the right amount of annoyance to seal it. "Now, can I please collect the children and get them to their appointments b'fo' it's too late?"

Sister Aloysius looked at her silently for another moment. Liz's nervousness heightened and she held her breath.

Finally the sister turned to her secretary. "Mrs. Henderson, please have the other Connor children sent to the office." Turning back to Liz, she smiled. "I'm sorry to have delayed you, Mrs. Baxter. Please let Mrs. Connor know I was just trying to do my job for the protection of the children."

"I undastand, Sister. I'll tell her."

With a sigh of relief, Liz sat back down in the chair next to a somewhat stunned Chrissy. She leaned over and whispered, "You know I love you, baby, and would do anything fo' you."

Chrissy, still not really understanding, nodded. She leaned in and planted herself against Liz's soft, pillowy body waterfalling over her chair. Chrissy let out a sigh of comfort, something she hadn't felt for a long time.

Chapter 12

Within a few minutes, the dutiful school secretary was leading my brother and me down the hallway into the school office. Mark looked alarmed, as if he thought he was in trouble. But I knew different. I impulsively ignored the admonition to walk down the hall and ran ahead to throw myself into Liz's arms.

When Mark nervously entered the office, she chuckled. "Hi, Mark. You look like you in trouble or somethin'. Nothin's wrong, child. We just goin' fo'...." Liz paused, noticing the secretary watching her closely and skeptically. "I've got to take you kids to some appointments. C'mon, now. We're gonna be late."

Once outside, Liz quickly ushered us to her car on the boulevard. "All right, Liz here now," she said cheerfully, as if nothing unusual was going on, after we piled into her old Chevy station wagon. "Now, you kids get yo' seat belts on."

"Where are we going, Liz?" Mark asked the question we all wanted to know. We sat quietly, waiting for her to explain.

Liz stopped still, reality suddenly returning to her mind. Like a mother hen she had instinctively gathered her endangered chicks close around her. But that, she now realized, was where her instincts ended. She had no further plan. Wide-eyed, she stared over the steering wheel through the windshield, at a loss for what to do next. After a second she turned the ignition. "Well, we're goin' on a trip," she responded vaguely.

Chrissy and I didn't care where that trip would be. Just being with Liz was all that mattered. Liz could drive into the pit of hell and that be would fine with us as long as we were with her. We had felt her warm flesh pressed against us once more. We could hear her sweet, comforting voice. Absolutely nothing else mattered.

Mark, being older, was more curious. He asked innocently, "You said we're going to the doctor's office. Dad's office?"

"No," Liz explained hesitantly. "We ain't goin' to yo' daddy's office today, Mark. And we're not goin' to another doctor's office either. I'm sorry you saw me tellin' stories back there to yo' principal."

She gave a small sigh of relief when Mark simply turned to Chrissy and me in the back seat and said, "Hey, want to play I Spy?"

Liz turned back to her worries. Lord, what fool thing did I just do, she asked herself. Her mind quickly argued, what was she supposed to do—leave her babies to keep getting hurt by their momma? Knowing her logic could not possibly hold water and allowing herself for just a moment to realize this might not end well, Liz wiped the struggle from her mind and drove down the long boulevard. For now, knowing her babies were safe was enough.

Rounding the final corner of Golf Links Road at the intersection of 98th Avenue and the interstate, she wrestled with her next move. She could take the children to her home, maybe hide them out with some of her neighbors in The Flats. Or she could get on the highway and usher them far away. She imagined for a moment that she could make them safe in a distant place, maybe with her kinfolk back in Arkansas. Unfortunately, she could now see neither maneuver had any hope of success. As the car idled at the intersection she tried to convince herself to take the children home to Woodland Estates.

Car horns began to honk after the light had turned green, then red, and then green again. Mark, Chrissy, and I gazed with puzzlement at Liz, who was hunched over the steering wheel. I couldn't make out all the words she murmured but I heard her say, "I can't do that, Lord. They may lock me up. But I can't."

"Liz?" Mark finally asked. "Are you okay? Did the car break down?"

His voice jolted Liz back into reality. She stomped on the gas, spun the wheel, and the car lunged to the left towards her home.

Within a few minutes, we had come over the hill and down the long slope of 98th Avenue, past Bancroft Avenue, to Birch Street. I was noticing, as I had on other visits to Liz's house, that the farther down the hill we went, the smaller the homes became. Also, the poorer they all looked. Once she turned right onto Birch, we knew we were close.

Both Chrissy and I perked up because we loved going to Liz's. She'd often taken us home with her, especially when Mom seemed to be slipping. Liz's place was so much smaller than our two-acre spread in Woodland Estates and I wondered why she didn't just buy a bigger one like we had. While most of the homes around Liz's were rundown and deteriorating, her white bungalow always looked as fresh as if Claman had just painted it the previous weekend. The front yard had flowers and a neatly cut, small lawn, and there was a vegetable garden in her back yard. In fact, the garden took up nearly all of the backyard. But Chrissy and I loved playing out there, where our imaginations ran wild. Rather than being hindered by the smaller space, we were liberated by the overwhelming joy-filled feeling of safety provided by being with Liz. How big her house was didn't really matter. It was full of love. And it was quiet—not with the silence of fear, but the delightful hush of peace.

Liz also had a cellar with shelves packed full of canned preserves and homemade jams and jellies, most of the fruit harvested from what she grew. "How come she has so much food in her cellar, Chrissy?" I once asked.

"She must be rich," Chrissy theorized with childhood logic. "I've never seen so much food in my life!"

"Then how come she doesn't have a bigger house?" I still wondered.

I didn't realize that Liz was poor until I was much older. I never had any notion that she and Claman must have struggled to pay the bills each month. I also never knew her neighborhood was dangerous, especially for whites.

As we pulled up to Liz's, she noticed Claman's car parked in front and knew his workday had ended early again. Her already confused emotions now mixed with both relief and fear, as she realized she had to explain herself to her husband. On the one hand, she mused as she let the children out of the car, he was a pillar of wisdom who could help her think through her next move. On the other hand, she knew he was going to be disappointed and upset by what she'd done. She braced herself for the upcoming conversation.

Liz walked up the few steps to the front door, opened it slowly, and ushered us inside. "Claman? You home?" she called from the small front room. "Claman, where you at? I know you're here."

"Huh? Liz, that you?" came his muffled voice from the bedroom.

Turning to the three of us, she instructed, "You kids go on out back and play fo' awhile. I need to speak with ma husband. I come getchya in a few minutes."

Excited, Chrissy and I dashed toward the back door. Liz cautioned with a chuckle, "Don't run now! You get there soon enough. An' show yo' brother around. Mark ain't been here as much as you two."

After we all disappeared outside, Liz went into the back bedroom. Claman was slowly bringing himself out of an afternoon nap.

"What you doin' home?" she asked.

"They let us go early today." Still waking, his voice was sleepy. He stretched his arms and yawned. "Who are them kids I heard?"

"Oh, that's the Connor children," Liz said as matter-of-factly as she could.

"The Connor children?" Claman's eyes snapped open in surprise. "I thought you didn't work there no mo'."

"Oh, I still ain't workin' there. I just picked up the kids from school." Liz spoke nonchalantly, avoiding his gaze, while she moved to the closet to hang up her coat.

"Hold on now. You're not workin' for the Connors but you picked up their kids from school? How'd that happen?"

Still looking away from him, Liz didn't answer.

Claman looked at the clock on the nightstand as he sat up. "An' how come them kids are outta school at two-fifteen? It don't end 'til three o'clock."

Liz slowly turned to look at him, tears forming in her eyes.

"You didn't! Oh Lord, please tell me you didn't! You picked up them kids from their school without they momma and daddy knowin'? And you brung 'em *here?*"

Liz slumped onto the bed beside her husband. "What was I supposed to do, Claman? I can't leave them with their momma. I just can't!" Her words faded as Claman rose, dumbfounded and motionless, towering above her. Regaining a burst of fervor, she tried to convince him of her thinking. "I drove by the school after I'd been to the police, and ..."

"You been to the po*lice?*" Claman's voice rose.

"Well, what else could I do? But I know they ain't gonna

do nothin'." She turned her face away, not wanting to see the mounting horror and shock in his eyes.

Claman sat down beside her. His shoulders slumped and his hands hung limp between his knees. He stared down as if peering into the abyss of problems ahead of them.

Liz stared straight ahead, facing her reflection in the mirror on the dresser. She willed the tension from her face and tried to convince herself of the words she said next.

"So, I drove by the school. Just to see 'em, Claman. That's all. All the children were out playin'. An' then I saw Todd. He was off by himself, just starin' through the fence like he was sorta dreamin' or somethin'. Well, I had to stop. So I went up an' talked to him. But he wasn't the same, Claman. He wasn't the same at all. He hardly knew I was there, even when I was talkin' to him. An' then he started cryin'."

Turning to face her husband, she placed a hand on his knee. "Oh, Claman, it was the most pitiful sight I ever did see. I had to get him outta there. I just had to."

Claman turned his face toward her, fear and disbelief in his eyes. He slowly shook his head but said nothing.

"Well, I was just gonna take Todd outta school an' hold him in my arms a while," she went on, hoping to make more sense to her husband. "You know, make him feel better."

Wordlessly, Claman dropped his head and raised his hands to massage his furrowed forehead.

Knowing he still did not understand, she appealed to her mirrored reflection once more to help her feel better about what she had done. "So, I tol' him to go on back to his class and I'd come get him. Then I went 'round toward the principal's office. An' on my way, Chrissy saw me. She was hurt bad again." Liz stared into the reflection of her face as she told him the rest of the experience.

As she talked, Claman shook his head back and forth slightly and murmured, "No, no, you didn't ..." When she finished, he rubbed his jaw hard as if to scrub the scene away. Liz's eyes were closed, tears leaking down her cheeks.

He reached an arm across her shoulders and pulled her close. "You've really done it now, Bert. Lord a'mighty, you've really done it."

His calm voice reflected the total defeat he felt. Claman knew there was no use scolding her. Not only would that not achieve anything, but in a way, he understood. The Elizabeth Baxter he married was the kindest, most compassionate person he had ever known. If anything, over the years, she had become even more compassionate, sometimes too compassionate for her own good. He knew this was one of those times. And when he considered how much she loved the Connor children, her impulsiveness actually made sense. It just didn't make good sense.

Claman rubbed her back while she continued to cry. "You are one crazy woman, Elizabeth Baxter. I sho' do love you, but that don't make you any less crazy." He finished with a slight chuckle.

With the backs of her hands she wiped the tears from her face, then looked up at him. "What are we gonna do now?"

Not surprised by his wife's question, but completely resolved as to the next step, he guffawed. "What are *we* gonna do? No *we* in this, Bert. What *you* gonna do is take 'em back to their momma an' daddy."

Liz's eyes widened as if she were in pain. "Claman, ain't you heard none a what I been sayin'? Their momma is gonna kill 'em. I can't never take 'em back ..."

Claman interrupted sharply. "They ain't yo' babies, Bert. No matter how crazy their momma is, that don' make 'em yo' babies. I know you love 'em like they are, but they ain't yours."

"I can't do it, Claman. I won't!" Liz stood and strode out of the room like a warrior woman. In her head, she knew he was right but her heart was in no way ready to accept or admit it.

After a moment Claman followed. He found her at the kitchen table, staring out the back window watching "her babies" at play. Without turning, she said, "Their momma don' love 'em like I do. She can't. Shouldn't they grow up with a momma that loves 'em, Claman? Doesn't the Lord want me lovin' 'em like that? If not, then why did He bring 'em into my life? I just can't let them go back there. I can't."

Claman stood next to her as another wave of grief passed over her. Once it had, he reasoned with her. "You've got no rights here, Bert. You've got no way to care fo' them kids. An' you know what else? They've got no rights, either. Their momma can do whatever she does to 'em an' ain't nobody gonna question that rich white doctor an' her. It ain't right, but it's the way it is. The only thing you're gonna get from takin' them children is jail time. There ain't no other way. You simply got to bring 'em back, right now, to they momma and daddy."

Defeated, Liz sat watching the children laugh and play in the safety of her backyard. Then she stood, pulled an apron off the hook, and defiantly announced, "Well, at least I'm gonna give 'em dinner b'fo' they be goin'."

We played in Liz's yard for some time while she fixed a feast of fried chicken and mashed potatoes and gravy, and warmed an apple pie she'd baked the night before. We laughed in her small kitchen as she fed us, teased us, and took turns tickling our sides while we talked. The sun began to set just as we finished. Even though Liz did her best to hide it, a somber face was slowly replacing the joyous countenance we laughed with over dinner.

Claman finished eating and wiped his mouth with his napkin. "Well, Liz, looks like you've done a good job at fattenin' up these children. My, my, I think these kids are fatter than them kids in that story about Hansel and Gretel. You fixin' we should eat 'em for breakfast?"

Todd Connor

He reached over and lightly pinched Mark's side. Mark jumped and Chrissy and I squealed while Liz smiled contentedly.

As our laughter died down, Claman's face grew serious. "Yo' family's gonna be wonderin' where you kids run off to." He looked pointedly across the table at Liz. "Seems like you'd best be takin' these kids home now, Bert."

The mood changed quickly as we all realized we were going back home. Liz didn't delay at this point, knowing that Mom would have found out what happened earlier that day. We all got into the car and rode the fifteen minutes back to Woodland Estates without saying much. We were all preparing for our re-entry into the Connor home.

I remember thinking Liz seemed very sad. She wasn't the only one. So was I. So were we all.

As Liz turned the corner into Woodland Estates, twilight was descending. We wound through the turns of Woodland Estates Road, passing finely manicured lawns and large sprawling homes, when our eyes were drawn to a blinking glow, as if a lantern were flashing on a pole, near the final turn before our Shady Hills Lane cul-de-sac.

No one spoke. Liz, steering slowly, kept glancing up at the eerie red-orange luminescence flickering in the distance. As we climbed the last winding hillside turn before reaching our home, Liz gasped. The reason for the glow became apparent: police cars, red lights whirling, were clustered around the entrance of our driveway.

"Oh, Lord, what's goin' on here?" Liz asked, surprise and trepidation in her voice.

The police cars hadn't completely blocked the road, so she wove between them slowly. She pulled into her usual parking spot in the driveway, just off to the side of the garage. Mark, Chrissy, and I couldn't believe what we saw—more than a dozen police officers and men in suits were all on our front lawn. Mom and Dad seemed to be at the center of their attention. A growing crowd of neighbors was congregating across the street, gawking at the activity.

Mom and Dad were each talking to police officers, who diligently took notes. Off to the right were two large vans with TV station names on the sides. Chrissy, Mark, and I watched the frenetic scene with amazement. As we opened the car doors, we heard a reporter speaking to a camera a few feet away. "There has been no sign of the children or Elizabeth Baxter …."

"There she is," came a shrill scream as Mom spotted us. "That's her! She stole my children!"

"Oh, Lord." We heard Liz sigh from the front seat as we slowly stepped out of her station wagon.

The next few minutes were a blur. Police and reporters and others ran to the car. Each of us children was swept up by someone and rushed up to the front lawn. Mark, Chrissy, and I were placed in front of Mom but she gave no indication she was even aware of our presence. Fixating a venomous attack on Liz, she kept screaming, "That's her! She stole my children! She's the one! That's her!"

In seconds, a throng of police surrounded Liz. We heard her high-pitched voice, nervous and strained, cry out, "All right now. I'm comin'. Ow!" She shrieked when handcuffs pinched her wrists. From the massive cluster of police, we saw a ruffled Liz emerge with her hands bound in front of her.

"I can explain. I didn't harm the children," she protested as she was escorted toward the spot where Mom stood victoriously like a vicious queen. Dad stood silently beside her and barely glanced at Mark, Chrissy, or me.

"That's her, officer. I want her arrested!" Mom roughly pushed Chrissy and me aside to lunge forward.

Chrissy cried out when I lost my balance and stumbled into her, driving my elbow into her side. We both fell, hard. Mom stepped over us without noticing.

"That's the woman who kidnapped my children," she screamed again as she rushed to confront Liz.

"Now, Mizzuz Connor, I can explain ..."

"You took my children!"

"No, Mizzuz Connor, I did not take yo' children. Here they are right now."

"And look what you did to them! You horrible woman!" Mom stepped back to Chrissy, who was still on the ground. She grabbed Chrissy's arm and yanked it upwards as if it were not attached to the rest of her body. Chrissy screamed.

Shaking Chrissy's arm as if it were a damaged trophy, Mom yelled, "Look at my daughter's hand!"

Chrissy screamed again as her body was pulled up like a ragdoll. Mom grabbed Chrissy's head by her ponytail and pulled her face around to display the black eye that was squeezed shut as Chrissy continued to scream. "And look at her eye!"

"I think you should put your daughter down, ma'am," a startled officer said.

"She did this," Mom continued to shout. "She's been abusing my children all along!"

The concerned officer, more commanding now, ordered, "Let the girl go, ma'am. Now!"

Mom gave no indication she heard him as she continued yelling, "You did this!" With her other hand she grabbed a fistful of my sister's hair and pulled, dragging Chrissy forward.

The officer bolted in front of her and grabbed her hand so hard she had to let go of Chrissy's hair. Mom winced for only a split second as she looked at the officer. Her face registered scant acknowledgment. As if Chrissy were irrelevant, Mom let go of her arm and the officer released Mom's hand.

Without hesitation, Mom strode toward Liz. Liz raised her

handcuffed arms as if to shield herself from Mom's eyes, now more crazed than she'd ever seen. A shouting match ensued between Mom and the police officers as Liz tried, in vain, to explain herself to all of them. All this madness was taking place at the back part of the sprawling front lawn. Closer to the street, a calmer negotiation was transpiring as another officer listened to Dad's appeal that Liz be arrested immediately.

Mark and I stood motionless between the two zones of activity, watching in disbelief. Chrissy crawled back to us but didn't rise from her knees. No one seemed aware we were even there. I felt as if we'd been sucked into a surreal whirlwind. We had no choice but to stand there, surrounded but all alone. We did what children do in times of overwhelming confusion—we cried and searched for a glimpse of something, anything, that made sense. No one seemed to be managing the situation nor getting a grasp of the mayhem.

Unbeknownst to us, someone was.

Chapter 13

Captain Thomas Whitmore arrived at the scene just before Liz Baxter pulled into the Connor driveway. He had been on his way to a neighborhood watch meeting to give a presentation and talk with a group of residents about growing concerns over Oakland's increasing racial tensions. A report came across the police radio as he drove: "Officers called to the Frank Connor residence. Possible kidnapping."

Whitmore mentally snapped to full attention, shifting from vacantly rehearsing his upcoming speech. He'd not been able to put his morning meeting with Liz completely out of his mind, and now this. He radioed dispatch to send another officer to the neighborhood watch meeting, even though he knew it would be frowned upon—keeping the mostly white population comfortable was the reason he'd been hired. But, he thought as he turned his car toward Woodland Estates, I'm sure not going to miss this.

After arriving and seeing too many officers on-scene already, he decided to stand off at a distance and watch, as he was not officially on the call. When Liz pulled up with the children and the real turmoil erupted, he stationed himself anonymously among the neighbors watching from across the street. He saw Liz handcuffed and trying to explain herself. He watched as Dr. Connor, in agitation, buttonholed an officer with great intent on making a case about something. Then

Whitmore focused on the doctor's screaming wife, who no longer was the confident bombshell he'd met at the party. Even from his distance, he noticed the crazed look in Mrs. Connor's eyes that Liz had told him about.

He found Mrs. Connor amazing to watch, as something very dark was exploding out of something very beautiful. It was as if a Hollywood B-movie starlet had swallowed Dr. Jekyll's mixture and Mr. Hyde was rapidly seizing control.

The neighbors gasped when Jane Connor yanked her daughter's arm and then grabbed the child by her hair. From the distance across the wide street, it looked as if a very pretty girl was mistreating a toy doll—except for the girl's piercing screams. Those were quite real. The neighbors reacted with emotional gasps but remained eerily immobile, as if watching a frightening movie in which they were the audience and could not intervene.

"I have heard that scream before," murmured a woman standing next to Whitmore.

He turned and looked at her. "You've heard that before?"

A look of embarrassment crossed the woman's face. She sounded flustered as she said, "Oh, I hear things sometimes. You know, neighbors can hear things."

Whitmore was glad he was not in his dress uniform. His badge was concealed inside his left coat breast. In his business suit, white shirt, and dark tie he looked like any other professional man who lived in Woodland Estates. For all intents and purposes, he could be another inquisitive neighbor. He introduced himself. "I'm Thomas Whitmore. We haven't met."

The woman gave him a grim smile. "I'm Kay Wagner."

Whitmore asked casually, "You hear things like that little girl's scream?"

"Oh, I don't mean to gossip," she responded. "I guess some mothers are more harsh with their children than I'd be."

She turned back to the scene unfolding across the way. After a few moments she pointed to the house down the hill. "I live next door, down there."

"All the way down the hill?" Whitmore asked with surprise as he gazed down the long hill to the Wagner home. "And you hear screams from this house, that far away?"

The look of alarm on Kay Wagner's face told him she realized she'd said more about the Connor family to a complete stranger than she should have. She turned, scanning the crowd, and quickly moved away as she called, "Flo! Flo, dear!"

Whitmore watched the Wagner woman weave her way to someone on the opposite side of the crowd. He turned back to the drama at the Connor home.

Liz continued protesting her innocence, crying as she spoke, but also sweating profusely. To Whitmore, she looked like she was begging mercy from an angry judge. Jane Connor, he thought, played that role well. With her arm outstretched, she pointed her finger at Liz as if it were a gun and continued to scream, "You stole my children. You abused them. Look at my daughter. Just look at her!"

"Now, Mizzuz Connor," Liz appealed repeatedly, "you know that's not true. You know it ain't."

Whitmore noticed the officer talking with Dr. Connor break away and walk to the two officers on either side of Liz, restraining her by the arms. He said something to one of them, who nodded to the other. In unison they began pulling Liz to a squad car.

With nothing more to lose, Liz began resisting vigorously. She raised her voice at the two officers. "You can't arrest me! I ain't done nothin' to them children! I ain't! Dr. Connor! You know it ain't true! I ain't never hurt ma' babies! You know I ain't the one hurtin' them! You know that. Dr. Connor, please. Dr. Connor, you know she's gonna hurt them babies mo'! She's gettin' worse! You know she's gettin' worse, Dr. Please!"

She screamed louder and with more passion as she struggled with the police who were slowly pulling her, unwillingly, to the police car. In a panic, Liz was fighting hard now. The officers were having difficulty holding onto her. She squirmed as she protested, now appealing to the officers on both sides of her. "No, you don't undastand! She's gonna kill them babies!"

As she pulled and tugged, she lost her balance and the officers could not keep her large body from crashing to the ground. Two other officers rushed to restrain her kicking legs. Whitmore heard a nervous snicker ripple through the crowd as everyone watched four police officers, holding all four of Liz's limbs, drag her to the police car. All the while, Liz's repeated screams filled the evening air of Woodland Estates, "Dr. Connor, she's gonna kill yo' babies! Dr., you know she's gonna kill 'em! Dr. Connor, please!"

Finally, the slamming door of the squad car muffled her cries. Whitmore watched Liz turn toward the three abandoned children in the middle of the yard. He could make out her words as she cried out, "I love you, babies! I'm always gonna love you! You mind yo' momma. You be good now. Don't get hurt no mo'. "

As if a flock of birds reacting to a secret signal, he saw all three of the crying children race toward her. They stopped short as the police car backed out of the driveway. Whitmore saw Jane Connor turn, oblivious to her children's presence, and take two long strides toward the house. She shoved both hands through her hair and uttered a guttural sound. Then she looked up, noticed the crowd of onlookers, and froze in place. Whitmore let out an almost silent snort—she looked like a deer on the highway, stunned by car lights. After a second she looked back at the children, then at the crowd, and back at the children. She rushed toward them and knelt down to grab the youngest, smoothing his hair and kissing his tear-stained cheeks. Very loudly, she said, "Are you okay, honey? Did she hurt you too?"

Whitmore snorted again. She may look like Jane Russell, he thought, but her dutiful mother act wouldn't even pass muster on the stage of a community theater.

Whitmore was just as shocked as the rest of the neighbors, who were beginning to disburse. Their basic belief about Woodland Estates had been shattered: that what they just witnessed could never happen there. But his shock was solely due to a different realization. What Elizabeth Baxter had told him about the Connor family earlier that day was the absolute truth.

After the squad car with Liz left, things quieted down somewhat. Jane Connor whisked the children into the house and shut the door so furiously that Whitmore was surprised the adjacent picture window did not shatter. Dr. Connor appeared to be holding court with a television news crew and other reporters who surrounded him. Two of the remaining officers headed across the street to break up the remaining crowd of neighbors. When they approached, Whitmore carefully showed them the badge on the inside of his coat and made his way across the street.

From what Whitmore overheard as he approached, it was obvious the good doctor enjoyed the limelight. He boastfully took full credit for having Liz arrested, as if he, himself, had single-handedly made the streets safer by putting away such a hardened criminal.

"We all know that Negro violence has been escalating," Connor pronounced. "I am gratified to have been part of helping curb the blight on this fine city of ours, especially now that racial violence is being turned against our white children."

Whitmore stepped between the doctor and the cameras. He extended his hand and said, "Hello, Dr. Connor."

"And you are?" Connor's voice and gaze conveyed annoyance at being interrupted during his grand presentation.

"Captain Whitmore, Oakland Police," he responded in a monotone intended to clearly communicate the doctor was not impressing him.

Whitmore opened his lapel to briefly reveal his badge. The reporters, apparently having had enough of the doctor's self-importance, took that as their cue to pack up for the night. Connor nodded. Both his face and chest seemed to deflate, as if air was slowly leaking from his inflated ego.

"I'd like to ask you a few questions."

Trying to recover, Connor said haughtily, "Oh really, Captain? Now? I think my family and I have all been through enough for one day, don't you?" Connor turned and began to walk away.

Whitmore had encountered pompous men before. Running the fine line between rudeness and appropriateness, he knew exactly how to enrage Connor without getting himself in trouble. He was going to enjoy the next few minutes.

" 'Enough for one day' or not, Dr. Connor, I still need to complete my report. Now, I have spoken with Mrs. Baxter and ...."

"What?" Connor turned and snapped. "You talked to that woman? When? About what?"

"I'm the one asking the questions, Doctor." The edge in Whitmore's voice matched the doctor's irritation.

Dr. Connor took a step closer to Whitmore to tower over him. He narrowed his steely blue eyes. In a low, disdaining growl he said, "Do you know who I am?"

Whitmore could see why the man was able to sway so much favor his way. He'd clearly perfected the ability to intimidate and to make people feel exposed and unnerved.

It was obvious he expected Whitmore to react the same way. Whitmore stared calmly back at the agitated doctor for a long moment, then pulled a notepad from his breast pocket and flipped it open. He thought, yeah, I know exactly who you are—a pompous ass, a nobody I wouldn't even give the time of day if it weren't for those kids.

"I said, do you know who I am?"

"I heard you the first time. I know exactly who you are, Dr. Connor." Whitmore moved his face defiantly close to Dr. Connor's, which was red hot with anger, and spoke forcefully. "I know exactly who you are. You're a guy with a story about his kids that doesn't add up. Based upon my extensive interview with Mrs. Baxter, it seems a lot of strange things go on in your home. And you are a guy who is going to answer my questions. Now, we can do it here, or down at the police station. Your choice."

The doctor's eyes flashed from anger to fear, as if the bolt of lightning he was trying to pierce Whitmore with had recoiled back onto him. He abruptly took a step back.

Whitmore had Connor exactly where he wanted him. "So, as I was saying, I have some questions, and you do need to answer them."

Before Whitmore could say anything more, a black blur sped around the corner of Shady Hills Drive and a car screeched into the Connor driveway. The back door flew open before the car even came to a halt. The mayor leapt out, calling, "My God, Frank! What you've been through!" At each rushed step of the politician's approach, Whitmore watched the doctor again expand like a clown's balloon.

Whitmore smiled and nodded to the mayor as he approached. He knew his time tormenting the doctor was over, at least for now. "I'll contact you in a few days to continue our interview, Dr. Connor."

Reinvigorated by the appearance of his political friend,

Connor ignored Whitmore. So did the mayor. "Rest assured that woman will rot in prison, Frank," Whitmore heard him promise as the two men walked into the house together.

Dr. Connor glanced back at Whitmore with a confidently satisfied grin.

"He who laughs last, laughs best, Dr. Connor," Whitmore murmured as he returned to his car.

Chapter 14

Claman woke abruptly from a peaceful sleep in his easy chair in the small front room of their Oakland Flats bungalow. He had stationed himself there after Liz left with the Connor children, committed to waiting up for her return. For a while, he kept himself awake by turning the TV volume up louder than necessary. But eventually the stress of the day's events overtook him and he drifted off.

"See Ellis Brooks today, for your Chevrolet, on the corner of Bush and Van Ness," blared the TV jingle of a San Francisco car dealer. Startled awake, Claman called drowsily toward the darkened hallway that led to their bedrooms. "Bert? You in there?"

Poor thing, she must've gone to sleep, he thought as he rustled from the chair.

A shrill voice of an energetic television news reporter called out, "Yes, Jim. I'm here! At Dr. Frank Connor's home in Woodland Estates ...."

The words slapped Claman out of his sleep-induced fog like an icy cold wave had splashed over him. "The children were abducted earlier today by a Mrs. Elizabeth Baxter, who took them from their classrooms at Blessed Child Academy."

"Say what?" Claman hollered back at the TV.

"Mrs. Baxter turned herself in to authorities this evening," the reporter continued, "as she returned the children to Dr. and Mrs. Connor."

"Bert?" Her name roared out as Claman spun around in disbelief and rushed down the short hallway to their bedroom.

"Where're you at, Bert?" he called as he feverishly scraped his hand on the wall for the light switch and snapped it on.

Their bed was empty, the pillows fluffed and the bedspread neatly tucked in, just the way his wife had left it early that morning.

"Aw, no!" Claman reversed direction and headed back to the TV in the front room. "Aw, hell no! This ain't happenin'!"

He stood and stared at the television. The caption at the bottom of the screen blared "Prominent Children Kidnapped." The reporter was in the middle of his story. "The authorities asked that the children be taken to Mercy Medical Center to undergo a complete physical examination. The little girl looked like she had been beaten. She also was wearing what looked like crude bandages on her hand. However, Dr. Connor insisted that he would examine the children and assess the injuries."

"I'll bet he did," Claman muttered as disgust briefly overwhelmed his fear.

The reporter continued, "Dr. Connor said he would deliver his full medical report to the police tomorrow. He stated that the children had been through enough of an ordeal and needed to remain home in their mother's care."

Claman ground his teeth. Fear turned to anger as he listened, and he growled at the set, "Someone best examine you and yo' mizzuz, you summabitch!"

The televised scene abruptly changed from the Connors' home to show the mayor in an earlier press conference inside the lobby of City Hall. "This is just one more example of growing Negro violence here in Oakland. Rest assured, in spite of the Negro claims of police brutality, this kind of violence—

murder, assault, and now even the kidnapping of our innocent children—against our white citizens will not be tolerated. I assure the world that there is *no* police brutality in Oakland. Such behavior would never be tolerated. Our city's finest are only trying to keep the angry Negro population from tearing our city apart with their own racial hostility."

"Mr. Mayor," a reporter yelled from the crowded foyer, "is this the work of the Black Panthers?"

"Well, we don't know that ... yet." The mayor paused, obviously for effect. "But the Black Panthers, as we all know, are bent on violence, targeting peaceful white citizens and businesses. Every possible lead is being investigated. We have not yet ruled out their participation, or possibly even the planning and execution of this abduction."

Stunned, Claman's mind reeled as he tried to process what he was hearing. Apparently, his entire world had completely altered in the few hours he had dozed serenely in his easy chair. For a moment, he hoped he was caught in one of those nightmares that seem more real than real life. His mind raced in disbelief as he reflected back on the delighted laughter from the yard as the Connor children had played, and the happy dinner they'd shared. He remembered the anger that had boiled silently in him as he saw Christine come in for dinner, with her black eye and bandaged hand. Then, like a hurricane blowing debris through the air, scenes of Liz's sleepless nights, of her tears and worry for those children came whirling back, overwhelming him. But overriding all else was a single thought roaring inside him—what had they done with his Bert?

The ringing of the telephone interrupted both the noise from the TV and his racing mind. Claman grabbed the phone in near panic, hoping it was his wife. "Bertie?"

"Claman!" the urgent voice belonged to Clara Weaver, the church choir director and Liz's closest friend. "What on earth's goin' on? I've been watchin' the news and they're talkin' 'bout

Liz. They say she took some white folks' children. What in heaven's name are they talkin' 'bout?"

Claman tried to form a coherent response. His mind refused to obey. All that came out was, "I've got no ... I mean, I ain't seen her ..." Claman sighed in frustration.

"The news said she's been arrested, Claman," Clara nearly shouted. "She call you? She gets one phone call, you know."

"I don't know, Clara. I've been sleepin'." Claman wished he hadn't said that—admitting he was sleeping while his wife was hauled off to the police station, accused of kidnapping. Trying to regroup, he said, "I mean, we all had dinner togetha'. Then she went to take the children home, and ..."

"What children?" snapped Clara. "You mean she took them little white children like they said?"

Shock waves resonated from her voice and Claman realized how bad this all sounded. "No, you don't undastand. They was just visitin' for a while."

"They sayin' Liz stole them outta they school in the middle of the day without they momma knowin'," Clara informed him, and pressed Claman to tell her what had happened.

"Well, yeah, she did that. But they was fine. They was just fine when they was here." He paused while Clara sat in stunned silence on the other end of the phone. "She ain't done nothin' bad, Clara."

Claman realized he was digging a big enough hole for him and his wife to fall into head first, creating the potential they could both go to prison for the rest of their lives. He stopped, took a deep breath, and regrouped. "Now, Clara, you are my wife's best friend in the world, and know she's never hurt no children in her whole life. She sure as hell ain't gonna hurt them Connor babies. She loves them like I've never seen her love any little children."

"Sho' 'nuff, Claman." Clara's voice was calmer. "You're right, I know. I've seen her with them kids when they was over

Todd Connor

to yo' house b'fo'. She loves them little ones. Then what is all this goin' on, on the TV? What all this talk about? Where is Liz at, anyway?"

"I don't know, Clara. After we fed them kids, Bert went to take 'em home. That's the last I seen of her. I fell asleep in my chair and just woke up to the news."

"They say she's been arrested." Clara's voice was hushed in fear.

"I heard. But I ain't heard from her. I don't believe she called while I was sleepin'. I woulda woke fo' that."

"What're you gonna do, Claman?"

"I don't know fo' certain. I guess I'd best get down to the police station. I expect they're holdin' her there."

"You ain't in no state o' mind to be drivin'," Clara stated flatly. "I'll call Pastor Williams, to see if he can drive us."

"Thank you, Clara, but I don't want you goin' with me down there. This town ain't safe fo' Negros anyway, 'specially this late at night. Now they're saying Bert is mixed up with some kinda plot by the Panthers or somethin'."

Clara laughed. "Yeah, I heard that—like our Liz is gonna overthrow the U.S. gov'mint. Now, Claman, from what I seen of the Panthers 'round town, none of 'em ain't nowhere near so fat. How Liz gonna overthrow the gov'mint when she movin' so slow? Or maybe she gonna sit on 'em till they stop oppressin' us coloreds?" She burst into a loud guffaw.

Claman managed a smile. "She does seem kinda fluffy to be part a them Panthers, Clara. Ain't that the truth?"

Clara sighed and said, "I guess you're right, Claman. It probably ain't safe right now. B'sides, you know my husband. Gus ain't never gonna let me out this late neither. But I'll call Pastor Williams and see if he'll bring his car over for you."

"Thank you, Clara. I'll call you when I know somethin' mo'. G'night now." After Claman hung up the phone, he went to change into his Sunday suit.

Pastor Williams made it to the house about twenty minutes later. For Claman, the wait felt like twenty hours.

He had never been a praying man. Praying people—other than his wife, always seemed weak to him. People who didn't really believe always started praying when life got bad. This annoyed him. He felt you either believed in God all the time, like his Liz did, or you didn't pretend to when you needed something. So it seemed hypocritical to pray to God only when you had no other way to fix your problems. But today was changing that and here he was, doing what annoyed him about others. Now, while he waited, Claman implored divine intervention.

"Lord, I know you ain't heard from me in a long while." Hearing himself say the words out loud embarrassed him, but he continued. "I know you hear from Bert a lot. I guess I've no right to ask you nothin'. But I expect you've got a lot of good feelin's for her. I know she must be talkin' to you right now. And I'm askin' too—please don't let the police hurt her, and, Lord, fo' sho' don't let 'em keep her locked up. Not 'cuz a me. But 'cuz a her. 'Cuz you and me both know how good she is, and how much she's done fo' you."

He paused, not knowing what else to say. He took a deep breath. "That's all, Lord. I just want her back and want her safe."

He tried to swallow his fear as he thought of how the Oakland police might be treating her. Feelings of being powerless overwhelmed him. He was surprised to notice his praying somehow made him feel less that way, like he was doing something that might help her. That, somehow, made him feel more powerful. Yet the truth remained. He was powerless and in great need of help.

Claman, like most Blacks, knew too well what it was to have no power—no political power, no social power, no power as a man. Powerlessness at the hands of whites had been deeply ingrained since his earliest memories. Claman remembered walking through his hometown, Jasper, Arkansas, with his dad one Sunday on the way to church. He was four. He and his five-year-old brother, Jimmie, each held their dad's hands as they walked along the sidewalk. Both boys were dressed in borrowed clothes, right down to bow ties and little suit jackets that matched their dad's dapper look. Claman felt so proud. He wanted to be just like his daddy—a big, strong man with a beautiful singing voice who led music at church. That day, Claman and Jimmie were going to sing all by themselves. They'd practiced for weeks learning a song. As they walked, their daddy helped them practice—"Why should I feel discouraged, why should the shadows come, Why should my heart be lonely, and long for heav'n and home, When Jesus is my portion? My constant Friend is He: His eye is on the sparrow, and I know He watches me, I sing because I'm happy, I sing because I'm free, for His eye is on the sparrow, and I know He watches me."

Before Claman had been able to repeat the last line of the chorus, he felt himself yanked sideways. His dad had launched himself and the boys into the gutter. It had rained all the previous night and the jolt of jumping off the sidewalk splashed all three of them with muddy street water.

"Hey!" Jimmie shouted in protest. Claman looked down at his soaked pants and muddied shirt and started to whimper.

"Hush now," came the stern rebuke of their father. As Claman lifted his head to complain, his father jolted both boys' arms. "Keep yo' heads down. And hush!"

Being four, Claman looked up instead of down. Coming toward them on the sidewalk was a fat white man, walking with a woman and a teenage girl. They too were all dressed up, obviously on their way to church. As they passed, the man gave Claman a sour glare.

After they passed, Claman, his daddy, and his brother

stepped back onto the sidewalk. His daddy said, "You see white people comin', you get off the way. No matter what's in the gutter—rain, mud, snow, garbage or horse foul, you step off that sidewalk and let the white folks pass. And you never, ever look a white lady in the face." He shook the boys' arms and looked hard at them. "You undastand?"

Claman never forgot the lesson—that even a man as proud and physically powerful as his father had no power at all, simply because of the color of his skin. Claman also never forgot the irony of being in church and singing to a powerful God who watches sparrows, but feeling the fear and powerlessness inflicted on his people. Even at that young age, Claman theorized that sparrows had to be white for God to take notice.

By the time he reached his teens, he had stopped going to church. "He be watchin' sparrows. But He sure as hell ain't be watchin' colored folk. I guess he got so many white sparrows, he ain't got no time fo' the colored ones," he used to say sarcastically to his friends, enjoying the laughter his mocking comment provoked.

He used that line once on Liz when they first met, thinking she too would laugh. Instead, he was surprised that she gave him a tongue-lashing. "Claman, you best watch yo' mouth," she said, and went on to lecture him about the ways of the Lord. It was then he realized how deeply religious she was. Even though he didn't share her devotion, he loved it about her. He could see from the beginning that her faith made her something greater than she could have been on her own. Claman didn't much like church or most of the church people Liz befriended, but he knew his Bertie was the real thing, and when he watched her pray he knew her belief was real. Even though he had given up on God back in Arkansas, Liz did make him wonder if maybe there was a God.

Now, the events of the day brought back his old questions

that were never answered about God. Sitting on his front steps waiting for Pastor Williams, he said aloud to no one, "He watchin' sparrows? Seems He still forgettin' to watch the Black ones." He chuckled briefly in a desperate attempt to release his pent-up tension. But all of a sudden the sarcasm turned to raging anger. "You've got to be watchin' over my Bert today, Lord," he shouted at the night sky. "If you're watchin' anything out there, you'd *best* be watchin' over my Bertie. Hell, she's way bigger than any sparrow! That ought make it easier fo' ya. Unless you're blind." Shaking his head in anger he added, "And just as powerless as me right now."

He was surprised at how deep his bitterness was towards God. In that instant, he realized he had always been angry with the God he was raised on. When he had made up his mind that God was weak, he never was able to discuss it with anyone—his religious parents would not tolerate such talk. And when he tried to talk about it with Liz, she simply could not comprehend his doubts.

Pastor William's car pulled up in front of the house. As Claman walked out and opened the car door, he felt the full weight of the years of unchecked, festering bitterness was about to burst out of him. He regretted agreeing to let Clara call the pastor. He should have just driven himself to the police station.

"How are you doing, Claman?" Pastor Williams asked with compassion.

"Oh, I've had better days, I 'spect." Claman said nothing else, not wanting to engage in conversation for fear his anger at God would make this man think less of him.

The pastor was a quiet man, and seemingly gentle. The few times Claman had accompanied Liz to church, he decided he liked the pastor. Williams wasn't like most preachers Claman had seen growing up—those flamboyant personalities who expected him to not think, just accept. They all seemed to answer every question or doubt with "You gotta trust the Lord, now. Don't be doubtin'. Just trust the Lord." Pastor Williams seemed to talk to God when he prayed, instead of just spouting words and working himself into a lather of emotion like so many others. He struck Claman as less dogmatic. His sermons also seemed to have more thought put into them. And, like Liz, the pastor seemed to live what he said he believed.

The car was quiet. Claman preferred it that way.

Pastor Williams broke the silence. "Do you mind if I pray, Claman?"

Claman sighed loudly. "No, I don't mind," he said without much enthusiasm. Frankly, he thought, he was surprised the pastor wasn't already spewing prayer and flowering up ridiculous words like "Lord, I know you've got a plan" or some other nonsense he'd heard too many times before in completely hopeless situations. There were plenty of hopeless situations and, from what Claman could see, not a lot of "plans" from God. Just chaos and pain. If He's been plannin', Claman thought, then He's pretty bad at it.

"Lord, I know you got a plan here," started Williams.

Oh here we go, thought Claman, twisting in his seat.

"Yes, Lord, I know you have a plan," Pastor Williams continued, "but I have to tell you I sure don't see it. And, Lord, being honest now, I am angry. I am angry because it feels as if you have no plan here at all, and our beloved sister is the one being harmed."

"Say what?" Claman interrupted. "You're angry? You talkin' to God, or to somebody else? 'Cuz there ain't nobody else in here but me, unless you hidin' somebody in the trunk."

"Of course I'm angry, Claman. Aren't you?" The pastor's voice was forceful.

"Hell yes, I'm angry. But you can't talk to God that way." As the words came out of his mouth, he laughed at himself, realizing he sounded more like a preacher than the man beside him.

"Well, I am angry, Claman," the pastor said in a gentle tone. "God already knows that. You know He already knows what we're both feeling. Now, I don't want to stay angry. So the best way to get the anger out of me is to tell Him, and turn it over to Him. I find that when I tell Him about my anger, my frustration, I don't usually stay that way."

"So you think God's got no problem with you bein' angry at Him," Claman challenged. But he also realized he had never considered it was acceptable to be angry with God. He'd always figured that once his anger drove him from God, God simply returned the favor and had nothing to do with him either.

"No, I don't think there's a problem with that."

"So God wants the truth? Well, I got a lot a truth fo' God. I ain't sure He wants to deal with all my truth." Claman seemed to spit the words.

"We're all angry," Pastor Williams said. "Everyone who knows your wife is angry. My phone began ringing off the hook as soon as the news came on, with angry people trying to figure out how this could have happened to Elizabeth and asking where is God in all this. But that doesn't take away the truth: that God has a plan."

Fuming now, Claman barked, "You're sayin' God planned fo' my wife to get arrested fo' somethin' she never done? She's the only one tryin' to save them kids. Do you know what their momma's been doin' to them children? Do you?"

Pastor Williams turned and looked at Claman, taking his eyes off the road longer than was safe. "No, I don't believe I do."

"That Mizzuz Connor is crazy. She's been hurtin' them kids fo' years. And she's gettin' worse. Bert thinks that woman gonna kill them kids someday. And that rich doctor daddy of theirs just bandages 'em up and hides the problem. My Bert's the only one who knows. And now, he and that crazy mizzuz of his say Bert's done all the hurtin'." Claman voice rose. "So

God's been plannin' those kids to be hurt by their momma? And He's planned fo' *my* wife to get arrested for it? If this yo' God's plan, He sure as hell don't know what He's doin'."

Claman crossed his arms over his chest and glared silently out the passenger window, blind to all but his rage. The pastor was quiet. The car's engine and the spinning tires on the freeway pavement were the only sounds.

After several minutes, the pastor spoke. His voice was so low it was barely more than a whisper. "Claman, you probably don't know, but my father was killed by the Klan. They hanged him right in front a me, my sisters, and my mother. I had just turned nine." After pausing to choke back his own emotions, he continued. "So yeah, I know what anger is."

Claman turned. In the semi-darkness, he could see the pastor's clenching jaw and the vein throbbing in his neck.

"I had anger in me big then. But I had an uncle who had it even bigger than me. You see, my aunt Minnie took a job keeping house for a white man, after his wife passed. He was in the Klan. One day she came home beaten up and crying. The man had done things to her. Nobody would tell me what, but later I figured it out."

The pastor gave Claman a short, knowing glance. He went on to tell how his uncle snuck into town that night and strangled the man in his bed. A neighbor found the body in the morning and called the police. Because Minnie hadn't shown up for work that day, the police assumed her husband was the culprit. A posse, mostly made up of Klan members, found him hiding in the mule barn behind the Williams' house.

"The police backed off," Pastor Williams said softly. "The Klan lynched my uncle in front of that barn. They made my daddy watch them kill his only brother. Then, for good measure, they hanged my father, too, before they set fire to every house on the street. We all ran. My mother got us onto a train and took us to her people up in Memphis. So yes, I know what anger is, Claman."

Silence hung heavy for a moment before he spoke again. "My grandma saw the anger in me and was patient as long as she could be. Finally, she grabbed me by the scruff of the neck one day and sat me down. She said, 'Anger ain't never done nobody no good, and it ain't never fixed nothin'. If you don't change your way in this world, you gonna end up dead like your daddy.'" The pastor chuckled softly. "Grandma made me sit there while she gave me what-for. First she told me I didn't understand what was going on in this life. She said evil is always working against God, and we're the ones caught in the middle of that battle. It wasn't our fault, and it wasn't God's fault. It was the fault of the evil. God still loved us, even when He couldn't always protect us."

Claman tried to process what the pastor was telling him.

"You fought in the war, right, Claman?"

"Yes. Well, no ... I drove supply trucks in France."

"Okay. Did you ever get mad at the U.S. government because the Germans were shooting at you? Of course you didn't. Because you knew they were the evil force working against you and the government—the right side, that sent you there. And the important part is, you continued risking your life because you knew you were on the right side, and you wanted to be part of the right side." The pastor's voice was now full of the passion he showed in the pulpit. "So just like when you were in the war, there's no point asking why you're being shot at. You were caught in a fight you didn't start. That's the way it is with God. We are in the middle of a fight we didn't start. The only question worth asking is, are you going to give in to the enemy, or you going to stand with God?"

The pastor let his question linger before saying any more. "It took me a long time to stop demanding a perfect world and start accepting the world as it is. And that I need God to help me through the battle. He doesn't always fix things, but He is with me through it all. I know that now. I think you'll come to see that too, Claman. Just give it time."

Claman sat silent as they took the downtown off-ramp and turned left onto Broadway. When they pulled up at the police station, Pastor Williams said, "I'll let you out here. I'll find someplace to park the car and come find you."

Claman got out, a bit foggy from the mix of his fears and the heavy theology he hadn't planned on listening to during the ride. He made his way to the front of the police station, which was ablaze in white light. Crowded about were news reporters, photographers, and others waiting for more information on the Connor children's abduction. The mob of people was thick. As he made his way through, he heard a montage of voices.

"Mrs. Baxter was arrested and brought to a holding cell here at Oakland Police Headquarters," one reporter announced into a microphone. A reporter in front of a different camera said, "Black Panther involvement has not been ruled out. Police report they are questioning anyone they believe is a member of the Black Panthers, but have not determined if there is any evidence of their participation." And another voice: "The status of the Connor children is unknown, as they remain at home with their parents. Dr. Connor stated he will issue a full medical report on their status in the morning."

As Claman pushed forward, he heard words that sent a shudder through him: "She appeared battered and bruised when she arrived. Police stated her injuries were incurred during a struggle with officers at the time of her arrest."

Claman finally reached the double glass doors leading into the building. Through the second set of locked glass doors he saw two officers standing guard, carefully watching the media crowd outside. He motioned to them. Neither moved. Claman motioned again. This time one of them shook his head, indicating Claman was not about to be allowed in.

"I'm her husband," Claman hollered. Almost instantly, he was engulfed by reporters shoving microphones at him. One hit him hard on the upper lip. The reporters pressed

Claman against the glass so hard he feared it would break. Voices screamed at him. "Did you know anything about her kidnapping plans?" "How long had she been planning this?" "Was she asking for ransom?" "Is your wife in the Black Panthers? Were they involved?"

Inside, the two officers became alarmed. They quickly unlatched the deadbolt and opened the door enough for Claman to squeeze in. Several reporters' arms followed, pushing microphones through the narrow opening. "Did you know your wife was abusing those kids?" came the last question.

Claman spun around with an enraged look, searching the sea of faces for the man who had asked this insulting question, as the officers managed to close and rebolt the door. Just then Pastor Williams started pounding on them. "Claman! Claman, tell them to let me in."

The two officers looked at Claman. "He's with me."

One of them sighed and went back through the process of unbolting the doors, fighting back the crowd as Pastor Williams slipped inside, and securing the building again. The other officer grabbed Claman by the arm and started ushering him down the hall. "We have some questions for you."

Pastor Williams spoke up. "Wait. I think this man is entitled to see his wife first, before any questions."

The officers both paused and glared at him.

"I don't think she has had her phone call yet because Mr. Baxter has not heard from her. That's a violation of her rights. Correct?"

One of the officers chuckled. "'Rights.' Yeah, she'll get to make her phone call when we say she can. Just about the same time we let him see her."

The two men turned and moved Claman down the hallway. Pastor Williams followed in tow, protesting relentlessly, albeit vainly for his friend's release. Pushing through the large wooden door, about halfway past a collection of desks, now vacant because of the hour, a voice came from off to the left. The man's tone was commanding. "Just a minute. Where are you officers going?"

"This is Mr. Baxter, Captain," one of them answered. "We're taking him to the cell for questioning."

At the word "cell," Claman's body tensed. Was he being arrested?

"Questioning about what?" the captain's voice demanded.

"His involvement in the kidnapping." The officer's tone clearly implied "you stupid idiot."

"I'll question him. In my office."

The officers continued holding onto Claman, as if he might run. Feeling dazed, Claman stood stock-still. As the man with the commanding voice moved closer, Claman read the name pinned to his sport coat: Whitmore.

"I said," Whitmore repeated, "let him go. I will be questioning him, not you."

The officers scowled at Whitmore as they kept their hands locked on Claman's arms. They'd been looking forward to getting Claman in a cell for a little "attitude adjustment" before interrogation. It was standard practice with Black detainees, and had been for years. Mostly it was used by the beat cops, who took out their aggression, unimpeded. By the time a detective would arrive, the accused was already sufficiently "adjusted." Investigators who questioned a suspect's injuries were met with such excuses as, "He fell when we brought him in," or "She resisted arrest" or—one of the most popular—"He took a few swings at us and we had to restrain him."

Whitmore had begun fighting the mindset from his arrival and was glad to spare Claman this experience. "Please, gentlemen." Whitmore motioned toward his office door. The pastor moved forward but Claman was still being held by the two officers. It took one more angry look from Whitmore before they released him, one of them mumbling under his breath.

"I'm a *what* lover? You are *never* to use that term again! Hear?" Whitmore's roar caused every officer within earshot to go silent. He looked around at all of them and continued. "From now on, *anyone* uses that word, and I'm writing you up. Got that?"

He turned back to Claman and said, "Gentlemen, this way please."

Claman and Pastor Williams followed Whitmore into his office and sat down as he took his place behind his desk. "So, you're Mr. Baxter. And who are you?"

"I'm Mrs. Baxter's pastor," responded Williams.

"I see." Whitmore turned his attention to Claman. "Well, it seems your wife is in quite a mess right now. Did you know she came to see me?"

"Yes, sir, I know. I told her not to." Claman turned his head away to hide his disapproval.

"She told me quite a tale. About Dr. Connor and how his wife is unstable and hurting her children." Whitmore watched carefully for any reaction on Claman's face. All he could discern was a deepening sense of worry.

Pastor Williams, on the other hand, was obviously stunned. "Say what?" He looked between the captain and Claman. "Elizabeth went to the police?"

Claman looked at him and said, "Yes, she did. I didn't know 'til after."

Ignoring their interaction, Whitmore said, "I told her that was a very serious charge to make against a prominent citizen of our city."

"Yes, sir." Claman responded obediently, hoping this would soon end and he would be allowed to see his wife.

"Do you believe Mrs. Connor has been hurting her children?" Whitmore asked.

Claman battled how to respond. If he told the truth, how could he trust that this man wouldn't throw him in jail too?

He'd be even more helpless then. Deep down, he feared he was never going to see his wife again. His admonishment to Liz rang in his head: "Ain't nobody gonna believe no colored maid over that rich white doctor and his mizzuz."

But he was undone. He couldn't hold in the truth his wife was now paying dearly for. Claman took a deep breath and gripped the arms of the chair. He looked Whitmore in the eye, man to man—hoping, even praying, Whitmore would see it that way.

"I've seen them kids with cuts and bruises almost every time my wife brings 'em by fo' a visit. But I've never seen the worst of it. Sometimes their momma hurt 'em so bad they couldn't get outta bed. Those times, I just watched my wife cry all night long, wonderin' how she was gonna save 'em, 'cause she's sure Mizzuz Connor's gonna kill 'em someday. An' Dr. Connor knows all about it, but does nothin' but bandage 'em up."

He paused for a minute to see how much damage he was doing with this white officer. Whitmore's face showed no expression. Claman shook his head in defeat and continued, "And I know she tol' you all that. An' still nothin' was gonna happen to save them children. So when she took 'em from school it was 'cuz she knew nobody, including the police, was gonna help, 'cept her. My wife. That much is clear." Anger had seeped into his tone before he ended.

The captain studied him for a long moment. Claman stared silently at Whitmore, holding the man's gaze.

"Aw, shit!" The captain pushed back his chair, got up, and walked to the window. He stared into the night as if the answer he was looking for was on the other side of the dirty pane that brought in no light at all—no streetlight and no metaphorical light to illuminate him with solutions.

Whitmore turned to face the two men. "Yeah, I know, Mr. Baxter. I know your wife loves those kids. I am certain she would never hurt them. Or any other child, for that matter." His eyes widened as he tried to lighten the mood with his next words. "Now, me? I thought she might take a swing at me once or twice this morning. Hell, maybe I deserved it. She could tell the only reason I didn't do anything was because she's Black and poor, and Dr. Connor's white and rich. Truthfully, I am ashamed of myself."

Both Claman and Williams felt a rush of relief deep in their lungs.

"The problem," Whitmore said as he returned to his chair, "is that she did take those kids from school without permission. So, now I don't know what the hell to do. If the Connors press charges, that's kidnapping, straight and simple. And you're right, Mr. Baxter. That means whatever the mother is doing to those kids, she's going to keep on doing it and Dr. Connor will keep on hiding it. At least until we can find some way to prove otherwise. But what in hell got into her that she took those kids out of school?"

"I know it don't sound right to you an' me, sir," Claman said. "She said she just wanted to go by their school. The kids was at recess and she saw Todd, so she stopped. She knew something was very wrong, so she started to the principal's office. The little girl, Christine, saw her and came running. That's when she knew Christine was hurt bad, too. I think when she saw that little boy and little girl hurt so bad, she didn't know what else to do but to take 'em away."

"The boy?" Whitmore asked. "I thought the girl was the one injured."

"Yessir, on the outside. But Bert—I mean, that's what I calls her, Bert. Anyway, when my Elizabeth found the boy with his legs all cut up, she knew he'd been hurt bad, not just on his legs, but ..." Claman struggled to find the words to describe what he was trying to express, "but inside. He was hurt inside his heart, worse'n ever befo'. That's why Liz went to scoldin' Dr. Connor so bad. He got so mad he hit her. And he fired her. That scared her so bad for the kids, she took to her bed for nearly a month. She didn't know what to do. So she finally came and talked to you."

"Wow." Whitmore shook his head at this new information.

Pastor Williams looked at Claman in horror and said, "That man laid a hand on your wife? You told us she was sick with the flu."

"I'm sorry, Pastor, but she didn't want anyone to know."

"Okay, Mr. Baxter." Whitmore stood as he spoke. "I know what I need to do. Right now, let's get you down to see your wife. Remember, I can't promise anything. She did take those kids."

With that, he ushered the two men out of the office and back to the waiting room. "Pastor, you need to wait here because only next of kin can see her right now."

Pastor Williams clasped Claman's hands. "I'll be waiting right here for you. Just remember, you're not going into battle alone."

Whitmore took Claman down the hall and into a side stairwell. As they rounded the corner of the room they entered at the bottom of the stairs, Claman noted the clock on the wall. Two-fifteen—twelve hours after all this trouble began. Claman thought about how tired he was in that moment, about how much he wished he had slept, back on that easy chair, and awakened to find it was just a nightmare.

Whitmore opened a door marked "Prisoner Holding Area." Before them was a long, white, brightly lit hallway with large, solid doors spaced along one side. Each solid metal, white door had a sliding window at about eye level.

Todd Connor

The whole scene appeared sterile, and eerily silent. It was hard for Claman to believe that human beings were behind those doorways. There was no noise other than their own footsteps as they walked down the corridor to a single guard, obviously asleep, in a chair.

As the sound of their footsteps approached the deputy, he rustled awake. He looked up at Whitmore and Claman standing over him and shook the sleep from his head. Registering who he was looking at, the guard's sleepy voice was apologetic. "Sorry, sir. I must have just slipped off."

Whitmore gave him a glare. "This man is here to see his wife. Mrs. Baxter."

"She's in cell four, sir." Glancing at Claman and then back at Whitmore, he added, "But the visitor booths have been closed for some time now, sir."

"I'm aware of that, officer," Whitmore responded curtly. "Open cell four and let this man see his wife."

"I can't do that, sir," the nervous guard responded. "You know the chief wouldn't like that, sir."

"The chief isn't here. I am. Now open the cell and let this man in." Whitmore stared down at the young guard. "Or should I write you up for sleeping on the job?"

The guard nervously fumbled with his keys for a few seconds while searching the right one, then opened the door. In the cell was a toilet, a cot, and next to that, one single wooden chair where Liz sat. Her head was down, her shoulders slumped forward. At first Claman thought she was asleep. But as they moved into the room, she slowly raised her head and looked up.

Claman gasped as he looked at his wife's face. He barely recognized her. Her upper lip was swollen to three times normal. Her lower lip was covered in blood, which oozed down her chin. There was an enormous gash over her left eyebrow, and the badly bruised eye was swollen shut.

Letting out a tearful sigh, she whispered, "Hi, Claman." Unable to form any more words, she held out her arms to her husband, who crossed the cell in two strides. He was fearful of hugging her, afraid he would add more injury to her badly beaten body. Instead, Claman clasped her hands as the pastor had clasped his, squeezing as much love into them as he could. They seemed to be the only parts of her that could sustain an embrace. Without letting go, he lowered himself on the cot next to her.

"Oh, Bert. What have they done to you?"

Whitmore wheeled on the still groggy guard standing behind him. "What the hell happened in here?"

The guard jumped back at the captain's ferocious voice. "I ... I don't know, sir. She came in like that. I swear."

Whitmore was about to upbraid the guard, but realized the wrath he needed to let loose on this young man was best taken outside. He motioned the officer to move into the hallway and followed, closing but not locking the cell door behind him.

Claman paid no mind to Whitmore's rant, which started immediately. All that mattered to him was his badly wounded wife. "Oh, Bert, I am so sorry I wasn't there fo' you." Liz stared at him, unable to speak. He could see in her eyes she was trying to let him know it was okay. "You know me, I can't sit in front of that TV without fallin' asleep. So I didn't know what was goin' on 'til I woke up and the news was on. I am so sorry, Bert."

Liz muttered something through her swollen lip but he didn't understand her. She took a few deep breaths to calm herself and tried again.

"I give up." There was total defeat in her voice and her eyes. As her tears mixed with the blood still seeping from the gash over her eye, she repeated it. "I give up, Claman. I failed ma' babies. I can't fight no mo'. I give up." Liz began to sob.

He didn't speak. Staring into the exhausted and devastated face of his wife, he wished he could find the words to tell her how proud he was of her. He had never realized until now that she was his hero, the strongest, most beautiful person he had ever known. And she had never been more beautiful to him than right now. He felt overwhelmed with pride and love for this woman, so much so that he thought he would burst with the powerful combination.

He gently placed three fingers under her chin and lifted it so she would look at him. Softly, he said, "You can't quit, Bert."

She slowly shook her head back and forth, making her resistance clear.

"You can't quit, Bert. You know that. An' I know you. You ain't gonna quit. Most anybody woulda quit, what with all you been through. But you ain't just anybody, Bert, an' you ain't never gonna quit. You can't. You won't." Claman rubbed his wife's hands tenderly. "You ain't gonna quit 'cuz you love them kids too much, Bert. Even if you tried to stop fightin', you can't stop lovin' them."

He paused for a moment, knowing she might well lose this fight and that he might lose her. He saw it clearly now. Her love for those kids would do her in. It had already gotten her arrested, beaten, and, for the moment, broken. Nonetheless, like a prizefighter-hero in front of screaming fans gets up for another round after a knockout, he knew this woman would do the exact same thing for those children. Even though she would not win this fight, she would do the exact same thing. She would lose her fight, and he would lose her. There was nothing he could do about it, and he knew it.

He knew the truth. He couldn't stop white America from rejecting her truth about the Connors. He couldn't stop the law from convicting her of a crime she did not commit. But Claman knew what he needed to do. Like the coach in the corner of the ring, he needed to strengthen his wife, his hero, this prizefighter of a human being.

His voice faltered as he started to speak, then gained confidence. "I don't know how you're gonna keep on, Bert, but I know you will. 'Cuz you know you're the only one fightin' fo' them. An' they need you fightin', 'cuz they've got no one 'cept you."

Liz dissolved in tears as she let go of Claman's hands and reached up to hold her aching head. "Oh, Lord, how am I gonna help 'em now?"

Claman waited patiently for his wife to slow her tears. When she looked up at him again, he nodded at her and said nothing more.

She took a big breath, shook her head, and sighed, "Oh, Lord."

The cell door swung open. Captain Whitmore entered. "I'm sorry, but time's up."

Claman gave Liz's hands one last squeeze and said, "I love you, Bert. Always have, always will. But now more than ever before."

She tried to smile, as much as her cracked lip and swollen jaw would allow.

Captain Whitmore motioned for Claman. Without words, they walked away, hearing the guard slam the cell shut, and the clack of metal against metal as the latch locked into place.

"She's in yo' hands now, Lord," Claman murmured.

Whitmore nodded. Trying to extend some hope, he said, "I have a plan, Mr. Baxter. I'll admit it's not much of a plan. So if you believe in God, I suggest you do some praying." He paused. "Because my plan … well, it's got about as good a chance of working as a prayer in hell. So if your God is listening to you, maybe you can convince him to give me some help."

Claman didn't respond, still wondering if God was listening at all, to Liz, to him, or to anyone.

They reached the waiting room where the pastor was waiting. The three men shook hands with nods of silent goodbyes.

Chapter 15

Captain Whitmore fell into bed around three-thirty in the morning. Three hours later his alarm clock announced the onslaught of the new day. It was not a day he was looking forward to. Most of the few hours he'd had for sleep were spent not sleeping. He'd lain awake trying to answer the critical questions that had festered inside him since he met Elizabeth Baxter. The previous twenty-four hours had been a complete whirlwind—for him, for her and her husband, for the Connors, and the whole San Francisco Bay Area riveted with the news media's notion that the race war in America might be heading in an ominous new direction.

Whitmore turned on the TV to listen to the morning news while he shaved, as he did every day. He was surprised to realize that the Connor kidnapping case had made national news. Riveted in front of the TV, he turned the dial to each of the five local channels. Both CBS and ABC had replaced their usual programs with news airing clips from the night before. Reporters added their own commentary on the repercussions being implied across the nation. One announced, "J. Edgar Hoover's office declined to comment on the events until further investigation can be made by the Oakland Police Department and the FBI office in San Francisco."

"Aw, shit!" Whitmore hollered at the screen. "Hoover? Who the hell called him?"

As incredible as it seemed to Whitmore, FBI Director J. Edgar Hoover had become increasingly concerned about the Black Panther movement, birthed in Oakland only months earlier, in October of 1966. Martin Luther King's leadership in nonviolent resistance had been successful in creating social and legal change but, all along, Hoover viewed Dr. King's nonviolent movement as a national threat. The Black Panthers' newer movement, although peaceful in its beginnings of reacting to police brutality against Blacks, was now blatantly preaching a violent overthrow of the U.S. government. Huey Newton, one of its co-founders with Bobby Seal, was publicly renouncing Dr. King's nonviolent approach. Newton and Seal often referred to Blacks as "colonized people," for having been brought to America against their will to help settle the continent. Just as the white Europeans eventually rejected their colonizing parent, so the Black community was rejecting its colonizing parent, the white man. Underscoring the barbarism of slavery, the white man had been far more cruel than the U.S.'s own parent, England. Whites had enslaved Blacks for centuries and still, even one hundred years after the Emancipation Proclamation, enslaved them socially. Newton and Seal argued that just as the white Europeans ousted England through violence, Blacks should do the same to the white-controlled U.S. government because of its continued mistreatment of their race.

What neither Whitmore nor anyone knew at the time was that within a year of Liz's arrest, J. Edgar Hoover would claim the Panthers represented the "most serious threat to national security." The Black Panther movement was quickly spreading from a regional, Oakland-based movement into other major cities around the country, with chapters in Chicago, Detroit, and elsewhere.

Whitmore knew his history. He had to, in order to do his job of trying to reconcile Blacks and whites, first in Chicago and now here in Oakland. The TV news was slamming Elizabeth

Baxter as an example of the race struggle in America. He fully agreed, but from a totally different perspective. He knew she was innocent of the abuse charges. On a moral level, he questioned how anyone who knew the real truth could blame her for taking those kids from school out of desperation?

The trouble was, besides Elizabeth Baxter, only he—and the Connors—knew the real truth. The system still treated dark-skinned human beings as sub-human. It felt, to him, that the system was mocking him with its power, sneering at him, knowing there was absolutely nothing he could do about it. It was taunting him with Liz's impossible situation, daring him to find a way to beat the ingrained bigotry that began when the first brown-skinned victim was kidnapped from Africa and brought to America more than three hundred years earlier.

"Aw, shit!" Whitmore exclaimed again. But this time, the expletive did nothing to release the frustration and anger he felt inside. This system guaranteed that Elizabeth Baxter, probably the most courageous person he'd ever met, would spend years of her life incarcerated for something she had not done. Not only that, but that same system guaranteed that a psychotic mother, protected by her arrogant bastard of a husband, could continue to abuse her children, while the only person who truly loved them rotted in prison.

The worst of it, for Whitmore, was knowing he was part of the system allowing this to happen. His stomach sickened at the thought. He was as powerless as Elizabeth Baxter and those Connor kids, and he knew it. He had no proof of the truth. All he had was the convincing passion that radiated from Liz as she spoke of the children, the wildly angry eyes he saw in Mrs. Connor, and the pompous posturing of Dr. Connor.

As a trained detective, he knew instincts didn't matter. Hard, cold facts did. He had to devise a way of proving the truth he knew to be true. And there lay the problem—how to prove a truth in a system that flourished on lies?

He wrestled with these questions all night, as he got ready for work, as he drove to the police station from his apartment, and as he walked through police headquarters to his small office. Oblivious to everything he'd passed or heard, he finally reached his desk and plopped himself down in his chair.

"Whitmore!"

He looked up to see his secretary at his door.

"What's a girl got to do to get your attention?" Madge asked in an exasperated tone. She set down a mug of coffee for him. "I've been talking to you. What planet are you on?"

"Huh?"

"What's gotten into you this morning? You act like my teenager, an expert at tuning me out," Madge said with mild sarcasm. When he continued to stare at her and didn't say anything, she asked, "What? No smart-ass comeback like you usually give me? You turning into one of the stiffs around here that I don't want to work for?"

He still didn't respond to her jab.

"Hey, Earth to Whitmore!" She shoved his shoulder.

"Oh, sorry, Madge. I was just thinking …."

"No, no. Don't you start that again." She snapped her fingers in his face, getting his attention. "Seriously, you sick or something? Because if you get me sick, I swear I'll poison your coffee."

"Yeah, you probably spit in it already."

She raised her eyebrows and smirked. "You'll never know. Listen, some guy named Rainsworth has been ringing my phone off the hook. He's called at least five times since I got in, and that wasn't even an hour ago. Says he's from the FBI in San Fran and needs to talk to you. Right away."

The mention of the regional FBI field office jolted Whitmore back to attention. "Why? What's he want?"

"Didn't say. But I'd guess it's about that Baxter kidnapper lady. Here's five copies of his phone number." She tossed several message notes on his desk and left the room.

"Aw, shit!" Whitmore sighed, depressed over the fact that, in spite of his intense thinking through the night, through his car ride, down hallways, and into his office, it yielded no ideas as to how to break the system that was suffocating him under this problem. And now he had the FBI to deal with.

The only notion he had was to stall the agent until he could come up with a plan. He brushed some papers aside on his desk to find the buried phone, dialed, and waited for an answer.

"Hello? Yeah, this is Captain Whitmore of the Oakland Police. A Mr. Rainsworth called?"

When Rainsworth came on the line, Whitmore sized him up in about thirty seconds. He was everything Whitmore expected: arrogant, condescending, claiming authority over the investigation based solely on the media's rumors of Black Panther involvement. Whitmore evaded Rainsworth's pressure to involve the FBI but, by the end of the brief call, had managed to hold him off only for a day, claiming that Mrs. Baxter had not yet been processed. Until that happened, Whitmore explained to the increasingly argumentative agent, the FBI, Rainsworth, and J. Edgar himself would just have to cool their jets.

As soon as the call ended, Whitmore dialed another number. While the phone rang, he wondered how much he could accomplish in the one day he'd managed to stall the FBI. The first thing he needed to do was get inside the Connor house.

"Hello. Dr. Connor? This is Captain Thomas Whitmore, Oakland Police. I'd like to come by in about half an hour to take a report from you and your wife." Whitmore paused, listening. "Oh, I see. Well, even if she's not able to talk to me, I need to talk to you. I'll see you at ten."

Whitmore grimaced as Dr. Connor started a tirade. He interrupted, "Yes, I know you're a very busy man. But this is of utmost importance if you want to see justice done. I will not take much of your time. You do want to see justice done, don't you? ... I thought so."

Whitmore grabbed his keys and headed out the door. "Madge, I talked to Rainsworth. If he calls again, tell him not to call me again before tomorrow. I'm heading to the Connors'."

As he drove, he wondered how doped up the doc had gotten his wife, if she hadn't been able to get out of bed. When Dr. Connor opened the front door, Whitmore greeted him as pleasantly as he could, considering his growing disgust for the man.

"Captain. Welcome! Please come in." Connor's invitation boomed with enthusiasm that struck Whitmore as too friendly for the situation. He motioned for the captain to sit on the sprawling, L-shaped couch adjacent to the front door.

Whitmore noted the doors from the living room to the rest of the house were closed. His eye caught the difference in paint color between those doors and the walls of the room. Paint was faded, meaning those doors were normally open, allowing a tremendous amount of sunlight into the room each day. It was obvious to Whitmore that Connor was intentionally restricting his access to this room only.

Whitmore ignored Connor's motion to sit on the couch and headed for the big picture window across the room. "You have a lovely home, Dr. Connor."

"Yes. It is."

"Pretty big, too. How many square feet is it?"

"I don't really know what that has to do with this visit," the doctor said, clearly annoyed. "Captain Whitmore, I need to get on with this. Patients will be at my office in an hour."

"Yes, of course, doctor." Whitmore took his seat and pulled out his notepad, still looking around the room for any sign of something he could use as evidence.

"Well, then. My wife is unable to get out of bed today to meet with you, due to the trauma of yesterday's events."

Whitmore sat back and listened to what he knew was obviously a rehearsed speech.

"The children have been kept home from school," Connor continued, "until we can guarantee procedures are in place to assure their safety there."

"Oh?" Whitmore asked, seizing on a glimmer of opportunity. "Where are they? I'd like to talk to them."

"I'm afraid I can't allow that. They're downstairs, watching television, to keep their minds off the horror they went through."

"I see," Whitmore said, while his mind silently added "you pompous ass."

"I have examined the children and have found that they are generally in good health. Except for the injuries to my daughter, which that nig ... I'm sorry, Captain. I have never used that invective before in my life. I am just extremely angry at that woman for the harm she caused my children." Connor paused, with a carefully formed look of concern on his face. "I'm sure you can understand my anguish, Captain."

Whitmore stared back blankly, not willing to give the man any notion that he was buying into that story at all. "Oh, yes. I understand quite well.

"Overall, the children will be fine and, with time, should heal up nicely. Now that that ... that *woman* is out of out of our lives, hopefully they will recover emotionally as well. What is the status of her prosecution?"

Whitmore paused before responding. For the first time since this ordeal began, he had an idea. He must have lost his poker face in that moment. Dr. Connor looked at him, puzzled, and asked, "Captain Whitmore, is everything okay?"

Whitmore's eyes brightened and a wry grin crossed his face. He realized he'd unnerved Connor, who preferred to be the one making other people uncomfortable. It gave him a feeling of superiority, Whitmore knew, and usually assured the doctor would get what he wanted.

Whitmore quickly resumed his poker face. "No, everything is fine. Actually, the investigation has taken an interesting turn I felt you should be aware of."

"Investigation?" Irritated, Connor's voice grew loud. "What's to investigate? This should be an open and shut case. That woman kidnapped my children and harmed my little girl, plain and simple. I want to know when she's going to be prosecuted and how long she's going to be put away, preferably forever."

"Well, I don't think there is any cause for alarm, Dr. Connor."

"I'm not alarmed. I just want to know when that bitch n ..." Connor stopped and composed himself. "I mean, when that woman will be brought to justice."

"That's why I'm here, doctor," Whitmore said. "To see that justice is done."

Connor leaned forward in his chair. His eyes narrowed, and his voice became menacing. "I spoke with the mayor last night. He's a personal friend of mine, you know."

Whitmore stared back at the doctor blankly, letting him know he didn't care.

"He assured me this would be handled swiftly. Has the mayor called you, Captain?"

"No sir. I have not heard from him, but ...."

Connor interrupted. "I also talked to Judge Lowry last night. He said he would personally see to it that Baxter woman is locked up for a very long time."

Not surprised or impressed by Connor's calling in favors from his crony friends, Whitmore did his best to not roll his eyes in a show of disdain. Whitmore knew Connor wanted Liz convicted in a hurry. But, Whitmore also knew, like most desperate men, Connor was overplaying his hand and showing how nervous he was. Enjoying seeing the man so off balance, Whitmore wanted to savor the situation, watching the doctor squirm for a bit longer. He decided to keep the conversation going, to see if he could make Connor struggle even more in the web of lies he had been weaving for some time.

"Well, as I was saying, the investigation—and that's what this is, Dr. Connor, an investigation. Remember, this is still America. Everyone is innocent until proven guilty."

Connor sat motionless, without response.

Whitmore went on. "As I said, this investigation has taken a turn in an unexpected direction."

"What?" Connor barked. "What are you talking about?"

Enjoying the doctor's increasing tension, Whitmore leaned back and stretched an arm across the top of the sofa. "Just before heading over here, I got a call from the FBI. Seems J. Edgar's concerned about the news allegations that Mrs. Baxter is connected to the Black Panthers, that this is the beginning of a wave of kidnappings of other white children around the country. The FBI will take over the case. I'm sure justice will be swift. Just not as swift as you'd like."

"What do you mean?" Connor asked cautiously.

Whitmore knew he had Connor sufficiently worried—his network of local cronies couldn't possibly help him with the FBI—so he moved in for the kill.

"Once we turn this over to them, well, you know, the FBI will conduct a deep and thorough investigation. That will, of course, extend far beyond an interrogation of Mrs. Baxter. It will include complete, independent medical exams of the children. As well as psychological evaluations." He paused, watching tension turn to fear on the doctor's face. He went on, stretching the truth as far as he dared. "And they will, of course, look carefully into everything about you, and Mrs. Connor too."

Whitmore stopped talking. He waited for Connor to ask what he meant by that. But Connor stared off into space.

Whitmore leaned forward. "That's too bad, because if the Oakland Police maintained jurisdiction, none of that would happen. Especially because of how prominent you and your wife are. But the FBI—well, they don't know you like we do. They'll dig into everything. I'm afraid that's likely to make things pretty uncomfortable for you for a while."

Connor turned to look at Whitmore. "This isn't what we expected."

"No, I'm sure it's not." Whitmore knew he had the doctor where he wanted him, and took the opportunity to draw lines to the exit. He chose his next words carefully. "If you ask me, I think the media's got this whole thing overblown, and you and Mrs. Connor just got caught in the middle. I mean, to me, it just looks like Mrs. Baxter, who'd been their caregiver since they were all babies, just picked the kids up at school, fed them a nice meal at her house, and then brought them home, safe and sound. Yes, she should have called so you and your wife wouldn't worry. That was foolish. But to me, this doesn't look like kidnapping at all. But that's just me."

He paused briefly, then laid out a clear strategy for getting around the abuse charges. "And as for your daughter's injuries? Well, to me, it looks like she just had an accident. You know, probably running with scissors, which we keep telling kids not to do. And she probably tripped and fell. Wouldn't surprise me that's how she got that black eye, and cut her hand."

Whitmore delivered the final blow with great, though undisclosed joy. "But the good news is, the FBI is highly trained at getting to the truth of such matters. They'll get to the bottom of this in no time. And the criminals—Mrs. Baxter, the Panthers, or whoever else is involved in hurting your children, will soon be brought to justice. So not to worry, Dr. Connor, justice will be served."

Connor still said nothing. Whitmore noted the blankness in his eyes and wondered what wheels were turning in the man's head as he was contemplating the ramifications of what he'd just heard. Whitmore let silence hang in the room, waiting for some reaction. When none came after several minutes, he glanced at his watch and stood.

"So anyway," Whitmore said cheerfully, "I guess I will be off. You've got patients to see, and I've got to get Mrs. Baxter processed for the FBI. Please give me a call if anything changes on your end." He tossed his business card on the coffee table.

"Changes? What do you mean?" Connor sounded a bit like a scared child.

"Well, like I said, to me this all looks like a big misunderstanding. When you and the missus talk about it, you might feel the same way. If you should decide that this is just a mistake ..." He paused one more time, choosing his words carefully to make the exit plan perfectly clear. "Or simply a misinterpretation of events, well then, that changes everything. There'd be no crime. Therefore, the FBI, the Oakland Police ... well, we all just go away."

As Whitmore turned his back to the still seated Dr. Connor and walked out the door, he allowed the sardonic grin he had been holding in for so long to finally show.

Driving back to police headquarters, Whitmore pondered the wisdom of having manipulated Dr. Connor. On one hand, he wanted Liz released from jail immediately. He had seen the beating she had taken. The presence of the racist Southern cops, recruited to Oakland in the last twenty years, was pervasive—a rotting pustule of bigotry in the department. Whitmore had no power or authority to change things, and he knew it would continue until either someone far higher up than he demanded it change, or until those men retired. Since many of the officers were getting older, they mostly worked at headquarters in places like the holding tank and the adjacent jail, which was where Liz would spend many weeks until trial. He knew she'd never be able to raise bail, even if it were set. He shuddered at what might happen to her there if more time elapsed. The only way to free her from jail was to have the Connors drop the charges.

On the other hand, his mental debate continued, he relished the notion of the Feds investigating the Connor family secrets. However, he knew the FBI guys—they were interested in the big, flashy cases and were only involved in this one because some idiot from the press stretched the story to suggest the Panthers were involved. He knew the FBI would soon discover Liz had nothing to do with the Panthers. Then the investigation would get dumped right back on his desk and he would have to clean it up. Also, it would take any agent about thirty seconds to perceive that this overweight Black woman couldn't possibly hurt a child.

He shook his head at the ridiculousness of it all.

Then he came to the real issue. He was pretty sure he had scared Connor into dropping charges against Liz. That would free her from jail, but what about freeing the Connor kids? How could he investigate and ultimately prove who really was harming them? The wife might be psychotic, he thought, but Dr. Connor has been cleverly hiding this for years. He was smart, very smart—they both were, and very well connected.

Whitmore filled the rest of his ride back with strategizing how to expose the Connors. He still had no answers as he pulled his unmarked police car into the city garage across from the Oakland Police Department. He remained engrossed in his thoughts until he reached the front door and saw the gaggle of reporters with lights blazing and cameras rolling. He pushed through the crowd toward the front counter, hoping to make it back to his office without answering their questions.

Officer Smeagel, again working the front counter, was shouting at the crowd. He looked rattled and annoyed. He hollered, "I've told you, we don't have any more information on the Baxter woman. And even if I did, I am not authorized to tell you anything."

The din of the reporters' loud questions continued: "What about the Panther involvement?" "Is the FBI still involved?" "Are the Connor children being hospitalized?" They were too focused on harassing Smeagel to notice Whitmore slip down the hall.

"The chief wants to see you right away," Madge barked as he rounded the corner towards his office.

"What's he want?" he snapped back, venting his annoyance on her.

She glanced over her cat-eyed reading glasses with raised eyebrows, and answered sarcastically, "Well, the chief *always* asks my permission before he calls someone into his office. And of course he tells me all about what he wants. But, gosh, for some reason, this time he didn't."

Whitmore grunted with frustration and reversed direction. He was being thwarted from what he really wanted to do: hide out in his office for a while, thinking of what to do next to expose that doctor and his psycho wife. When he reached the chief's office, Gloria Martin nodded her head toward her boss's door. The chief's secretary, just as sassy as Madge but not quite as pretty, whispered, "He's been waiting for you."

"Any chance he's in a good mood?"

"Yeah, sure—for a man-eating tiger that hasn't eaten for a while," she answered with a smirk.

"Everyone's a comedian today." Whitmore smirked back at her. "What's the tiger hungry for today?"

"Raw Whitmore." She chuckled.

"Aw, shit," he muttered.

"Don't you ever get new material?"

Deadpan, he looked at her and said, "Why? The old shit's so perfect for today."

Whitmore took a deep breath and strode into the tiger's lair. He didn't particularly like Chief Hudson. The man was political—a friend of the mayor, which also made him a friend of Dr. Connor. While Hudson himself hadn't hired the Southern boys on the Oakland police force, he did little to curtail the actions of those who brutalized Blacks. Hudson also wasn't thrilled that the mayor had ordered him to create Whitmore's position as police forces across the nation came under mounting social pressure to stem brutality against Blacks. Whitmore especially resented the chief for misrepresenting himself when he recruited him. Hudson had acted as if he was politically progressive and truly wanted to reconcile the rift between the Oakland police and the Black community. Upon Whitmore's arrival, however, it became clear that wasn't the case. In fact, the chief did his best to ignore every effort Whitmore made to improve community relations. Whitmore felt nothing but disdain for the man.

When Whitmore stepped into the chief's office, Hudson was on the phone, talking animatedly to someone. He motioned for Whitmore to take a seat across from his desk as he listened to whoever was on the other end of the call. "Yeah, yeah, you'll have the case today," Hudson said after a minute, then slammed down the phone receiver.

Hudson turned his eyes onto his new prey—filet of Whitmore. "What the hell is going on with this Baxter woman? That was the FBI. They want the case *now*."

"I'm not sure I know what you mean, Chief." Whitmore cocked his head and opened his hands palms up, as if to say, "What do you expect me to do about the FBI?"

Changing the subject, Hudson asked, "What about this Baxter woman's involvement with the Panthers?"

Whitmore took a deep breath and curtailed his impulse to tell his boss he was a complete idiot. With only mild sarcasm, he asked, "Chief, have you even met this lady?"

"Why should I? I don't meet every g-d criminal we arrest."

Whitmore flushed the disdain from his voice this time. "Well, sir, there is no possible way she is involved with the Panthers. She is a kind, middle-aged, church-going, extremely overweight woman who worked as the Connors' maid for more than a decade. Before the thugs in the holding cell beat her up, she was really quite presentable."

"What?" The chief lurched out of his chair in alarm and began pacing behind his desk. "Who beat her up? How come I didn't hear about it?"

"The official report says that she struggled and resisted arrest, requiring the arresting officers to use force to subdue the suspect." Whitmore's monotonous voice could have been reading from any number of police reports. "I think you know that phrase, Chief. And its usual context."

The phrase Whitmore quoted could have been in the police handbook, it was used so often. It was the ultimate out for police brutality. Cops could do anything, short of killing Black prisoners once they were arrested, under the claim the perpetrator resisted arrest, allowing the use of violent force at will.

Whitmore didn't like the chief, but he knew the man wasn't an overt racist. He just wasn't interested in shaking up the status quo. Hudson had inherited the bigoted police officers, who were tenured by the time he got the post. He couldn't easily get rid of them. Plus, he didn't hear about everything that went on. Thanks to the fraternal bond of the cops, even the more moderate officers were not going to inform on their brutal brethren.

The chief looked at Whitmore knowingly but ignored the comment. "Well, I want to hold the Baxter woman, to get the Connors justice. And now the FBI's on my ass to turn her over immediately so they can begin investigating any Panther involvement."

The door to the office opened and Gloria poked her head in. "Chief. Call for you on line two."

"Not now! Take a message. And if it's that damned Rainsworth again, tell him I'll call him back when I'm damned good and ready."

"Uh, sir, I think you'll want to take this call. It's Dr. Connor." She retreated and closed the door.

Hudson shot Whitmore a glance as he grabbed the phone and lowered himself into his chair. "Frank, old buddy." His voice was compassionate. "How's the family doing? The kids okay?

Hudson listened a moment, then glared at Whitmore. "He did what?" As he listened again, he put his hand to his forehead and rubbed hard. "I see ... uh huh ... I see ... yes, I understand. I'll take care of it. You just take care of those kids and that sweet wife of yours. Bye."

Hudson hung up, leaned back in his chair, and glowered at Whitmore. "I didn't give you authorization to talk to Connor."

"I didn't need it," Whitmore said. "My position here gives me the authority. It was just a courtesy call."

Hudson clenched his jaw several times before saying any more. "The Connors are dropping the charges. Frank says he and his wife had a talk after you left. Seems her hysteria last night was because she was so worried about the kids. Seems Frank hadn't told her about the girl getting hurt that morning. Happened before Jane was up. He patched the kid up and sent her on to school. Now that Jane's in a calmer frame of mind, they decided they overreacted. Seems the kids insist Elizabeth Baxter just took them to her house for a visit and dinner. They're dropping all charges."

Whitmore bit the inside of his lower lip hard, to keep from

bursting into gloating laughter. His bluff had actually worked. "Well, that's good news."

"For who?" Hudson spit back. "Not for you, Mr. Interracial Community Relations. You clean up this mess. First you get the FBI off my back. Then you get that Baxter woman out of here. And get the press to shut up. Now get out of here."

Chapter 16

Back at his desk, Whitmore hung up the phone and sighed. Rainsworth had made his displeasure abundantly clear upon learning Liz was to be released. Whitmore couldn't care less about what Rainsworth wanted. But there was something the FBI investigator said that he could not get out of his head: the FBI field office was still under orders to prove the Black Panthers were out to incite racial violence through kidnappings. Among other things, Rainsworth made it clear they'd be taking a very long, hard look at the two Baxter boys in college. Whitmore rubbed his hand across his face and thought that maybe the kids out protesting in the streets had it right with the slogan, "Just because you're paranoid doesn't mean they're not out to get you."

Madge walked in with a sheaf of papers. "Boss, these reports are due and I need your input."

"Not now. Listen, bring me a cup of coffee and then close my door. No calls, no interruptions."

"Hold on, tiger. Before you bite my head off, just know I can't keep everyone out. I'll try, but ...."

"No buts. I don't care if Hoover himself calls. Got that? I need time to think."

Madge raised her eyebrows, pursed her lips, and emitted a soft whistle. "Got it. If Hoover calls, I'll tell him you'll bite his head off too. I'm sure that'll scare him off."

Whitmore looked up and they exchanged familiar teasing grins.

On her way out, she paused. "Listen, it's after one. I'm getting you a sandwich. Can't think straight without reloading that thick skull of yours." Madge watched as his teasing grin grew into an appreciative smile.

"Yeah, that'd be good. Thanks."

Two hours later Whitmore emerged from his office, briskly gave Madge instructions on how to respond to the messages that had come in, and told her to process the release forms for Elizabeth Baxter. "Again with the eyebrows, Madge?" he asked when she gave him a startled look. "The Connors dropped all charges. I'm going down now to tell her. When I get back, get her husband on the phone so I can fill him in on my plans."

Madge nodded and asked, "Anything else?"

He thought a moment. "Yeah. Don't file the release papers yet, and not a word to anyone. Got that?"

"Got it, Captain."

No guard was on duty when he reached the holding area. In the distance, down the long hallway of holding cells, Whitmore heard an argument coming from behind one of the bolted metal doors. The sound of a hard slap followed a shouted expletive, then silence.

Smeagel emerged from behind the cell door, slammed it hard, and locked it. He turned and smugly strutted back down the hallway. When he saw Whitmore standing at the desk, Smeagel's self-satisfied smirk broadened. "Guy needed a little attitude adjustment, Captain. Nothing to concern yourself with. That one's a *white* guy."

Whitmore narrowed his eyes, raised his chin slightly, and spoke sharply. "Is that so? Why aren't you still on the front desk?"

Smeagel tossed the cell keys on the guard's desk. "Covering for Mason. Took sick."

"Pick those keys back up and unlock cell four."

Smeagel sighed heavily but did as instructed. Without opening the cell door, he returned to his chair, sat down, crossed his arms over his chest, and put his feet up on the desk.

Whitmore turned the cell door handle and stepped into the barren room. Liz was still hunched in the chair where she'd been the night before, still staring despondently at the floor. She didn't acknowledge Whitmore's entering, pulling a chair from the hall along with him.

"Mrs. Baxter?" he said softly as he moved into the cell towards her. "Mrs. Baxter, I'm here with good news."

Liz looked up at him, puzzled. He suppressed a gasp over how much worse she looked. He hadn't focused on the extent of her injuries the previous night, when he brought her husband in. Now he could see clearly. The swelling around her eyes was so severe it looked as if they had sunk into her skull. Both eyes were bloodshot and swollen nearly shut, but he couldn't tell if it was from the beating or from crying. The gash over her left eye, only partially scabbed over, continued to ooze. Her upper lip was distended, and as purple as the outside of an eggplant. Whitmore thought she was the most pitiful sight he'd had ever seen. The "boys" must have beaten her face like it was a piñata.

Placing his chair close to her, he sat down. "Mrs. Baxter, look at me please."

When she turned dully toward him, he continued. "I'm sorry about what happened. What I came to tell you is, Dr. Connor has dropped the charges. As soon as the paperwork is done, you'll be free to go. But I've got to ask a favor. The press is still swarming this place. They won't leave until after the late news deadline. I want to keep you here until they're gone, so they can't accost you on the way out. Do you understand?"

Liz nodded slightly.

"Have you had anything to eat?"

She shook her head. "Hurt too much," she whispered.

"Anything to drink?"

Again she shook her head.

"Okay." He sat silently, thinking. He knew Liz needed medical treatment for such severe injuries. But there wouldn't be a white doctor in town willing to cross Frank Connor to treat her. A Black doctor could be found, but that would open a different can of worms. Whitmore envisioned that doctor leaving, encountering the reporters outside, unleashing his anger over the brutality she'd been subjected to by the police, the reports going out, and The Flats bursting into fiery riots. Hell, Whitmore thought, if they did he just might join them. After several minutes pondering what he might do, he finally had a solution. He laid a hand on Liz's knee and said, "I've got to step out to make a call. I'll be right back."

Out in the hallway, Whitmore picked up the desk phone and dialed the extension to his office. Smeagel, feet still up on the desk, watched him.

"Madge, you got that paperwork on Mrs. Baxter finished yet? ... Good. Listen, she's in pretty bad shape. We can't call in a doctor so I need you to play nurse ... Look, you've patched up your kids, you can do this, so get the first aid kit. Bring it to cell four. I'll be in there with Mrs. Baxter. Door'll be open."

Smeagel glared at him as he hung up the phone and murmured something.

Whitmore snapped, "What was that?"

With a sneer Smeagel said, "Nothing. Not a damned thing. Boss."

Whitmore shook his head and walked away. Smeagel, and those who thought like him, were a battle he wasn't about to bother with right now. He returned to Liz's side. "Mrs. Baxter, my secretary's on her way with a first aid kit. We can't do much about the wounds, but we'll do what we can. It'll be a few minutes, and I'm going to wait with you, okay? Then I'll take you home after the press is gone, so they won't bother you."

If Liz heard him, she gave no indication. He sighed and leaned back in his chair. Protecting her from the glare of flashbulbs wasn't his only reason for keeping her away from the press. If pictures of Liz in this condition made the news, the risk of calling in a Black doctor would be moot—the racial tinderbox in The Flats would explode.

Whitmore sat quietly while they both waited for Madge. It was the first time that day he noticed the knot in his stomach. He had seen racism before and its ugly spawn of violent brutality.

The first time was as a kid, growing up in Nashville. Although an outwardly moderate city, the Klan maintained a large, if hidden, presence there. Because he lived near the "dark" part of town, he often saw the results of the Klan's violence. One particular beating he would never forget. In high school, Clarence, a Black boy he had played with when they were both little, was beaten within a thread of his life. Clarence was a foster child of Miss Nellie's, who would bring Clarence over when both boys were too young for school. As prescribed by social custom, he and Clarence stopped playing together when they were about six. Social pressure in the South simply prohibited the two from maintaining an open friendship. The boys, however, liked to fish and had a secret fishing spot. Neither ever told any other friends about it. Over the years, on occasion they'd find the other one there with his pole. Whitmore liked it when that happened. It was the only acceptable place he and Clarence could continue to be friends.

One day when he was home watching his younger brothers after school, Nellie came rushing in through the back door. She was panting under the weight of the clean laundry basket she carried in the autumn heat. "Tommy!" she shouted at him. "Tommy, I need bandages! Quick! You got any bandages?"

Without asking why, Tom rushed to gather everything he could, then he and his brothers followed Nellie to her house. Clarence was on the front room floor, writhing in pain. His jaw was broken, his lip was swollen—much like Liz's was now. Blood gushed from a deep gouge above his right ear. Tom got so sick he thought he would throw up. His younger brothers, behind him, both screamed.

Nellie turned around, noticing for the first time she had been followed. "Oh, Lord. Tommy, get them boys and you outta here! What's a matter w'ich you? These younguns ain't 'spose to see nothin' like this."

Taking the scolding as an excuse to escape, Whitmore shepherded his traumatized brothers home. He turned the radio on loud, hoping the sound of the Cincinnati Reds game would drown out what they had just seen.

Tom Whitmore learned a deep lesson that day: that what he'd previously thought of as the benign Jim Crow he'd grown up under was really a vicious raptor of racism. Those around him had deemed his friend as sub-human, unworthy of peace and safety, but instead deserving of cruelty and abuse. All simply because his skin was browner than theirs.

Of course, there would be no justice levied against the perpetrators. The beating would never be reported. If it were, it would only invite more violence. Besides, Whitmore knew, no white man would ever be charged for, let alone found guilty of, beating any Black—man, woman, or child.

That experience had forever changed him, scarred him. Racism was no longer an abstract concept. The effects of that day ultimately shaped Whitmore for the career he had chosen. More than a career, he felt a calling—that he would do whatever he could, no matter how little, to prevent such things from happening. He had failed Clarence. The pit in his stomach grew larger as he realized now he had failed Liz.

"Oh my God." Madge's murmured exclamation drew

Whitmore back to the present. She looked at him in shock and whispered, "What did those cretins do to her?"

"It's obvious." Whitmore stood up. Turning to Liz, he said, "Mrs. Baxter, this is my secretary, Madge. She's going to get you cleaned up and bandaged."

Madge sat down in the chair Whitmore had vacated and began opening items from the first aid kit. Liz raised her head. She tried to smile and softly said something that Madge took to mean, "Pleased to meet you." Madge gently responded, "It's nice to meet you too, Mrs. Baxter."

"When you're finished here," Whitmore said, "I want you to get her out of this cell. But I don't want the press to see her. Take her the back way to one of the victims' families' rooms. In fact, put her in the one that's got the sofa, so she can lay down. See that she has something to eat, if she can. And something with a straw to drink."

Madge looked up at him quizzically. "Uh, boss..." She rose and moved closer to whisper, "You know the 'City's Finest' consider that to be for whites only."

Whitmore's eyes went cold. "Not any more. Jim Crow never should've migrated out here. He's on his deathbed and I plan to bury him."

Madge burst into a laugh. "Okay! Glad to carry the shovel for you, Captain America!"

Hours later, once the last of the news media hangers-on finally departed, Whitmore made his way back to the room where Liz had been moved. He wasn't surprised to see that Madge had drawn the blinds and posted the "In Use" sign on the door. Liz pulled herself up to sitting on the sofa as he entered.

"Come on, Mrs. Baxter. It's time to get you home now." He spoke gently as he helped her to her feet. He held her arm by the elbow, supporting her as they slowly left. He led her the back way to the enclosed parking area where he'd moved his car so her release wouldn't be witnessed.

Todd Connor

As he helped her into the car, she saw kindness in his eyes. She began to feel she could trust him. She had not felt that way the day before when he was stonewalling her. She didn't really understand why today he was being so nice to her. But it didn't matter. She was glad she didn't have to fear him. Her head was still foggy from the pain of the beating she'd endured. All that mattered now was she was on her way home.

In the darkness of the moving vehicle Liz stared straight ahead silently. She faintly understood as Whitmore explained to her the details of the last twenty-four hours as best he could: the media frenzy over her alleged kidnapping of the Connor children; the wildfire of media that ensued; the rumor of Panther involvement; the FBI's insertion of itself into the case. At that bit of information, Liz looked over at Whitmore, her swollen eyes opened as wide as possible, and her head tilting in disbelief. "Say what now?"

"I know, Mrs. Baxter." He chuckled as he continued. "According to the news hounds, you became quite the notorious criminal while you were locked up."

She shook her head slowly in stunned amazement and returned her silent stare straight ahead. He went on to warn her that the media would not go away anytime soon, and told her that refusing to talk to them was the best way to get them to go away. Liz nodded but still did not speak. He also filled her in on why the Connors decided to drop all charges.

"Believe me, it was not benevolence on their part. The media frenzy attracted the interest of the FBI and that scared the doctor and his wife. Dr. Connor may be able to sway a local investigation, but the FBI doesn't care who he is. The family secrets might be fully exposed," he explained. "Dropping charges against you makes both the police and FBI probes go away."

Whitmore cleared his throat. "There's something else I should inform you of. You have the legal right to retain an attorney and press charges against the Connors for both slander and false arrest." He said nothing about the fact she could also sue the Oakland Police Department for brutality.

For the second time Liz responded, this time with shock in her raspy voice. "Sue the Connors? Oh, no sir, I can't do that. I can't hurt my babies' family."

Whitmore wondered, why does that not surprise me? "Well, that leads us to the next pressing problem: the Connor children," he said somberly. "I want you to know I believe your story—all of it. I am sorry I resisted believing you when you came to my office yesterday morning. Truth is, I actually did believe you by the time you left. I just didn't know what the hell to do about it."

Liz nodded and murmured, "Mmm-hmm. I kinda thought you did. We're both caught in a hard place, ain't we, Captain?"

Whitmore felt himself flush with embarrassment and was glad the darkness of the car hid that from her. "I still don't know what to do about it," he admitted. "With the investigation ending before it started, Dr. Connor maintains his good ol' boy position in town. Unfortunately, that means nothing changes for the Connor kids. They're still in danger, with no way to get away from it. I'm sorry. I truly am."

"Thank you." She sniffled and dug a tissue out of her purse. "I know you is."

Neither of them spoke again during the rest of the trip. When Whitmore pulled in front of the Baxter home the car's headlights revealed Claman waiting on the darkened front porch. He was quickly down the steps and opening Liz's door before Whitmore could come around to do it. The men shook hands.

"Captain, I appreciate your secretary lettin' me know when you'd be bringin' my wife home. Thank you for not makin' her go through those news people. They've been here all day. The vultures finally left about ten-thirty. Drove me nuts banging on the door and windows 'cause I wouldn't answer."

"I'm sorry you're being subjected to this," Whitmore said. "I told Mrs. Baxter they'll give up soon. The story will die down in a few days, so it's just best to ignore them."

Claman stepped off the curb to help Liz as she exited the car. He leaned close and whispered, "I love you, Bertie. I am so proud a you."

For the first time all day, Whitmore saw Liz break into tears. She quickly took a breath and composed herself, then looked over at him. "Thank you again, Captain," she said kindly.

Claman nodded his head in silent assent, then put his arm around his wife's shoulder as they turned and walked away. Whitmore watched as they slowly moved up the walk and into their small home. He wished he had what they had—a connection that could withstand anything, even this. His career had killed his marriage back in Chicago. He especially wanted a woman in his life with qualities like Liz Baxter's. She seemed to hold them in great abundance: integrity, courageous strength, and gentleness all wrapped up in that enormously large but tender being. He found himself wishing he could be the Baxters' friend.

Back in his apartment, he plopped onto the bed. He was glad the day's ordeal was over. Tomorrow he'd deal with the next tribulation—how to break through the sealed vault of the Connor family's dark secrets. Before he finished that thought, sleep welcomed him to blessed oblivion.

At the Baxters' bungalow, Claman helped Liz into bed. She stayed there for the better part of the two weeks it took for her to heal from the beating she'd endured at the hands of the "peace" officers.

During the first week, the media frenzy outside their door continued. Claman had no choice but to face them on his way to and from work every day. Head down and pushing through the group that surrounded him each time, he ignored the questions and taunts they hurled like a pack of barking dogs: "Can we speak to Mrs. Baxter?" "What is her involvement with the Panthers?" "Why is she hiding from us? It makes her look guilty, you know!"

After a few days of frustration, Claman decided if he couldn't get rid of them, he would have some of his own fun with them. "Panthers? Well, we got a cat, but he's pretty small. An' he ain't even black. No, we got no panthers 'round here."

Another day, a newspaper reporter hounded him onto the porch as he came home, demanding to speak to Liz and refusing to hear Claman's repeated "No." Finally, Claman stopped, looked the chubby young man in the eye, and said, "Okay, I'll tell you the truth 'bout why you can't see my wife. She ain't here."

"What? She has to be," the fellow shot back. "We haven't seen her leave."

Claman pushed his hands deep in his pockets and rocked back on his heels. Knowing Liz could now hear him from the other side of the front door, he said, loudly and clearly, "Well, see, I'll tell ya how it happened. Little green men came and stole her away in the night. Yeah, they snatched her away. Now, I tol' 'em to leave her and take me. But they wouldn't listen. Said they wanted her 'cuz she's so big. They're gonna feed they whole planet fo' a week on her."

Claman put his key in the front door lock as he looked the pudgy reporter up and down. "Best be watchin' out. They may be comin' back for a snack."

Closing the front door on the clench-jawed young man, Claman was greeted by a burst of laughter. "You're awful." Liz called to him from the sofa.

He grinned mischievously at her as he locked the deadbolt and walked over to her.

"That po' kid is just tryin' to do his job," she chided with a giggle. "You are strange. I don't even know why I loves you. I guess somebody's got to. But you sho' is strange." Liz's full-throated laughter filled the room.

Claman bent down to kiss her on the lips. "An' it sho' is strange to hear you laughin' again. It sho' is good to hear."

Chapter 17

By the end of the third week at home, Liz had recovered from most of her aches and wounds. She became restless, and knew it was time to start looking for another job. Claman hadn't said anything, but she knew the burden he felt trying to cover their bills without her help. One Saturday morning as they got up, she asked him to buy a newspaper for her before he went to work.

"You sure you ready? Not gonna be easy findin' another day job, what with all we've been through."

"I know," she said, "but I've gotta do somethin'. Sittin' here worryin' about my babies ain't doin' anybody no good. Time for me to start scourin' the want ads. Maybe I can get somethin' in a hospital or school. I can't hide here forever. I'll have yo' breakfast ready when you get back."

As she made her way to the kitchen, she instinctively reached her hand up to the wall just outside the kitchen door, above Claman's easy chair. She brushed her hand along the space where her grandmother's cross should be. In the still darkened living room, she was momentarily confused about why she couldn't feel the cherished icon. Flipping the light switch, she again saw the blank space where the cross had hung for so many years. Its faint shape lingered like a ghost where the paint had not faded like the rest of the room during years of sunlight. A sense of sadness filled her, as it had every time she realized the cross was gone. Every time she was aware of its absence, her heart sank. How could she have forgotten to take it the day Dr. Connor fired her? How could she have been so careless as to leave it behind?

She pondered calling the Connor home. Maybe they had hired another maid who would answer the phone and retrieve the cross for her. She reached for the phone on the kitchen wall and dialed the memorized number as fast as she could, before she lost her nerve. After several rings, a voice answered. "Hello?"

Liz froze at the sound of Mrs. Connor on the other end of the line. She didn't know what to say, so she said nothing.

"Hello?" came the question again. Then, angrily, Mrs. Connor shouted, "Look, if this is another news reporter calling, we're not giving any statements. And if you don't stop calling, I'm calling the police!"

The phone slammed down loudly and the line went dead. Liz's hand shook as she slowly replaced the receiver on the hook. She took a deep breath. While putting coffee on the stove, she spoke aloud, as if Claman were there to hear. "Of course the Connors won't get another maid. They can't keep their secret safe if someone like me shows up again." Pans rattled as she continued, "Well, I can't leave Grandma's cross there. I'm just gonna have to get it back myself." Usually, such statements drew Claman's wise, cautioning counsel.

"What's that you say, Claman? Nothin'?" She chuckled, then briskly brushed her hands across her apron and grinned. "Well, if you ain't gonna talk me outta it, I guess that's just what I'll do."

Claman strode into the house, paper in hand. "Who you talkin' to?"

She smiled slyly over the little game she had just played with herself, glad that her imaginary version of Claman always remained mute. She knew what she had to do and, as with all other times before, when she set out to do something, there was no stopping her. "Oh, just talkin' to myself. 'Cause I got me a new mission."

Claman smiled and gave her a peck on the cheek. "Good. If you're that anxious to get a new job, it sounds like my Bertie is fully recovered."

Liz's grin grew wider. "Yup."

After Claman left for work and the kitchen was cleaned, she put on a nicer dress and headed toward the Connor home in the Oakland Hills. Soon she turned the car off the main boulevard and passed between the broad, oversized gatepost sign that proudly proclaimed "Woodland Estates." The gateway separated the neighborhood within from the rest of the outside world. The posts seemed to announce that if you were crossing through, you must be somebody, and if you weren't somebody, you didn't belong. Liz had missed driving through those posts. She thought about how she felt like somebody each time she arrived, even if she was only the maid of a "somebody."

She let her mind fill with pleasant memories of coming to the Connor home for so many years—not on the days after periods when Mrs. Connor's eyes had flared, but just the times she came in the back door and her babies ran into her fat legs to bury their little faces deep into the folds of her skirt. She smiled as those selectively pleasant memories swam in her mind. Being Saturday, she knew Mark, Chrissy, and Todd would not be in school; maybe they'd come running like they used to. She decided that if she saw them, she would sit on the front steps and let them climb onto her lap to sit awhile, as long as possible before she was confronted by their mother. She knew her babies needed her. She needed them, too. She fought, somewhat unsuccessfully, to hold back the wave of grief coming on her.

But as she turned onto Shady Hills Drive and rounded the

Todd Connor

final corner into the Connor driveway, unpleasant memories came back as well: her fears as she came to work, especially on Tuesdays, not knowing what had been done to one of her babies over the long weekend. By the time she parked her car, she was fully sober about what she was stepping into. No matter. She needed that cross of Grandma's. She couldn't live with herself if she didn't at least try to retrieve it.

Mrs. Connor's car was parked in the garage. Hoping to catch a glimpse of one of the children, Liz peeked through the breezeway into the back yard as she slowly walked to the front door. At the bottom of the steps leading up to the door, she took a deep breath and raised her eyes to the gloriously blue sky. "Lord, I don't know if I can stand livin' without them kids. I know you can fix this, Lord. I sho' don't know how. So here I am, askin' you like I never asked nothin' befo'. Fix this. Please, Lord." She drew another deep breath and walked up to the front door.

She pressed the bell. From inside, she heard the eight chimes singing out Big Ben's melody. There was no response. She waited longer than usual before ringing again. Still no answer.

A horrifying thought struck her—what if Mrs. Connor was hurting one of her babies? Liz held her breath, listening for the sounds of screams or cries, but heard none. She looked around the front porch as if to find an answer for what to do next. Then she remembered—in his rush to fire her, Dr. Connor had never taken back her house key.

She rummaged through the clutter in her deep purse for her extra key chain. There it was, still on her key ring, where it had been for the decade she had worked for the Connor family.

Her hand shook as she slipped the key into the doorknob and turned it. A flash of fear jolted her as she again wondered if one of her babies was hurting somewhere in a dark corner of the rambling ranch house. Quickly, she whisked the thought away and focused on what she would say if she was confronted while inside the house. She whispered to herself, "I'll just tell her the truth, and ask fo' my grandma's cross. Then I be on my way."

Stepping inside, she was surprised to find the house completely disheveled. It confirmed that no other maid had been hired. She couldn't resist going down the hall to peek into the kids' rooms. Toys and clothes were strewn about, and the rooms were in complete disarray. She wondered if the extent of the mess might be an indication that Mrs. Connor's instability had grown even worse. Her nerves on high alert, she made her way down the long hallway toward the kitchen and laundry room. Rounding the corner to the kitchen, she gasped. The counters and table were buried under dirty dishes, cereal boxes, and spilled milk cartons. "Oh, Lord," she blurted. "An' how is the doctor puttin' up with this?"

Without pausing in the silent stillness, she made her way into the laundry room. She tried to come up with a story to explain the eerie silence surrounding her. "Maybe they all went over to a neighbor's house," she muttered. "Or somebody come picked 'em up and took 'em all somewhere."

Just as she began to believe her own narrative, she noticed the outside door to the laundry room standing wide open. Another chill ran through her. She knew that would never be allowed if no one were home. She knew the Connor's were nearly paranoid about crime in the volatile atmosphere of Oakland, and were adamant about locking all windows and doors before leaving home.

Liz opened the laundry cabinet and reached up to the shelf where she had hidden her cherished icon so long ago. She pushed aside several boxes of detergent, then slid her hand along the side to feel for the cross. A sigh of relief flowed out as her searching fingers found their prize. She pulled the old heirloom cross from the cupboard and clasped it to her breast as joy and relief washed over her.

The sound of a child crying and footsteps bolting up the stairs from the back patio shattered her peace. Liz wheeled to look out the open laundry room door. "Todd! Child, what's wrong?"

I couldn't speak. I was terrified, running at a full gallop. I'd almost reached the top step to the back porch as Liz hurried out to meet me. She appeared like an angel in a vision and I hurtled toward her legs at full force. Anticipating the impact, she quickly lowered herself to the cement steps and opened her arms to receive me. I crashed into her pillowy, soft frame and onto her lap without thinking. I didn't know why she was there. I didn't care. All that mattered was that she was. I closed my eyes and sobbed as she held me.

My tears were deep, mostly because it felt so good to be in her embrace again. All the pent-up hurt and emotion from living in the Connor home had a desperately needed outlet to drain off the fear and hurt. I cried as if I would never stop.

Liz didn't ask why I was crying. She didn't need to. She held me and talked to me softly. "Oh, Todd, it's gonna be all right. Liz here now. It gonna be jus' fine now."

Her voice cracked as she spoke. That surprised me. I briefly stopped my tears and looked up into her face. Her eyes were filled with tears too. She smoothed the hair back from my forehead. "I've been missin' you, baby. I've been missin' you real bad."

I put my head back down onto the soft cushion of her shoulder and continued to cry, washed by her comforting words. Liz cuddled me as if I were a much younger child. I didn't mind, even though I was now five and a half. "You jus' go on now and let it all out. Liz here now. It's gonna be all right."

Finally, tears spent, I straightened up and smiled at her

through my sniffling. She pulled a tissue from the deep pocket of her skirt to wipe my tears and nose. "It's so good to see you, Todd. I sho' been missin' you, baby," she said softly. Then, as awareness of reality replaced the dream we both floated in, her eyes darkened. "Baby, what happened to yo' face? How'd it get scraped up like that?"

My eyes widened in terror. I couldn't tell her. I had to keep the secret.

Liz knew. She asked, "Where yo' momma at?"

The memory of why I had come running crashed back. I began to shudder and couldn't stop. Liz, with growing concern, grasped me by the arms. "Todd, look at me." Her voice was still gentle, but was gravely serious. "Where's yo' momma at? You've gotta tell me, child."

My breath began to heave again, not from crying now but from the realization of why I'd run to the house in the first place. "Mom fell ... Chrissy and Mark trying ... Mark said ... I gotta get Mrs. Wagner ... I gotta get help ... gotta get her out."

"Outta where?" Liz asked in alarm.

"A hole. A great big hole. She's stuck. There's dirt all around her."

Liz quickly slipped me off her lap, stood up, and grabbed my hand. "C'mon, Todd. You show me where. Show me where yo' momma's at."

I didn't move.

"Don't be scared now, Todd." She leaned down and looked me in the eye. "Liz here now. Gonna be all right now. C'mon, Todd." Her hand coaxed me up. "Show me where yo' momma at."

Silently, we made our way down the many stairs of the three large patios where our family held barbeques and parties where Mom dazzled her guests, and money flowed at political fundraisers for Dad's friends. Our pace picked up as we crossed the fenced basketball court and passed through the side gate

Mrs. Wagner had used that day she heard Chrissy scream. I led Liz across the lower level, the open area with fruit trees and unmown grasses that extended over more than an acre.

As we descended toward the lowest part of the hillside upon which our home perched, we could hear Mom's angry shouts. But her voice was not the constant raging we kids were used to hearing. Her words were sporadic, interspersed with gasps and grunts.

I led Liz down a narrow path along the hillside to the small clearing near where an old barn once had stood when the property was a massive ranch. All we could see of Mom's body were her head, chest, and arms. The rest of her was buried in the ground, which was slowly pulling her deeper as she struggled.

Robert Wexler had developed Woodland Estates in the late 1940s. His family had owned the land, as well as much of what grew into Oakland and Berkeley, since the mid 1800s. Ranchers and dairy farmers, their cattle and dairy cows grazed on the grassy hillsides. Then came World War II. Wexler saw an opportunity to capture some of the millions of federal dollars pouring into Oakland for the war effort, mostly focused on shipbuilding. The herd that had grazed the surface of one large section of land was replaced by herds of men who used massive equipment to quarry rock and mine coal. When the war was over, Wexler's operations ended as abruptly as the federal subsidies that had made mining profitable. An inventive entrepreneur known for his creativity but not for his scruples, Wexler quickly converted most of the land in the hills above Oakland into the exclusive housing development, golf course, and country club he called Woodland Estates. Unfortunately, the mining operations left huge subterranean caverns below the surface. City officials believed they compensated for any potential dangers by requiring Wexler to drive each home's piers deep into the soil to assure a firm foundation. The homes were sufficiently secured, but everything else was not. What was not foreseen was that those large caverns would lead to sinkholes, occasionally collapsing large sections of people's expensive yards.

When Liz and I finally stopped our rush along the path, Mom was struggling to get free from the caving earth that engulfed her. A fifteen-foot swath of dirt surrounding her slowly moved and shifted, as if the Earth were alive. Mom's terrified efforts to climb out only quickened the pace of the collapsing soil. Caught in the center of the depression, she was slipping downward like the last bit of ice cream melting to the bottom of an ice cream cone. It was impossible to see, from where we were, how deep this hole would go or how far down Mom would be dragged. Mark and Chrissy were near the rim, struggling to extend a long branch out far enough for Mom to reach.

Liz stopped dead in her tracks and let out an audible gasp as she took in the scene. "Mark! Chrissy! Get away from there! Now!"

Startled at the sound of Liz's voice, my brother and sister raised their heads in shock, then immediately ran to our side. Mom didn't even notice as she writhed and sputtered expletives. "Get me out of here, damn it!"

Liz ignored her. "Mark, what happened?"

Mark's hand shook as he pointed to the hole. "We were playing. Mom got mad when we didn't come when she called us. She came down here. All of a sudden the ground was going down." He looked up at Liz, eyes wide in disbelief. "It's like that story we all heard. About how old lady Wexler's prize horse got swallowed up and died."

"That ain't quite true," Liz said. "That horse got saved. Now we gotta find a way to save yo' momma." When Mark turned to run back to the edge, Liz yelled, "You get back away from there. We don't know how big that hole's gonna get!"

Unsure of where the edge of the unstable ground was, Liz cautiously approached the loosely-defined rim of the cone. "Mizzuz Connor, what happened here?"

Mom looked up, now as startled as Mark, Chrissy, and I had been at seeing Liz. But she didn't react as we had. "You stupid bitch. What the hell does it look like happened? And what the hell are you doing here? You're never supposed to set foot on our property again, do you hear?" Mom continued struggling against the sands that slowly tugged her downward. Another lump of dirt gave way and she screamed as she sank further. "Get me out of here!"

Liz stifled a reflexive laugh at the absurdity of the situation. "Well, just what do you want me to do? Get myself out, or get you out?"

She turned to us and started issuing orders. "Mark, get up to the house and call the police. Then you and Chrissy wait out front 'til they gets here. Show 'em where we are. Todd, you just get back a ways for right now."

"Do something!" Mom yelled. She grimaced in pain. "It hurts, oh God, my legs hurt."

Not knowing how wide the hole could grow, Liz wasn't about to add the weight of her body to the crumbling edge. She scanned the area, looking for something that might help her breach the distance to Mom's futile struggling.

"Todd." She pointed to the flower garden about ninety feet away. "Run get that hose and drag it down here. Hurry."

Running as fast as I could, I raced up the incline and tried to pick up the coiled hose. I staggered under the weight, dropped it, and grabbed the nozzle end. It unfurled behind me like a writhing snake as I wrestled its increasing weight along behind me. Mom continued to yell and sputter in pain and frustration.

Liz silently considered the problem before her. The hole might be very deep. It might even swallow Mrs. Connor and suffocate her. The thought of conveniently not doing anything, but simply waiting for the police, flashed across her mind.

Her thoughts quickly scolded back, "Elizabeth Baxter, don't even think about it." But she couldn't help it. The obvious opportunity was screaming at her. She could simply do nothing. If help didn't come in time, would it really be her fault? After all, it would solve a problem. She couldn't bear the thought of her babies continuing to endure the violence inflicted by this woman, who was now, as fate would have it, in perilous danger herself.

I finally reached Liz's side. She took the end of the hose from me just as Mom yelled, "What the hell took you so long, you slow little brat? You can't do anything right. Get that to me! Now!"

Liz's eye's narrowed and her jaw clenched, righteous anger rising in her soul. She gripped the end of the hose so tightly her arm shook. She glared at Mom, still writhing and screaming insults. Then she turned that glare on me.

"Boy, you'd best get up to the house." Her voice was low, but powerful. "Now!"

Awestruck by the fury I'd never seen in Liz's face before, I turned and ran, as fast as I could. Behind me, I heard one last thing, Liz's voice.

"No! I ain't ready to help you, Mizzuz Connor. I ain't."

Liz tossed the hose aside as Mrs. Connor's angry face morphed into fear. She looked up at Liz with the terror of a criminal facing a firing squad. She sputtered a powerless, "Wha ..."

Liz glared back. She shouted, "Why you done all that?"

Mrs. Connor looked up as if facing her Judgment Day, without defense, unable to respond. Her hands started trembling and her terrified face pleaded, without words, for unwarranted mercy.

"Why did you do that to yo' babies?" Liz's voice growled

with God's own wrath. Her chest heaved as she fought to control her emotions. Tears suddenly burned her eyes. But these tears were not borne from sorrow. Nor were they out of pity, or fear for Mrs. Connor's dilemma. They were tears of pure, white-hot rage.

"They're yo' kin! Why you done all that beatin' and cuttin'? Why'd you do all that to yo' own babies? You're their momma. You 'spose to love and take care a them. An' then you put me in jail just 'cause I was tryin' to protect 'em!"

Briefly, reflexively, the indignant anger deeply schooled within Mrs. Connor took control as she yelled back, "You Black bitch! You can't talk to me that way. Get me out of here!"

Liz shook her head in disgust. Although she found the woman's delusion of power satisfyingly comical, her own rage kept her from enjoying the moment. Then the dirt gave way once again. Mrs. Connor's countenance quickly reverted to terror.

Liz still didn't move. She clenched her fists and raised them to beat the air. She screamed, "They're my babies too! I've been lovin' 'em since they was born. Why'd you do that to my babies?"

Except for the soft sound of slowly sucking sand, silence hung as both women glared in hatred at each other.

Liz pulled herself up as tall and straight as her short stature allowed. She crossed her arms over her chest. Her voice was calm when she spoke again. "Maybe God wants you in that hole, Mizzuz Connor. Maybe God done this to you so you'll stop hurtin' ma' babies. Maybe it's yo' time. Maybe it's time fo' him to take you."

For the first time ever, Liz saw tears flow from Mrs. Connor's eyes. Her face slackened, like that of a hurt child. Deep, heaving sobs began to wrack her. Her struggling stopped. Her arms went limp and her head sank into her chest.

Liz stood and watched. She felt no pity for this woman. But a small fear began to grow in her mind. A voice in her head told her this was not about justice, or even about Mrs. Connor. Liz realized it was about her. What kind of a person was she? The kind of person who would just let someone die?

Words flooded her mind, words she knew were not of her own conscience. Liz knew who had put Mrs. Connor in that hole, and who had put her beside it. She knew what was being asked of her. Liz buried her face in her hands and pleaded aloud. "Lord, you know this woman is gonna keep hurtin' my babies. How can I save her when you know she's gonna keep on hurtin' 'em like that?"

The voice inside was silent.

She looked up at the cloudless sky, gave a deep sigh, bent down, and grabbed the end of the hose. She tossed it as far out as she could, then pushed more of the hose until it was close enough for Mrs. Connor to grab onto. As Liz began pulling, more earth gave way behind Mrs. Connor. Liz fought back her alarm as she stepped back, picked up the other end of the hose, and dragged it to a young live oak tree nearby. She wrapped the hose around it several times to secure it. Then she called out, "Mizzuz Connor, you wrap the end around your chest and hang on with both arms. Then I'll start pullin' you out."

Another chunk of soil gave way just beyond Mrs. Connor's left side. Her body tilted left, her weight pulling on the now-secured hose. Then more dirt collapsed. Her feet dangled over the newly exposed crevasse. Both women stared wide-eyed at the precipitous maw that opened before them. The sinkhole dropped at least thirty feet, exposing a jagged, rocky surface below. Both knew the spit of surface dirt still holding Mrs. Connor would soon give way. Terror again flashed in her eyes as she looked into the open grave below her.

Liz's voice was unruffled as she instructed, "C'mon, Mizzuz Connor. You hold on now. We're gonna get you outta there."

Liz dug in her heels against the stable ground away from the cavernous edge. She wrapped the hose behind her back and grasped it on either side of her body. Leaning back, she used her massive weight to leverage Mrs. Connor partway out of the hole. Liz's foothold slipped and she fell backwards, but she didn't break her hold on the hose. Even more destabilized now, the dirt in the hole began falling away more rapidly.

"Hang on, Mizzuz Connor," Liz called out as she struggled to her feet. "We're gonna do that again."

Liz pushed backward with all her might. She fell again, but this time her weight succeeded in pulling Mrs. Connor's body up over the edge.

On her hands and knees, Liz inched her way close enough to grab Mrs. Connor's arms and drag her over the rim. As she did, loose dirt crashed loudly. Panting from exertion, both women stared at the pit that had opened, even deeper than before.

Chapter 18

The church was silent as my pent-up grief finally took control of me. I leaned on the podium that had been my steadying crutch throughout the entire story. Claman stood from his chair, walked to me, put his arm over my heaving shoulders, and stood silently as the relief of tears poured from me.

"We all wanted her gone," I finally blurted, not able to look at anyone. "I'm ashamed of that now. But it's true. We wanted Mom gone. We wanted the pain and hurt and all of that violence to stop. We loved our mother, but we didn't love the mom we had. We hated that woman." I paused for a deep breath, "We were just kids. We were too young to understand how love and hate can be so intertwined. We wanted that hole to take her away."

Claman's strong hand massaged the back of my tense neck. Never before had I uttered that truth to anyone. Now I was confessing my sin not only to God, but also to a congregation of strangers. My shame ran deep. Yet so did relief.

I took another breath and raised my head to look Claman in the eye before turning back to the mourners. "But that was not Liz. She could never execute a death sentence on anyone, no matter how deserving it seemed. As much as she loved us, as much as she longed for us to be safe, she could not bring herself to let our mother die. I know that now. For a long time, I didn't understand. That no matter what happened to Mom, Liz had to be Liz, that magnetically huge butterball of absolving love. We never would have survived if Liz had been anyone less than Liz. To Mark and Christine and me, she was the most compassionate, courageous person who ever lived."

Grief clutched me again, and my throat closed. I fought back tears as I remembered Liz's strength. Finally I was able to draw a deep breath and continue. "She always told us that everyone has a hero inside, but most didn't know it on the inside and so they couldn't show it on the outside. Elizabeth Baxter was a hero, my hero, inside and out. I will never stop loving her and thanking God for her in my life."

I nodded to the crowd and took a step away from the podium. Claman, however, held his grasp on my shoulders and stopped me. I was too exhausted to resist.

Leaning into the microphone, he said, "Thank you, Todd, for sharin' that with us. My Elizabeth never would tell it on her own, and she never let me tell a living soul. She'd never talk about herself like that. But, it's true. She was more than anyone in this church ever knew, an' Todd's made that clear."

He pulled a large handkerchief from his pocket and wiped his eyes and nose. When he raised his head, his face was stern. He said, "So many a you tol' her she was a fool to go back to that doctor and his mizzuz after what they'd done to her, sayin' she kidnapped those children. You hurt her heart, tellin' her over and over all those years that she shouldn't'a done that. Now you know. She didn't do it for the doctor or the mizzuz. She did it for those babies. My Liz raised our boys to fine men, and she raised the Connor children right too. Mark and Christine couldn't be here today. Mark's a music professor at Oberlin, and he's off teaching in South Africa. Christine, why, she's a surgeon at St. Jude's Children's Hospital. And Todd here, many a you know the good work he does, mentorin' young folk from The Flats."

He looked at me. "So you haven't just been tellin' a story about her, Todd. This's been yo' story. An' we need you to finish yo' story. We need to know what happened to you and yo' siblin's after that time. Please, son, I know you're tired a talkin'. But we ain't tired a listenin'. What happened after she helped yo' momma outta that hole?"

Everything inside me wanted to stop. I was emotionally and physically drained, beyond anything I had experienced before. Reluctantly, I agreed. The crowd rustled a little as they settled in again.

Liz grabbed Mom under her arms, pulled her safely away from the edge of the hole, and tried to lift her to a standing position. Liz was startled to see her dirt-covered legs flopping as limply as a ragdoll's.

Mrs. Connor whimpered in pain, then a new form of exhausted alarm filled her voice. "I can't move my legs. I can't even feel them."

"C'mon, Mizzuz Connor." Liz spoke reassuringly. "You're gonna be fine. I'll help you up. We just need to get you up to the house."

As Liz tried once more to hoist the woman's body to standing, Mrs. Connor screamed in pain. "It hurts! My back ... it hurts."

A deeper fear gripped Liz as she carefully lowered Mrs. Connor's limp body to lie flat on the ground. The sound of faint sirens rose from the distance.

Mark, Chrissy, and I trailed behind the fire department rescue team. We watched from a distance as they rushed down the hillside. They carefully lifted Mom onto a stretcher and carried her back up the hill. We followed them as they rushed her into the ambulance. Liz held us all close by her side as we watched it disappear on its way to the hospital.

Liz stayed with us until Dad came home late that night. We were all fast asleep when he finally arrived. We never saw her leave.

We didn't see Mom for a long time because children weren't allowed to visit patients in the hospital. Dad attempted to make our lives at home normal. He didn't do that by being home more—in fact, he was away as much or even more. He never came home until long after we were asleep. A parade of babysitters was hired from an agency, to see to it that we got to school and back home again. None of them ever stayed very long. Most of the sitters were old spinsters who acted like they hated children. Some seemed nice. We didn't like any of them. None of them was Liz.

We were told nothing of Mom's condition. Only later did I learn that the pressure of the earth that engulfed her had seriously damaged her spine. Doctors attempted several surgeries, which yielded no measurable success. After several weeks in the hospital, the specialists who'd rallied to help told Dad that she would be permanently impaired—she might walk again, but probably not.

What I also didn't know was that during those weeks, Captain Whitmore was continually harassing Dad. He had Madge call Dad's office at different times every day, trying to get him on the line. The office manager at the front desk had one consistent message: "I'm sorry, Dr. Connor is seeing patients right now. No, he will not be available later."

"Who is this guy? Albert Schweitzer?" Whitmore chortled at Madge's reports that she still couldn't get through to Dr. Connor. After about a month of this, Whitmore simply got in a squad car and drove to the doctor's office a few miles away.

As he stepped into the waiting room, the voluptuous nurse behind the office counter looked up at him and smiled. What a knockout, he thought, as he read the Nurse Callahan name tag on her lapel. He wondered if this was the woman Madge complained sounded like a drill sergeant.

"May I help you?" Her question came out sultrily through her lipstick-red lips.

"Yes, I am here to see Dr. Connor."

"Do you have an appointment?"

"No, but I'll take one from you," he impulsively flirted. Nurse Callahan laughed and turned her head teasingly, then suddenly drew herself up. Almost like a tornado, from the other side of the office came another, larger figure, making rustling sounds as it approached. Nurse "Ruby Lips" Callahan whisked herself off in the opposite direction.

"Thanks for covering my break, June." There was the raspy voice Madge had come to know over the phone. The brusque schoolmarm looked at him. "Dr. Connor only sees patients with appointments. I'm sorry, but he has no openings right now and is not taking new patients."

"Oh, I think he'll see my friend here." Whitmore pulled his badge out of his pocket and held it up to the rigid monitor behind the counter.

She grunted and scowled, then said, "Wait here." She evaporated out of sight down a hallway. Does this mean Nurse "Ruby Lips" comes back, he wondered hopefully.

Before that could happen, the marm reappeared and announced, "Please follow me." She led him past a scale in the hallway, a number of rooms that looked like exam rooms, and possibly an X-ray room to the doctor's personal office in the back. "You can have a seat. The doctor will be with you as soon as he's finished with his patient."

Whitmore knew that "soon," for most doctors, usually meant a half-hour wait. He sighed and settled in, and was surprised when Dr. Connor appeared barely five minutes later.

"What is the meaning of this?" Connor demanded loudly as he entered the room.

Whitmore turned in his chair with a big smile, not out of pleasantness but because the doc was sufficiently alarmed that a policeman had shown up unannounced. Whitmore was glad the schoolmarm hadn't bothered to ask his name. He grinned wider, enjoying the shock of recognition on Dr. Connor's face. Connor's arrogant countenance immediately changed. Whitmore thought he detected a flash of fear.

"Oh, hello, Captain Whitmore. What brings you here?" Connor cautiously walked behind his desk and sat down.

"Well, Dr. Connor, I'm just doing some follow-up on our last discussion." Whitmore's voice was neutral. "About Mrs. Baxter and your children."

"That matter has been closed," Connor snapped. "We dropped the charges. Mrs. Baxter was released from jail."

"Yes, that's true regarding Mrs. Baxter. But there was the other matter. Of the children being seriously, and repeatedly, injured."

Whitmore paused as the color drained from Dr. Connor's face. Connor said nothing.

"That matter has not yet been investigated."

Recovering quickly, Connor responded, "That is of no matter at all. I told you, my children are all accident-prone. Our daughter's earlier injuries were due to falling into some rose bushes in our backyard. That's all."

Knowing he had the man rattled, Whitmore skewed the discussion in the true direction he wanted to go. "Dr. Connor, I understand your wife was seriously injured on your property. I am very sorry to hear that."

"Yes." Connor's voice resumed its vigor, and Whitmore knew he was relieved to get off the previous topic. "Terrible thing. Apparently an old mining cavern opened up. She was nearly killed."

"She was saved by someone, isn't that correct?" Whitmore asked with feigned innocence.

"Yes." Connor's tone darkened.

"And who was that again?"

Connor's nostrils flared. "The Baxter woman."

"Ah, yes," Whitmore said. "And where were the children when all of this was happening?"

"They were at home with their mother." Connor spoke dispassionately, as if reciting from a medical file. "When Elizabeth, I mean, Mrs. Baxter arrived—unexpectedly and without prior authorization, I might add—she sent them to call the police while she pulled my wife from the cave-in."

"Yes, yes, I heard that," Whitmore said, almost pensively. "I read the report. It also stated that the youngest—Todd is it? It said that he had fresh injuries, as well. To his face and lip. Do you know how that happened? Maybe he fell into those same rose bushes as your daughter, perhaps?"

Connor didn't respond. He stared at Whitmore. Both men knew what Whitmore was up to, and Whitmore knew the doctor didn't know how to talk his way out of this without revealing the family secret.

Whitmore broke the silence. "Well, as I said, I wanted to follow up concerning your children. It really does seem like they have been injured a lot. And you know, with the press having been involved, nosing around ..." He let his unfinished sentence linger in the air between them, then added, "Well, you know how it is. The Oakland Police couldn't afford to miss anything that may be of concern."

Connor squirmed, but still said nothing.

"Well, I assume you will be hiring Mrs. Baxter again. That is, what with your wife's injury and the hazardous conditions around your home and all. You know, the rose bushes, cave-ins? As for the police, we'd just as soon not take this matter any further. But with all the press, and the repeated injuries of the children ..." He again let the unfinished sentence hang for a moment. "I know I'd feel a lot better closing out this file if I were sure the children had a steady caregiver again. You know, someone who truly cares for them. Someone who'd keep them away from all those potential hazards around your home."

Connor took a deep breath and exhaled in resignation. "Yes, that would probably be a good idea," he responded in an obedient tone.

The men stared at each other again, waiting for the other to make the next move. Whitmore finally said, "Well, you could call her now. I'll bet she's home. And if she's not—why, I don't mind hanging around until she is. "

Connor's eyes darkened and a vein along his neck throbbed. He buzzed the front desk and the schoolmarm's voice answered. "Mrs. Caldwell, please get Mrs. Baxter on the line for me."

Whitmore smiled with cunning satisfaction and thought, yeah, you jackass, you're finally going to do the right thing by your kids.

The intercom soon buzzed again and Mrs. Caldwell's gruff but businesslike voice announced, "Mrs. Baxter on line one."

"Put it on speaker," Whitmore said as Connor picked up the phone.

Looking like a scolded schoolboy, Connor did so and spoke sheepishly. "Yes. Elizabeth? How are you?"

"Fine, Dr. Connor. And how are you?"

Whitmore could hear a touch of caution in Liz's cheerful reply. She's a saint, he thought as he shook his head, wondering how she could restrain herself from not cursing Connor to hell and gone.

"Fine. Fine." Connor let out a sigh. "Um, I wanted to ask ... uh, well, I was wondering if you would be willing to come back and take care of the children again?"

"Oh, that'd be just *fine!*" came Liz's obviously elated reply.

Looking at Connor as sternly as if he were the school principal forcing compliance from a wayward child Whitmore instructed, "For a dollar an hour more."

"For a dollar an hour more," Connor repeated obediently.

"Oh, that's very generous of you, Dr. Connor," Liz chimed in delight.

Keeping his chokehold on Connor, Whitmore ordered, "Five days a week. And you pay overtime when you come home late."

The doctor shut his eyes in acquiescence. "I'll need you five days each week. Can you swing that?"

"That'd be fine. Ever since ..." Liz's voice trailed off for a moment. "Uh, that'd be fine, sir. I can be there every day."

Whitmore knew Liz didn't want to highlight the fact that since her arrest, even though she'd been fully exonerated, she had found it impossible to find any other work. Whitmore raised his chin and widened his eyes at Connor, signaling he expected full compliance.

"And if I have to work late at times, I want to be sure to pay you time-and-a-half. So don't worry about that." Connor held his hands up in the air as if to ask Whitmore, "Anything else you want, master?"

Whitmore nodded and smiled without a word.

"So I'll expect you tomorrow morning. Is that okay? Can you be there then?" Connor asked.

"Oh! Yessir, yes, I'll be there. Thank you so much."

"Uh, thank you, Elizabeth. Goodbye now."

As Connor hung up the phone, the captain smiled as if the school principal had successfully reformed a troubled child from his past errors. He stood and extended his hand to the doctor, who meekly reached up from his chair.

"I'm so glad we had this little chat, Dr. Connor. I can now put in my report that your children will be safe from all harm. I will be checking in with Mrs. Baxter from time to time to make sure it stays that way."

He let the veiled threat hang as he turned and walked out the door.

The next morning, Mark, Chrissy, and I were awakened by the familiar sound of Liz's sweet whisper as she came into our rooms with a huge smile on her face. "Time to get yo'selves ready fo' school."

I shot up in my bed, rubbing my eyes to assure myself I was not dreaming. I looked at her in disbelief and bolted out from under the covers to hug her pillowy legs. Mark and Chrissy did the exact same thing when they saw her.

She joked and laughed with us while making pancakes. We didn't ask how long she would be there. We just drank it all in, as if the parched land of our hearts was receiving desperately needed rain.

Finally, Chrissy asked innocently, with worry in her voice, "Will you be here when we get home from school?"

Mark and I both looked up from our plates with bated anticipation of the answer, fearing this was only a brief gift to be torn away from us again.

Liz turned from the kitchen counter and came over to the table. She reached her massive arms around all three of us, smothering us in her Jell-O-like softness. I was the lucky one in the middle, with her warm brown cheek pressed against mine.

"I'm gonna be here in the mornin' when you wake up," she said, "an' I'm gonna pick you up from school. An' every day, we're gonna do it all over again. Ol' Liz gonna be here fo' a long, long, long time."

After Liz took us to school that morning, she returned home to begin cleaning the mayhem that had accumulated in the Connor home over months of Mom's neglect. Around nine, she prepared a breakfast tray with a grapefruit cut in sections, a glass of milk, and a small carafe of coffee. She added a delicate vase with a rosebud and carried the tray down the long hallway to the master bedroom. Balancing the tray on one arm, she knocked lightly on the door.

"Come in," came a woman's groggy voice from inside.

"Good mornin', Mizzuz Connor," Liz announced with her usual cheerfulness, as if she'd never been away. She nodded a greeting to the private duty nurse reading silently in the light of the shaded window.

"Good morning, Elizabeth," slurred the semi-sedated voice. Mrs. Connor struggled to raise herself to a seated position in the bed.

Liz set the carefully prepared tray down in front of her. "Now, don't you struggle none, Mizzuz Connor," she said softly. "The doctors say you might make things worse if you try to move around too much."

"Move around?" Mrs. Connor cried out in frustration. She hunched forward as she began to cry. "I'll never move around again!"

"Now, you know cryin' doesn't do any good, Mizzuz Connor. It's gonna be all right. You still got yo' husband and yo' children."

Mrs. Connor was not soothed by this information. She flung herself back onto the overstuffed pillows dramatically, still the actress overplaying her role. Then she closed her eyes to block out the world. "I'm not hungry," she announced with a huff. "Leave me alone. I just want to sleep."

Liz gave a glance to the private nurse, whose expression said she had given up long ago.

"All right, Mizzuz Connor," Liz responded with calm compliance. "You just rest now. I'll set yo' breakfast right over here."

Liz moved the tray to the bed table, where it could be reached later. She smoothed the bedcovers gently, as if to communicate extra concern for comfort. "Everything's gonna be all right now, Mizzuz Connor. I'm gonna take care of everything."

As she turned and walked toward the door, a wide smile grew across her face, refusing to be suppressed. It came from somewhere deep inside her. She knew it would not leave her heart for a very long time. It was not a laughing smile or a mocking smile. It was simply one of deep satisfaction, as if to say all had been made right with the world, all the stars had aligned, the pain and fear that had once ruled had been overturned.

"That's right, Mizzuz Connor," Liz said, feeling the bubbling joy as she looked back before quietly closing the door. "You just rest. Everything's gonna be just fine. Liz here now."

Acknowledgments

For years I have tried to tell my story. When friends asked me for details about growing up well-off but in an abusive home, I would share some of the grave realities of my upbringing: the violence, the raging, the complete betrayal of parental love. I always expected the storytelling to bring me comfort, to lessen the weight of my scarred past and somehow find relief in not feeling so alone and trapped in the memories.

But those comforting feelings never came. Instead, I was rendered more alone and isolated. Sharing details only brought puzzled looks, as most people could not conceive of how bad it really was. The fear and despair could not be adequately described and, therefore, never be shared fully. The weight of the pain could never be unloaded, and the shackles of memories could never be removed.

As a result, I always halted the story before I could share how my life was saved, and by whom—the most unlikely savior: a short, heavy-set Black woman named Liz, during the most unlikely time, in the midst of the civil rights struggles of the 1960s.

Those problems have been resolved with this novel. I realized I had been doling out my story as one might present portioned ingredients of a recipe, separately, one at a time, like serving only the bitter lemons and not the whole Lemon Meringue pie. The bitterness could be noted, but the full taste would not be appreciated. Instead of parceling out my story, I needed to draw people into it—for them to truly understand, and for me to be truly understood. Just as a Lemon Meringue pie has a sweetness that tempers the sharp lemons, it is the full story of a seemingly powerless Black woman and her courage and unconditional love that overwhelms the bitter violence and despair in my own story. Without her, my story would have turned out far, far different. That is, if I had even managed to survive.

For me, remembering has been painful, but also therapeutic. Remembering Liz in the writing of this story, and how her love gave my siblings and me a reason to live, brought me the peace I long sought. I hope my siblings will tell their own stories someday, and experience this same release. To each of you, who endured the horror even longer than I did, I am so grateful for your helping me deal with these experiences over the years, for helping me not feel crazy in remembering the "crazy" we all survived, and for corroborating the saving love of Liz we all felt so deeply in our own ways.

Regarding my parents, who also could be described as my tormentors, I forgave them many years ago. This was no easy task, but it was not for their benefit as much as for mine. The clinching reality that pushed me across the finish line of forgiveness was to consider their own stories. I know only some details. I don't know it all, but can imagine the damage that produced two people who would treat their own children the way they did, the way this book describes. One thing about their childhoods that I know for sure—they never had a Liz. And for that, I can offer them compassion.

As for the truth of the story, it is biographical as to my childhood experiences. The abuse perpetrated onto the children in the story all happened to me in one form or another. Again, I leave it to my siblings to tell their own stories. The pendulum of our home during those years oscillated between sadistic, hidden violence and lavish public parties. The one stable force was Liz: always constant, always loving, and always attempting to protect us from our torturing parents.

My goal was not to tell all the exact details of my childhood. My goal was to communicate the feelings, and therefore tell a more accurate and deeper story than I had ever been able to convey before. Fiction can tell a truer truth, when at times non-fiction cannot accurately portray it. To that end, some details were modified. Names have been changed. Places have been obscured. My intent was to communicate, in a limited number of pages, many years of my childhood experience—the fear and despair—contrasted by Liz's deep and undying love, as well as the impact of her presence. Those were the two powerful forces that genuinely saved the lives of my siblings and me.

Her presence moderated our parents' actions. It always seemed mystical to me, as if she possessed a superpower over these two wealthy, white people in a world she was barred from entering in any way except through the back door. However, instead of a cape, she wore an apron. And instead of feats of strength, she displayed her power by being present and doing the mundane—the laundry, cleaning, and making meals. But she clearly wielded power over my parents. She scared them without needing to utter a word against them. She was always the first, in fact the only one, to find us after one of Mom's psychotic breaks. Within minutes of her arrival, my mother shifted from raving psychosis to abject fear. I was too small to fully understand what power Liz wielded, but it was palpable and forcefully weakened my parents' violence against us.

Yet because of the times, she had no power, at least no public power. I have been asked, "How could she have continued working in a home like that?" My response is embedded in knowledge of the dark history of U.S. racism. It was at a time of the civil rights struggle a century after the

Civil War supposedly settled the matter. What white person in any position of power in the 1960s would believe an African American maid accusing a prominent doctor and his wife of child abuse? Furthermore, child abuse was simply ignored—there was no government agency protecting children from domestic abuse until years later.

Also, one needs to remember that, when most of this story happened, African Americans were still in fear of being lynched in certain places of our country. For a poor Black woman in a bigoted society, there was simply no way to intervene on our behalf. Just like all Black women in the 1960s, she had very few rights. The one right she did have, and could have exercised, was to quit her job and end her own turmoil of watching her "little white babies" suffer. Then we would have lost her, and along with her, our entire reason for living. I thank God she did not exercise that right.

Then what was she to do? How could she save us? A more modern interpretation of this story would completely miss the force of her character that made her who she was: our savior. She did what a savior needed to do with the situation she faced at that time in history—she stayed with us and showered us with the power of her love.

We all learned in school that there are only five senses. I believe that is incorrect. There are six: sight, hearing, touch, smell, taste... and love, deep love. This sixth one is felt as acutely as the other five. It is experienced in real time, just like the others. It remembers. It teaches us to feel safe and valued. In many ways, it is far more powerful than any of the other senses because it reaches to our souls and has the power to direct our lives. It makes us want to live and to survive, even in the worst of situations. It saves those who cannot save themselves, like the little ones who lived in that home so many years ago. Liz loved us deeply. She washed our clothes, made our beds, and fed us meals. She held us when we were hurt and sad. But most of all, her deep, palpable love made us want to live, and for that, I am forever grateful to her.

Yet there are so many other people I am grateful for, people to thank in this process.

First I want to acknowledge and thank my wife, who has been an unending source of strength for me. Beyond that, she has taught me to laugh, a much needed element in light of my childhood. Also, she has been a model of normalcy that I had not experienced before knowing her. We have had nearly thirty years together and I thank God for her every day. Life without her is unimaginable. No matter how many days I have with her, it will still not be enough time.

My siblings deserve to be lauded at length, yet that will remain private between us. Todd's brother and sister in the story reflect only my experience and the tender love and appreciation I have for my true siblings. Their stories remain their own, to share when and if they may choose to do so. The love and bond we share will forever nourish our selves and our souls, and only we can understand the depth of the grief we share as a result of the destruction we endured during our upbringing.

I want to thank my friends who took interest in my story and tried to understand the trauma of my younger years, fully intent on easing the lonely burden I carried for so long. Especially my "wing-buddies"—Doug, Jeremy, Tom, and Jeff. Thank you, guys, for your patient understanding of me as the cracks, or more aptly fissures, of my wounded personality became hurtful at times. Thank you for your understanding, for your patient endurance, and most of all, for doing what Liz did: sticking with me through it all.

So many others gave me useful advice, provided insight, and were willing readers through the numerous drafts. I wish I could thank you individually, but you know who you are and know my heartfelt appreciation. You all came to love Liz as much as I did. To you all, I am forever grateful.

And most thankfully, I somehow was led to my editor Paula Stahel, who very accurately recognized early on that this was not just a novel but, in large part, a form of therapy for me. She was so gentle and kind to allow my process but still refine the words into a work that was far more than I could have ever done on my own. I am forever grateful to her.

And finally ...

I love Liz. She is why I wrote this book—to thank her and to tell the world about her. She is the kindest person I have ever known. If I have one hope for readers of this book, it is that you will come to love Liz as much as I do.

Made in the USA
Charleston, SC
23 October 2016